Bad Penny

STACI HART

Cover design by *Quirky Bird*

Photography by *Perrywinkle Photography*

Editing by *Love N Books and Jovana Shirley*

Book design by *Inkstain Interior Book Designing*

BOOKS BY
STACI HART

HEARTS AND ARROWS
Paper Fools

CONTEMPORARY ROMANCE
Hardcore
With a Twist
Chaser
Last Call
Wasted Words
Tonic
A Thousand Letters
Bad Penny

SHORT STORIES
Once
Desperate Measures
Nailed

*To all the girls who aren't afraid to be who you are,
even when the world would judge you.*

*And for all the girls who dream of throwing off the
yoke of expectation:You can. You should. You will.*

Dick Lips

-PENNY-

"**Did you know that a** man's lips are the same color as the head of his dick?"

I took a long lick of my ice cream to punctuate the question. Ramona choked on hers, and Veronica, our other roommate, laughed openly and a little too loudly for a public place. A few people in the ice cream parlor turned to look.

"I'm serious," I said. "It's a real thing. I can vouch for it. I've seen a lot of dicks."

Veronica snorted. "Oh my God. Stop it."

Ramona couldn't stop giggling. The three of us sat at a small table on the patio of our favorite ice cream joint, which was conveniently located around the corner from our apartment. It was *hot*. June in New York is no joke — though nothing compared to August — and that day was particularly humid without a cloud in the sky to give us reprieve from the blazing sun. Hence, the ice cream, shorty shorts, and tanks we all wore.

Curse of getting ready to go anywhere with your roommates. Everyone matched.

It happened more than I'd admit to openly. But we were attached at the hips: we lived together, worked together at Tonic — a tattoo parlor— and boy hunted together. Well, I hunted boys, Ramona played with her engagement ring, and Veronica rejected all potential suitors. The only difference in our appearance was the color of our messy buns: Veronica's was pitch-black, Ramona's was platinum-blonde, and mine was a silvery shade of lavender that I'd stuck with for three whole months. It was nearly a record.

"Like take this guy for example," I started, nodding into the ice cream parlor where a group of guys sat just inside the rolled up garage doors.

We all looked, not even pretending to be inconspicuous. Everyone knows no one can tell if you were looking at them when you have sunglasses on.

Two of their backs were to us, but the third faced our direction, and, boy, was he a looker. He was in a sort of muscle shirt, which sounds horribly douchey, but he pulled it off well enough that I wished he'd pull it off. He was tan and dirty blond with biceps that had curves like a rollercoaster and a tattoo on his shoulder that I couldn't make out from the distance. Black Wayfarers sat on his nose, and when he laughed at something one of his friends had said, I swear his smile blew a circuit in my brain.

"Wait, which one are we looking at?" Veronica asked.

"Blondie. With the arm porn," I answered. His lips were wide and full, a dusty shade of pink that sent a little tingle between my legs. "So, check his lips out — they're like the perfect pink. Like not *too* pink. You just want a nice, neutral shade, nothing extreme. Don't want any surprises when he unleashes the beast."

Ramona snickered. "*That* is a neat trick, Pen. I swear to God, I can picture it now. I bet it's pretty," she said dreamily before licking her ice cream.

My bottom lip slipped between my teeth. "Mmm, I bet it is too. Shaped like a pretty little mushroom with veins in all the right places."

Veronica groaned with her mouth full of ice cream. "You are so gross."

I made a face at her. "It's not my fault you don't appreciate the finer things in life. Like a gorgeous dick."

A laugh burst out of her, and I smiled. She could pretend she thought dicks were gross, but I knew it was a boldfaced lie. I'd heard her calling for Jesus behind the wall we shared — though it was rare enough that I found myself constantly on a mission to get her laid.

Blondie glanced over and caught all three of us looking. A slow smile lifted one corner of his lips, and I found myself mirroring him.

The girls and I didn't look away because we were utterly shameless. And with him looking at me like that, I did what any woman with a pulse would do: I held his gaze and did something blatantly sexual to my ice cream.

His eyes were on my lips. I was pretty sure at least — he had on sunglasses too, so he could have been watching the granny who sat behind me. But I knew I had him when his smile faltered, his brows rising just a hair, and a little shock worked through me, a rush that set my heart ticking a little faster.

Veronica hit me, effectively knocking my elbow out from underneath me and sending the tip of my nose into my cone.

"Hey!" I said with a simultaneous pout and scowl.

She only laughed and picked up a napkin to wipe my nose off for me.

"You are so fucking boy crazy," she said with a laugh. "Get serious."

"Never." I let her wipe off my nose. I'd earned that. "And what's wrong with being boy crazy?"

"Nothing," Ramona answered for Veronica and in my defense. "You're happy chasing all that dick, and it's super entertaining to watch."

"Thank you," I said gratefully and stuck my tongue out at Veronica.

"You're welcome. If we were on *The Golden Girls*, you'd be Blanche."

A laugh shot out of me. "Duh, she's my spirit guide. A different beau every episode. A drawer full of crotchless panties. A lot of dramatic flailing." I licked my cone with my eyes on Blondie, who was still watching me too. "And Veronica would be Dorothy. Forever single and an absolute killjoy."

Veronica rolled her eyes. I heard it from behind her sunglasses.

"Who would I be?" Ramona asked.

"Sophia, except taller. Or Rose but with less anecdotes about cows."

We broke into more giggling. Maybe the heat was making us punchy.

"Anyway, the dick-lip thing works for women too."

Veronica chuffed. "Oh? You can tell the color of our dicks?"

"I wonder if it would apply to a clit." I hummed thoughtfully. "But no, our lips are the same color as our nipples."

Ramona froze, her red lips dropping open in a little O. "Oh my God, it's true."

"I know it is." Eyes locked on Blondie, I stuck out my tongue to swirl around the top of my cone. I closed my lips over the top of it real slow, making a show of it.

He gripped the edge of the table.

Ramona shook her head. "I'm never leaving the house without lipstick on again."

Veronica snorted.

"Isn't it weird?" I asked. "It's like nature was like, *This is your mouth. It's for eating and putting genitals in. Let me color-code that into your brain, so you don't forget that lips are for food and fucking.*"

Ramona chuckled. "Only you, Penny."

I put up one hand and shook my head. "Blame nature, not me. Lips are so sexual. Why do you think women wear lipstick? We want men — or women, if you swing that way — to notice our mouths, but we don't really give their lips the consideration they deserve. Blondie's lips are soft and smooth, and I bet his dick is too. I bet he kisses like a god and fucks like a porn star."

Veronica laughed and stood. "All right, that's enough out of you. Let's go. If we stay any longer, you're going to face-rape that poor, unsuspecting man you've been taunting with your sexual salted caramel."

"Sexual a-salt." As she pulled me out of my chair, I licked my lips, my eyes still on Blondie. "I wonder what he'd look like under a little salted caramel."

Ramona playfully pushed me in the shoulder, and I followed the girls, twiddling my fingers at Blondie as we walked away from the shop, laughing.

– BODIE –

H*er hips swung as she* walked away, and I sat there like an idiot with ice cream dripping down my hand.

"Dude." My twin brother, Jude, slapped me in the arm, sending my cone teetering.

I scowled at him. "What the fuck, man?"

"You weren't even listening."

"You're right. I was too busy watching one of the hottest girls I've ever seen lick her ice cream like it was her job."

He looked around. "Where?"

"She's gone."

"Man, why didn't you tell me?"

I smirked. "Because I saw her first."

Phil rolled his eyes from across the table. "You guys argue like sisters."

"That's what happens when you share a womb for nine months." I took a bite of my waffle cone, still thinking about her.

Her hair was a soft shade of purple, tied up in a bun, and her face was framed by a blue bandana, tied on top. She looked like a pinup girl, and when she'd stood and walked away, I'd caught sight of the sweetest heart-shaped ass. I couldn't help but imagine my hands around it and my face buried in her—

Jude slapped my arm again. "You're drooling, asshole."

I punched him in the bicep. "Lay off."

He rubbed the spot where I'd hit him and frowned.

Phil shook his head and propped his skinny forearms on the table. "I miss the days when you guys were more worried about your *Magic: The Gathering* deck and binging on Snickers bars than girls."

Jude smirked. "Ah, the great sexual drought of our teenage years."

Phil made a face and pushed his glasses up his long nose. "Easy, guys. Some of us never outgrow that curse."

"Aw, come on, Phil. You've got Angie."

"True, and I love her. And, beyond all reason, she loves me too. Fortunately, Ang doesn't give a shit that I'll never be a blond, buff Bobbsey twin."

I shook my head. "You should have gotten into surfing with us, Philly."

He gave me a flat look. "First off, there's no real surfing in Berkeley. Second, sharks."

Jude laughed. "I get it, man. If Dad hadn't guilted us into learning before we left for college, we wouldn't have either. But even if we hadn't, you don't live in Santa Monica without becoming a surfer."

I nodded. "It's true. I mean, I hated surfing the pier, but the sound of panties hitting the ground when we came in from a session made it all worthwhile."

Jude sighed. "Ah, the good old days. It was so easy to get chicks. But I swear, when we started surfing, I thought I was gonna die. I could barely even paddle out past the breaks without having a coronary."

"Too many donuts." I took another bite of my cone.

"I think I lost thirty pounds in two months. And then came the girls," Jude said, his eyes all dreamy.

"So many girls," I added.

Phil made a face. "I hate this story."

"If you'd gotten into USC, you could have paddled through pussy with us," Jude said matter-of-factly.

"Please, UCLA would have been better," I shot.

"Whatever, dicks. Berkeley is better on all counts."

"Anyway," Jude started, "New York is a totally different game. In LA, if you have a BMW and surf, you can bag pretty much anybody on the West side. Here, the bar is high. New York chicks don't give a shit about any of that."

I frowned. "Sounds like a lot of work."

"Yeah, but it's worth it," Jude said with a smile. "You'll see tonight. We'll hit a couple of bars, see what there is to see. I'm so ready to get back into the game after wasting all that time with Julie."

He sounded flippant, but I knew just how much she'd hurt him. They'd moved out here together years ago, and just before I'd moved from LA a week ago, she'd dumped him.

I clapped him on the shoulder, hoping he could find a distraction at whatever bar we were going to that night. "Tonight, you get in where you fit in."

He smiled. "Hell yeah. And you'll see what New York is really like. We need a break. We've been locked up in the loft coding ever since you got here."

I shrugged. "We've been talking about this game since we were in middle school, and now that we have the tools and the degrees and we're in the same place, it's been good. We've been coding it for eight fucking years, and now we can really do it instead of just dicking around with it in our spare time."

Phil nodded. "Thank God you lost your job."

"Thank God for my severance and savings," I added. "And that your parents are Silicon Valley yuppies and pay for the loft."

He laughed at that. "Otherwise, us quitting to go all in on the game wouldn't have been an option."

"No pressure, right?" I joked, skirting the magnitude of the situation by pretending the risk we were taking wasn't a big deal.

Jude's face softened until he looked all sappy and sentimental. "Really, man, I'm glad you're here. I don't like being split up. It's been a shitty four years without you."

"It has," I agreed. "But we're back together now. And even though I hate being stuck in the city with the beach an hour away and no surf to be had—"

Jude's sappy face turned into a frown.

"—I'm glad I'm here. Now, show me this high-class ass before I head back to the land of a thousand bikinis."

After we finished our ice cream, we headed back to the loft, and I found myself thinking about the pinup girl, wondering if I'd ever see her again. I'd been a fool for not chasing after her, stunned stupid by her blatancy, knocked out by the boldness of her. She'd seemed like a girl who knew what she wanted, and that confidence, that forwardness of her actions, had lit a fire in me that no amount of mint chocolate could cool down.

Slideshow

-PENNY-

Courtney Love wailed about waking up in her makeup as I sat with my roommates in front of the long mirror hanging on my bedroom wall. I'd hung it sideways a couple of years before, low enough on the wall that we could sit at it, and framed it with lights, just like I'd seen on Pinterest, and I'd even used a drill, and nearly drilling a hole in my leg was so worth it. No one put makeup on anywhere else in the apartment.

The light was perfect, the music was perfect, and the company was perfect. I sat between Veronica and Ramona, singing along with Courtney, as I uncapped my lipstick, a dark red matte called *Heartbreaker*. It couldn't have been more accurate of a shade for me and not just because of my skin tone.

See, I didn't do serious or permanent, not with my hair color and not with my boys.

I'd been lollipop pink and shamrock green. I'd been fiery orange and cotton-candy blue. In fact, I hadn't really seen my actual hair color past a half-inch of roots since high school back in California. I hadn't had a serious boyfriend since then either.

Why choose one when you could have them all?

Veronica called me boy crazy like it was an insult, and I was. Every time I met a new guy, I would fall into easy infatuation, a giddy affair with a time limit. I wanted zero commitment. I wanted the fun and the thrill and to call it before things got messy. Sticky. I always skipped out the door before those pesky old feelings got involved and wrecked the whole train. I wasn't into napalm. I was more of a rainbows-and-ponies kind of girl — I wanted feelings, but only the good ones. And good feelings didn't last past three dates. After three dates, somebody inevitably wanted more. Usually, it was them. Every once in a while, it was me.

At that point, I didn't skip out the door. I ran like my hair was on fire.

You'd think it wouldn't be so hard to find guys who were cool with no strings, but this was shockingly untrue.

They would *say* they were fine with it, but I swear to God, at least a third of the time, we would hit that three-date mark, and they would profess their love. Date one would be easy, fun, always the best. Date two, I could feel those strings looming, hanging over me like a goddamn raincloud, but I'd just pop open my rainbow-striped umbrella and keep on skipping until date three when I'd get some variation of, *I think I'm in love with you.*

The last one was a perfect example.

As I had been getting dressed, he'd sat up in bed with eyes like the saddest beagle ever and said, *I feel like you're using me.*

I'd smiled and kissed him on the forehead and told him I'd call him.

I never called him.

I know, I know, trust me. I wish I could let myself fall helplessly in love, but I'd done that once, and when it had ended and I had been left alone to put myself back together, I'd known without a doubt that love wasn't for me. The reason: He had driven me crazy. And not the cute kind of crazy. The kind of crazy that earned you a restraining order.

Not that I was butthurt about what had happened — hanging on to things just wasn't my style. I looked forward, not back. Forward was easy. Forward was fun.

No point in lamenting all the things I couldn't change. Instead, I'd learned my lesson and kept myself blissfully unattached.

Once my lips were red and plump, my skin creamy and white, and my liner black and winged, I felt ready, getting up to inspect my reflection. My favorite black-and-white-striped bustier set off the tattoos across my chest with its sweetheart neckline, and I'd paired it with high-waisted black shorts with sailor buttons on the front.

I smoothed a hand over the wide finger waves in my purple hair as Ramona belted the last verse of the song, and I joined in with an air-guitar accompaniment that would make Lady Love proud.

Veronica swiped at the corner of her lips with the pad of her finger, inspecting her makeup. "Courtney Love was a badass. I don't care what anybody says about her."

"I mean, she was a hot-ass mess, but she got to bang Kurt Cobain on the regular. I miss him." I sighed and sat on the edge of my bed to put on my red wedges. "They were like the '90s version of Sid and Nancy. Totally, terrifyingly romantic. That's what love is. All-consuming, self-destructive, and absolutely not something I'm interested in experiencing."

Ramona laughed. "You're so dramatic. Shep and I aren't like that, and you see us all the time, so I know you know better."

I shifted my boobs around in the bustier to maximize my rack. "Yeah, but that's not how I love. You know me. Do you really think

I'm capable of doing halfway on anything? I mean, need I remind you about Rodney? I would have gone toe-to-toe with Satan himself to hang on to that boy in high school. This is the same guy who wouldn't let me speak when that commercial with Paris Hilton eating a hamburger came on. Like he would clap his hand over my mouth and force me to be quiet until it was over. He was a psycho, and for two years, I let him torment me."

"Ugh, fuck that guy," Veronica said. "Even if he is a rock star."

"Don't remind me." My face was flat. "If he hadn't dumped me, I probably would have hung onto him like a barnacle. A screaming, psychotic barnacle. Can you imagine me on tour? I really would have been like Courtney — lipstick smeared and mascara running down my face when I ran onstage and shoved him because he'd banged a groupie. But at least the three-date rule came from the whole mess."

Veronica rolled her eyes. "First of all, it's three bangs, not three dates."

My brow quirked. "Who doesn't bang on a date?"

She ignored me. "And second, that rule is so stupid. And I say that with love. Think of how many relationships you've missed out on."

"You say that like it's a bad thing. Listen, a multitude of things can happen after the three-date zone, and I don't want to deal with any of them. Either I'm bored or I try to climb up their b-holes like an enema. Either they blow up my cell phone or get stalky. Or they propose marriage, like Clay." I gave Ramona a pointed look.

"What? He flew here all the way from Italy to ask you to marry him. What was I supposed to do? Leave him in the hallway with two dozen roses and that look on his face?"

"No, you *should* have called the cops. The last thing I expected was him sitting naked on my bed looking like he'd delivered me everything I'd ever wanted via Lufthansa Airlines. I had to fake a headache and let him cuddle me, pretend all the next day that things were cool. I couldn't break up with the psycho until he left for the airport."

Veronica laughed. "Oh, which one was the baby-talk one?"

I groaned. "Derek. My God, he drove me nuts. We would get tacos, and he knew I liked the chips that were like three chips wrapped up together, so he'd dig through the basket, hand them to me, and watch me eat them."

They laughed, and I kept going, always happier with an audience.

"The baby talk though, that was the worst. *I wuv you a yacht. I wuv you a whole FLEET of yachts! Aw, schmoopsie-poo. Are you a sheep or awake?*"

Ramona waved her hand with the other on her stomach as she laughed so hard that she was barely making noise. "Oh my God!"

"Seriously. But he was so hot. I mean, how could I resist a firefighter? With that ass? And that smile? I was willing to overlook a lot for bunker gear and smelling like a campfire." I sighed. "But I mean, those guys are so much easier to deal with. The real kicker is when *I* go bonkers. Like when I was five dates in with Tony. Remember him?"

Veronica sighed wistfully. "The one who could cook."

"Right? Dude made his own pasta. Fucking dream guy. But, I swear, I was begging to meet his mother by date five — *after* I told him no strings, and he was so about it. He slowly backed toward the door, said he'd call me, and I never heard from him again. There's a chance he died in a gutter somewhere, but I'm pretty sure it was from his phone exploding from the eighty-four-thousand text messages I'd sent him. And that was just a mild case of stalking — I've crossed the line so many times, I'm surprised I've never had the cops called on me."

"You're too cute for jail," Veronica said with a laugh.

"Not when my crazy eyes get going." I crossed my eyes and drew a circle in the air around my ear. "Rodney trained me to trust no man, so ninety percent of the time, I convince myself they're lying to me about where they are, what they're doing, how they feel. I go clinger. I'd rather be clung to."

"I dunno. See, I disagree with Veronica," Ramona said. "I think the rule makes sense. Penny, you're larger than life. I've been friends with you for eight years, and I've seen how guys treat you. Every hetero man in the room notices you when you walk in. It's like every curve on your body is sending a signal directly to them. They want to know you, and some, like Rodney, want to control you. This is a way for you to protect yourself against the whole thing. You break hearts so yours doesn't get broken. And who knows? Maybe someday you'll meet somebody who changes your mind."

I laughed. "God, I hope not."

She smiled like she knew better than me. "How long have you been on the three-date wagon now?" Ramona asked.

"Two whole years," I answered, proud of myself. "Two years of normal dates with no crazy on either side of the line. Everything has been perfectly smooth ever since I really decided to stick to the rule. This is better for all parties involved, trust me. I'd rather not put my heart through the meat grinder again, thank you very much."

Veronica snickered. "She said to her friend whose wedding is in two weeks."

"Oh, stop it. That's what I'm saying — Ramona and Shep are perfectly perfect. I'm just a mess, like Courtney Love but with tidier makeup."

But Ramona's face had fallen into a sad expression. "Two weeks. That's all we have left for this."

Veronica looked the same. "Less than that. You're moving next week."

Ramona's eyes misted up. "What am I going to do without you guys?"

I knelt down between them. "You'll start your life with Shep, and it's going to be everything you ever wanted. We'll see each other at the tattoo parlor every day. And Ronnie and I will be here, doing our makeup and trolling for boys at *least* three times a week, so you can come with us anytime. Be our wing woman."

She laughed and rubbed her nose. "Ha. As if you need help."

I smirked. "I wasn't talking about me."

Veronica rolled her eyes. "Oh, ha-ha. You're a fucking riot, Penny."

I shrugged innocently. "I mean, if you weren't so picky, you'd be able to find a guy — at least for a night."

She made a face at me. "Maybe not all of us want a guy just for a night?"

"That's fair. But not even sometimes? I'd love to be your wingwoman, but it's exhausting, and I've got goals of my own."

"Yeah, to eat every dick in Manhattan," she shot, eyes twinkling and lips in a smile.

My mouth popped open, and I laughed. "You bitch. I don't have to eat them all, but having them in or around my vagina would be fine. You know, as an alternative."

"So slutty!" Veronica shook her head.

"Thank you," I said sweetly. "I love being slutty. I don't make any promises, and I know exactly what I want. What the hell is everyone's problem with that anyway? Who cares who I sleep with? Does it affect anyone but me and the guy involved? Answer: No. And I tell all the guys I *whatever* with what my expectations are, and they agree. It's not my fault if they catch feelings." I shuddered. "It's like the emotional equivalent of gonorrhea — the clap, but for your heart!"

Veronica laughed. "I mean, with that endorsement, why wouldn't you want a boyfriend?"

"Precisely my point. And anyway, it's such a fucking double standard. Guys are allowed to fuck whoever they want, and other dudes are like, *Way to go, bro,* and slap them five. Girls are supposed to be all demure and pure and rely solely on their vibrators if they're not in a committed, monogamous relationship. Fucking patriarchy."

"Fuck the patriarchy!" Ramona crowed as she held up her hand for a slap.

I obliged.

I rapped the chorus of "I'm not a player" like Big Pun. "Ronnie, you need to crush a lot. I'd even settle for a little crushing. You're too hot not to crush as much as humanly possible."

Veronica laughed. "Maybe tonight. Wing me."

My mouth popped open. "Oh my God, seriously?"

She nodded, closed lips smiling. "You won me over with your slut speech."

"Finally. I've been working on you for years. I can't believe I've seen the day. And I'm not even in Depends!"

She laughed and pushed me over, and I couldn't even be mad about it.

A half an hour later, we were walking into a bar on Broadway called Circus that had popped up a few months before. The thing about themed bars was that they were hit or miss. That was mostly because, in an attempt to be cute, the bars would end up overdone, and within a few months of the novelty wearing off, the bar would close and a new one would take its place.

Not Circus.

A circular bar stood in the center of the room, and it was made out of a small version of a carousel. It looked like someone had plucked the top off a carousel and hung it from the ceiling. Around the top, Edison bulbs lined the panels of alternating mirrors and vintage paintings of circus scenes, and long white bar lights spoked from underneath the center, like a wheel. Red-and-white striped fabric draped from the peaked top of the carousel and out into the darkness of the edges of the ceiling, and the barstools were all saddles.

Everything in the bar had a circus feel — from creepy-cool oddity art to brushed brass fixtures on everything. The bartenders were dressed up like ringmasters, complete with handlebar mustaches and red tails, and the cocktail waitresses were all dressed in tails too. Rather than shirttails, they wore black bras, and rather than pants, they wore high-waisted shorts and fishnets. They even had little top hats on.

I swear to God, if I hadn't had my dream job as a tattoo artist, I'd have dropped everything and joined the *Circus.*

I led the charge through the crowd and to the bar with my roommates behind me, squeezing in between two gigantic guys to lean on the bar.

They looked down at me.

"Hey, fellas."

They smiled.

The closest bartender set a drink in front of a girl down from me, and the second he saw me, he headed straight over, effectively skipping everyone ahead of me.

It might have been the fact that I'd hopped up a little, caging my rack in my arms to put it on display. Oldest trick in the book.

I told you — I was absolutely shameless.

With drinks in hand, I gave the bartender a smile, and the girls and I headed away from the fray to look for a table. A group was just getting up, and we swooped in like birds of prey just ahead of a pack of bitter chicks wearing painful-looking shoes.

I sipped on my tequila — it was chilled: I'm not that hard — looking around at the mass of people, soaking it all in, as "Pretty in Pink" by *The Psychedelic Furs* played.

And then time stopped, and the crowd parted like the universe wanted to point right at him.

It was Blondie from the ice cream parlor.

The music stretched out, people slowing under the red and white striped fabric, the naked bulbs of the carousel painting him in golden light. He stood right there like he'd been placed in that spot just for me, tall and beautiful, his skin tan and smile bright as he laughed at something his twin had said.

I almost fell out of my chair. There were two of them. My insides turned into raspberry jelly at the thought of what kind of damage they could do to a woman.

But my eyes found Blondie again — his twin was wrong somehow, which was bizarre in itself because they were identical. From where I sat, they were night and day. There was something about Blondie, some vibe that hit me even more now than it had at the ice cream parlor. He felt … *familiar*. Something about him I couldn't quite place caught me, something in the line of his profile and the curve of his lips. But I was certain I'd never seen him before — I remembered all of the Adonises I'd met and arduously logged them in my mental bank of spank.

He was tall and jacked with a smile like a lightbulb and hair like spun gold. It was a little long, curling around his ears, and I wondered if it was soft, wondered what it would feel like between my fingers as I rode his face like a pony.

I didn't realize I had slipped off my stool and was walking toward him — I had locked onto him like a goddamn target — until he met my eyes, froze for a split second, and then walked toward me like he was caught up just as much as I was.

I should have known right then that I was in big Blondie-sized trouble. But I couldn't seem to find a single fuck to give.

- BODIE -

The pinup girl from the ice cream shop had the reddest lips curled into an irresistible smile, and my feet, which had been moving entirely of their own accord, didn't stop until we met in the middle.

I knew her somehow, but I couldn't place her and wondered if it was just that I'd been thinking about her since I saw her a few hours before.

Shock and awe, man. She was standing there in front of me like a dream, but up close and personal where I could see her. In a split second, I'd catalogued everything about her — her gold septum ring, the black gauges with tiny cat ears, the curve of her plump red lips, the shine of her hair, and the tattoos across her chest, her shoulders, her arms, her thighs. I wondered where else she was tattooed and found myself smiling down at her, imagining the answer.

"Heya, Blondie," she said slyly. "Fancy meeting you here."

"If I didn't know better, I'd think you were following me."

One dark brow rose with one corner of her lips. "Who says you know better?"

I chuckled as my eyes combed over her face like it was the first face I'd ever seen. She was so familiar to me, but I'd have remembered the purple hair, the piercings, the tattoos. That smile.

I blinked.

I knew that smile.

"I'm Penny," she said, extending her free hand.

I took it, my smile spreading. "Bodie."

She showed no recognition at my name — when she had known me, I'd gone by a nickname. Her eyes were on my lips, and I realized fully that she had no idea who I was. I wondered if I'd really changed that much from when she'd seen me last, realizing I had. Sometimes I'd look in the mirror and barely recognize myself. And earlier she'd had on big sunglasses, on top of being far enough away that I couldn't tell it was her. Eight years had changed her too, but only the colors of her feathers. Everything else seemed exactly the same.

I considered telling her, but dismissed the thought. Because there was really only one thing to do: fuck with her until she figured it out.

"Good to see you again," I said ambiguously.

"You too, but I'm surprised. I mean, after going down on a waffle cone for you earlier, I figured you would have had plenty of me to last."

A laugh burst out of me. "Oh, I have a feeling your kind of ice cream is the kind you can't get enough of."

She shrugged and brought her drink to her lips. "It's been said." She watched me for a second again. "So what's your story, Bodie?"

"I just moved here from LA."

"For a job?"

"You could say that. I'm a software engineer."

She laughed. "Wow, not what I would have guessed."

"Oh?"

Penny dramatically looked me up and down. "Hmm. I'd say … personal trainer. No, no. That hunky moving company I always see commercials for."

"Manly Movers?"

She lit up and snapped. "Yes! You definitely look like the Manly Mover type. All those muscles."

I chuckled. "That's super sexist."

"Male model. That would have done too."

I couldn't stop smiling, and I hated thinking that my dimple was on display. "I guess I should be flattered that you think I'm hot enough to be a male model."

Her eyes twinkled. "Oh, you definitely are."

"How about you? What do you do? Where are you from?" I asked, baiting her.

"I'm a tattoo artist," she offered but didn't elaborate, and I sensed a story there. "I've lived in New York since I graduated high school, but I grew up in Santa Cruz."

"Me too."

Her eyes widened, and she smiled. "No way. I went to Loma Vista. What a small world."

She still hadn't figured it out, and I found myself grinning like an idiot, wondering how long it would take her to put it together.

"Ever surf?" I asked.

She laughed. "No way. Sharks."

"That's what my buddy Phil says too."

She glanced behind me, twiddling her fingers, presumably at Jude and Phil. "So, you're a twin, huh?"

I nodded and took a sip of my Maker's as "Rock the Casbah" kicked off, and everyone around us started bouncing and dancing. "Since birth."

She laughed. "What a win for the universe that there would be two of you."

"Double your pleasure, double your fun."

That caught her off guard, and her bottom lip slipped between her teeth as a flush rose on her cheeks.

Just like that, I had one objective, and it began and ended with her lips.

"Although I should tell you now," I stepped closer, slipping into her space, and her eyes widened, pupils dilating as she leaned into me, "I don't like to share."

The tip of her pink tongue darted out to wet her lips, and her eyes were locked on to my mouth.

"Are you thinking about kissing me?" I asked.

She shook her head, though her eyes didn't stray. "No, I'm thinking about what your dick looks like."

I laughed from way down deep in my belly, shocked in the best way and turned on in the worst. And as the ocean of people waved around us, she rose up on her tiptoes, grabbed a handful of my T-shirt, and pulled.

I caught the smallest breath — a surprised, satisfied gasp — just before our lips met, and fireworks exploded in my brain. The kiss wasn't soft or sweet; it was strong and determined, those red, red lips pressing against mine, opening to let me into her hot mouth, her tongue finding mine like she'd been looking for it her whole life.

The surprise left me as quickly as it had hit, and I leaned into her, my free arm winding around her back to press her body against mine. There wasn't an inch of space between us, and all the while, our mouths worked each other's in a long dance that left my heart chugging like a freight train in my chest.

She pulled away, her lips swollen and eyes lust-drunk as they met mine and held them while she kicked back her drink and grabbed my hand.

"Let's get the fuck out of here," she said.

And I smirked, breathless. "Your place or mine?"

Mr. Diddle

- BODIE -

For the record, I had every intention of telling her who I was. It was just that I was so caught up in her as we hurried back to my apartment that my brain had short-circuited, thinking only from my raging hard-on in my pants. I didn't have time to consider what it meant or what would happen, and I didn't have the will to break whatever trance I'd found myself in.

I should have been surprised to have her by my side. I should have been confused about how I'd ended up with Penny's hand in mine. But wondering felt like the absolute first and last thing I should be doing, so I didn't. And as I towed her toward my apartment, I was unable to consider anything other than the feeling of her fingers twined in mine and the sight of her smiling up at me, eyes shining and hot.

The loft felt like it was on Mars for as long as it was taking to get there.

I took the opportunity to kiss her as we waited for a stoplight to change, slipping my fingers into her purple hair, closing my lips over hers, and she tipped her chin and gave me her mouth, her tongue, with her hands clutching my shirt, pulling me into her like she was starving and I was a porterhouse.

My keys were in my hand before we hit the elevator — another opportunity to kiss her, my fingerips brushing her bare collarbone, down the curve of her breast, around her waist to her ass. I squeezed, pulling her into my cock, pleased with the whimper against my lips.

We practically ran down the hallway. She panted behind me as I unlocked the door, and we tumbled inside.

I closed it behind her and turned. "Hang on, there's something I need to—"

She launched herself at me, and I caught her, my back hitting the door with a thump, as she wrapped her arms around my neck. Her feet dangled off the ground, and I held her around the waist, kissing her deep.

In that moment, there was no point in stopping to tell her I was the chubby, nerdy kid with glasses she went to high school with. If she even remembered me.

But I remembered her. I'd imagined kissing her a thousand times, but never in my life had I thought I'd ever get the chance. Until now.

I turned her around, the decision made and my mission singular, and pressed her against the door. She pulled my lip between her teeth, and I growled, moving down her neck, nipping and sucking a trail past her collarbone and across the tattoos marking the soft skin of her breasts.

I wanted her naked. I wanted to see every tattoo, every inch of skin. I wanted her in my mouth. I wanted inside of her.

But first, this.

I dropped to my knees, my fingers working the buttons of her shorts. There were four — two on each side of a panel — and my heart thudded in my chest as I dropped that panel to reveal a rectangle of skin covered in tattoos. Flowers framed two pistols just inside her hip bones, barrels angled in a V, pointing down. I slipped my hands into her shorts and around her naked hips, pushing them down her legs, and as she stepped out of them, my eyes caught on the gold barbells above and below the hood of her clit.

"Oh, fuck, Penny," I whispered, my hands gripping her hips, my lips already on a track for it.

I closed my eyes and buried my face in the sweetness of her.

She braced herself with her hands on my shoulders, murmuring something I couldn't make out and didn't try. My tongue rolled against the bottom ball that rested right over her clit, circling until her nails dug into my skin through my shirt.

When I broke away and glanced up, she was looking down, her eyes half-shut and those red fucking lips hanging open in pleasure.

I smirked and lifted one of her legs, hitching it over my shoulder to spread her open. I trailed my hand down, framing her piercing in the V of two fingers, and when I squeezed gently and shifted in a circle, her eyes rolled back in her head that rested against the door, stretching her long white neck out.

For a second, I wished I could be everywhere at once, licking her neck, sucking her lip, my face in her pussy — everywhere. I wanted to devour her. So I started with what I had at my fingertips.

I moved my hand down to cup her, my fingers shifting against the slick line of her core.

"God, you're soaking fucking wet." My voice was ragged, my body coiled.

She whispered a plea, begging me with a single word, "*Please.*"

I happily obliged, licking my lips, bringing them just close enough to her hood that they touched only infinitesimally, waiting for a stretched out second before I slipped my fingers inside at the exact moment I closed my lips over her clit.

"Oh God," she whispered, bucking against me, closing around my fingers as they slid in, out, in, reaching for the rough spot inside.

Her fingers slipped into my hair and twisted, and mine matched the pace of my tongue.

She clenched around my fingers, pinning me between her thighs as I moved faster, harder, and then …

Then, she came with a cry to a higher power and a burst that I'd be thinking about on my death bed.

As she came down, I slowed, softly kissing and licking her, every flick of my tongue sending another pulse through her pussy around my fingers.

"Jesus fucking Christ," she breathed. "Where the fuck did you come from?"

I closed my lips, reverently kissing her once more before looking up at her with a smile. "Santa Cruz. Loma Vista, Class of 2009."

Her eyes went wide, and she blinked. "But there wasn't anyone named Bodie in my class."

"There was. You just knew me as Diddle."

Her mouth hung open, and a shocked laugh escaped her. "No way. No fucking way. Diddle was …"

I moved her leg, putting her foot back on the ground, but she still hung on to my shoulders. "Chubby? Glasses? Into Dungeons and Dragons? With an equally dorky twin? Friends with Rodney Parker since the second grade when he moved in next to us and gave me that stupid nickname?"

I rose, and her hands on my shoulders stayed put until I was standing before her with my hands on her hips, feeling ashamed of myself for not telling her sooner. She stood there, stunned and still blinking at me.

"Are you mad I didn't tell you?"

At that, a smile spread across her lips. "How could I be mad at a guy who just ate my pussy like it was his last meal?" And she laughed, pulling me down to kiss her, running her tongue across my lips to taste herself.

When she broke away, she looked up at me with the devil in her eyes. "Now, if you don't fuck me and show me what the rest of you can do, I might actually die."

I laughed and bent to sling her over my shoulder, smacking her bare ass once I had her where I wanted her.

– P E N N Y –

Everything was upside down — his apartment, his ass I was clinging to, my insides after the orgasm I'd just had.

I'd been diddled by Diddle.

I giggled at the thought of that and the fact that I was slung over his bohunk shoulder as he carried me down a hallway and into what I assumed was his bedroom.

He kicked the door closed behind us, and with his big arms wrapped around my legs, he tilted, dumping me on the bed with a bounce.

I watched him walk around the room, clicking on a couple of lights, as I stared at his face, looking for the kid I had known in high school. Rodney was my ex-boyfriend — the *last* boyfriend. And Diddle — Bodie — and his brother, Dee Dee, were always hanging around Rodney's band practices or at his house. I couldn't connect the dots that they were the same person.

When he reached back to grab a handful of his shirt and yank it off, I quit caring.

He had muscles on top of muscles, his arms touched with ink here and there. I itched to get a closer look. But that could wait. There were other things I needed a closer look at first.

I sat up as he walked to the bed, and I moved to the edge, parting my legs. My eyes were on his — his were between my legs.

His cock was right in front of me, tethered by his jeans, though I could see the bulging outline of it like a beast. I bit my lip and unfastened his belt with a clink, unbuttoned his pants with a soft pop, and dropped his zipper with a buzz I felt all the way up to my elbow.

He wasn't wearing underwear.

The sight of the tight skin so low on his stomach, the V of his hips, the shape of his cock still tucked into his pants — all of it hit me with a shock that hit me straight between the legs, so I reached out and freed him, leaving my fist closed around his base.

The head was the same dusty pink as his luscious lips, and I smiled, my pulse picking up and tongue sweeping my bottom lip, as I leaned forward and placed the silky-soft crown in my mouth.

Bodie hissed, his hands slipping through my hair as I grabbed his ass, pulling him to me as I leaned into him, taking him as deep as I could, which was deep. Perks of not having a gag reflex.

"Fuck, Penny," he whispered, his fingers tightening, pulling my hair just enough to sting.

I let his base go so I could grab his ass with both hands, guiding him, and he matched the rhythm with his hands in my hair, pushing me farther as my throat relaxed, his cock rock hard in my mouth.

He pulled out with a pop, and before I knew what was going on, his hands were on my face, his lips against mine, his tongue deep in my mouth, like he was trying to taste where he'd been.

"When I come," he whispered against my lips, "it's going to be inside you. Now, take your clothes off, Penny."

My heart thudded against my ribs as he backed away. I didn't have much on, just the bustier and my wedges, so I stood, smiling as I turned my back to him and folded over at the waist, unbuckling one shoe, then the other. When I peeked at him through my hair, his jeans were hanging off his hips, his hand was rolling a condom onto his cock, and his lips were pinned between his teeth, the line of his jaw hard and his eyes locked between my legs.

I turned around to face him and unhooked the corseted bustier one blessed hook at a time before letting it fall to the floor.

His eyes raked over my body for a long moment before he rushed me, grabbing me around the waist, and we tumbled into bed together as our lips connected. He nestled between my legs, and my arms wound around his neck, my legs around his waist. And when he shifted his hips, I felt the tip of him press against the center of me.

"Oh God, Bodie," I breathed. "Get your fucking pants off."

I scrabbled for his jeans that hung half off his ass, sliding them down enough to hook my foot in the crotch to push them the rest of the way until he was blissfully naked and lying on top of me.

He hummed against my neck, teasing me, as he moved down my body to my breasts. For a long minute, he cupped one, closing his lips over my tight nipple, sliding the barbell back and forth with his tongue, the sensation sending a pulse directly to my aching clit.

"Fuck, Bodie. Please."

He ran his teeth across the tip of my nipple, sending another shock down my spine as he brought his body to mine. And, when he pressed his wide crown against me, my breath froze in my lungs.

He propped himself up, his lids heavy. And when he moved, when he filled me up until he couldn't get any deeper, I thought I'd died and gone to heaven.

His hips rolled like he knew my body, rocking against my

piercing exactly where I needed, pressing against my clit, hitting me in the perfect spot, inside and out, with every pump of his hips. He stayed propped up, somehow maintaining his cool while I wriggled underneath him like my body wasn't my own.

With every slow wave of his body, I lost my mind a little more with no idea what to do with myself. The whole thing happened in bursts — his hand on my breast, kneading and toying with my nipple ring; his thighs pushing my legs open wider so he could get deeper; his lips on mine, not that I could kiss him back. Because I felt the orgasm building, the heat of it deep inside me, spreading through me, and when he took my nipple between his teeth and hummed, my body didn't know what else to do but explode. My heart, my legs, my arms, my pussy — everything flew apart and back together, pulsing and squeezing as I breathed his name on a loop.

I barely registered him coming — I was too high from what he'd done to me — but I could feel his fingers in my hair, the sting as he pulled, exposing my neck, making a space to bury his head as his body rocked, slamming into me with a guttural noise that made what was left of my insides turn into mush.

All I could hear was my panting and the thundering of my heart in my ears, a steady *da-dum* that matched the feeling of Bodie's heartbeat against my breasts. I was surrounded by him — his arms bracketing my head, his face in the curve of my neck, his fingers threading into my hair, his body pressing me into the bed — and it was absolutely and utterly glorious.

It was the feeling I lived for, everything I wanted. Who needed love when you could just have the good? The rush, the easy rightness of being together without demand? Love only complicated things, weighing down the good until the high was gone. I never wanted the high to end.

After a little while, he shifted his face to kiss my neck, sending a warm tingle up to my ear and down to my nipple like some sort of sorcery. I smiled out of sheer instinct from the sensation, bending my neck to press my cheek to his head.

"Mmm," he rumbled.

I clenched around him, still inside of me, and he twitched in answer.

"Seriously, where have you been hiding?" My voice was rough and lazy against his ear.

Bodie kissed my skin again. "LA. I've only been here a week."

He twisted, rolling us onto our sides so he could pull out, leaving me empty. I didn't like it, not one bit.

"What brought you?" I asked, propping my head on my hand to admire his back as he turned away.

He sat on the edge of the bed and cleaned himself up. "I got laid off."

"Oh God. I'm sorry."

He smiled over his shoulder at me. "Don't be. That just made the move about a hundred times more worthwhile."

I smirked as he lay back down next to me, mirroring my posture. "So, what did you do?"

"I was a software engineer for a start-up that was bought out. They canned all of us and replaced us with their own people."

I chuckled, my eyes raking over his gorgeous face, his massive body. "You don't look like a computer geek."

He laughed at that. "Maybe not now, but back in my Diddle days, you wouldn't have thought twice."

"True. I still can't get over it. I can't even see Diddle in there."

"You sure?"

He leaned a little closer, smiling that brilliant smile of his that forced the sexiest dimple I'd ever seen. I didn't even know dimples could *be* sexy.

It was his eyes, electric blue and sparking with intelligence — that was where I saw the boy I used to know.

Just like that, I was taken back years to the boy who would pick up my pen when it rolled off my desk, the boy who would share his notes with me and give me rides home when Rodney had left me somewhere. His braces were gone, and the softness of his face had filled out into hard lines and full lips. I was left wondering just how I'd missed it, how I'd missed *him*.

My smile stretched wider along with my heart. "Oh, there you are." I cupped his cheek and laid a little kiss on his lips.

But then his hand found my naked hip and pulled, bringing me closer, and the kiss wasn't so little anymore.

I broke away after a moment, breathless. "Jesus, Bodie. I don't even know if I could have another orgasm."

"Is that a challenge? Because I really, really love to win."

His hand trailed to the back of my thigh and pulled, slinging my leg over his hip — his cock was already hard again against me.

"I didn't get to take my time," he said, his eyes darkening as his pupils shot open.

So I did the only thing I could with him looking at me like that, with the hard length of him shifting against my piercing — I let him.

- BODIE -

An hour later, **I found** myself trying to catch my breath, lying flat on my back with a sweaty Penny splayed across my sweaty chest.

"I can't feel my legs," she panted, her voice gruff.

I couldn't wipe the smile off my face to even pretend to be cool. "Then my work here is done."

She laughed, and all I could think about was the feeling of her nipple rings against my skin.

Get a fucking grip, man.

Of course, then I imagined her gripping me, which didn't help me stave off another boner. I wasn't even sure how it was physiologically possible, yet there it was.

She noticed and propped herself up to look at me, incredulous and amused. "I don't think my vagina can take any more tonight, Bodie."

I smirked. "I can't either, but it's got a mind of its own."

She laughed as she slid off me — literally, we were soaked — and starfished out next to me on her back. "God, that was good. Can we do it again?"

I chuckled. "Anytime you want."

Penny turned her head to look at me, and I did the same, resting my hand on my chest.

"I have to warn you though …"

One of my brows rose. "You come with a warning label?"

"No, I come with your face between my legs."

A laugh burst out of me.

She smiled. "I don't date, Bodie. It's not just for me — I haven't been serious with anyone in a long time, and … well, that's not what I'm looking for. I need you to know and agree to it before we go any further."

I watched her for a second before answering. Her purple hair was fanned out all around her, her naked, tattooed body stretched out next to me, and right then, I knew I was in trouble.

The first problem: I'd been crushing on her since I was sixteen.

The second problem: I was officially obsessed with every inch of her body.

The third problem: There was no way I would walk away from her after that. Not without putting up a fight.

But the biggest problem of all was this: I couldn't put up a fight, or I'd spook her.

I knew Penny well enough from high school to know that I was playing with fire. And I knew I'd probably get burned if I fell for her, but if I could hang on to her? Well, it'd be worth the risk. Because I wanted more Penny. I wanted more of her smiles. I wanted to know where she'd been and what she wanted out of life. I wanted her in my bed and in my shower and anywhere I could get her. All I had to do was convince her that she wanted the same.

So I made up my mind and stepped into the lion's cage with a chair in one hand and a whip in the other.

"I'm in. No strings."

That ruby-red smile widened. "Good. And if you catch feelings, I need to know."

"Deal," I lied, "and you do the same."

She laughed at that, a sound that hit me right in the chub. "Oh, I don't catch feelings. On account of my black heart and all."

By the way she was looking at me, I didn't believe her for a second. But if that was what she thought … well, like I'd said, I loved to win.

What Would Blanche Do?

- PENNY -

I **skipped down the stairs of** our building the next morning, whistling "Yankee Doodle" with Veronica and Ramona in my wake.

"'Yankee Doodle'? Really?" Ramona called after me.

I jumped off the last step and spun around, making a whistle show of calling it macaroni, complete with jazz hands.

Veronica laughed. "I still don't get why Yankee Doodle would call the feather in his hat pasta."

They caught up, and we started down the sidewalk, heading for Tonic — the tattoo parlor a couple of blocks away where we all worked.

"Well," I said like the know-it-all I was, "that's because macaroni used to be a term for fashionable."

"How do you know shit like this?" Veronica asked.

I shrugged. "I just remember useless stuff like that. I hear it once and *bam*." I tapped my temple. "Steel trap. Problem is, it doesn't actually hold important information. Or numbers. Don't make me try to remember numbers, or math. I cannot math."

"We know, honey." Ramona smiled and patted my arm. "We've all seen you try to split a check."

I rolled my eyes.

She didn't wait for further response. "So, are you going to tell us what happened last night? If I hadn't woken up late, I would have alarm-clocked you so hard. I need answers."

"I can't say I'm bummed to have missed you jumping on my bed to harass me before I had to be up."

Bodie crossed my mind — flashes of his hands and lips and smile and *God*, I was about him. I smiled to myself.

I'd left his house sore in all the right places and knees about as stable as quicksand. Once I'd floated home, I'd sunk into my bed and slept like I was dead — no dreams, nothing. I didn't even think I'd rolled over once.

I hadn't been nailed that well in a good long while. And when I'd woken, he had been on my mind.

I was infatuated. Smitten. Giddy and grinning and gone.

"Earth to Penny. Anybody in there?" Veronica pinched my arm.

"Ow!" I rubbed the spot and stuck my tongue out at her.

"You deserve that. So much for a wingwoman. Your ass barely hit the seat before you disappeared with Blondie."

I wrinkled my nose, but I was smiling. "Yeah, sorry. And you're never going to believe this; I fucking know him."

Ramona's brow quirked. "Well, I mean, that was the guy from the ice cream shop yesterday, wasn't it?"

"Yes, but also, we went to high school together. I didn't even recognize him — he looks completely different."

"I'd imagine so if you didn't recognize him," Veronica said. "No way Blondie wouldn't have made it onto your radar."

"Right? The guy went from Chris Pratt in *Parks and Rec,* dumping Skittles into his mouth, to Chris Pratt in *Guardians of the Galaxy*, shirtless and ripped and orange and all mad because they stole his Walkman. Except it's even less obvious than that. Like, he had glasses and braces and … I don't even know, man. He was hidden inside of there that whole time. I remembered his eyes the most. Is that weird?"

"Not at all," Ramona answered. "When did you figure it out?"

"When his face was between my legs."

They both busted out laughing.

"Just kidding. It was actually post-face-between-the-legs."

Ramona frowned a little. "He wasn't, like … stalking you or anything, right?"

"I don't think so," I said, considering it again. "No, I mean, he seemed just as surprised to see me as I was to see him. But, man, let me tell you, the dude went downtown like it was his only purpose in life."

Veronica sighed. "I need to find a boyfriend."

"No, you *need* to find a fuck boy," I corrected. "Anyway, his name is Bodie, and he has a twin brother named Jude. Maybe his pussy-eating is a genetic trait." I waggled my brows.

She laughed and shoved me in the arm. "Ugh, you."

I just smiled.

"Are you going to see him again?" Ramona asked hopefully.

"I want to." I felt high, my body still humming and purring his name. "Guys, he kinda blew my mind. I can't believe I went to high school with him."

"So, what's the story?" Veronica stuffed her hands into the pockets of her black romper, her heels clicking on the sidewalk. Hair in a French twist, high on top, she looked totally elegant and gorgeous and classic, offset by full sleeves, a septum ring, and gauges like mine. I swear, she was the most badass of us all and the least emotionally available.

"Well, he was friends with Rodney—"

A collective groan passed over the peanut gallery of two.

"Just hear me out, for chrissake," I huffed. "*As* I was saying, he lived next door to Rodney, and I guess they'd been friends since the second grade or something. But when we hit high school, Rodney turned into a fox and started his band, and Bodie and Jude … well, I guess they were late bloomers. They were always so cute — you know, in that, like, puppy sort of way where you go *Aww*. But I didn't even know their real names. I knew them by Diddle and Dee Dee."

Veronica's mouth popped open. "Those nicknames are fucking awful."

I chuckled. "I know, trust me. I meant to ask him the story there, but I was way too busy with his dick."

They giggled.

"Guys," I said on a laugh, "I got diddled by Diddle."

I got a solid cackle for that one.

I shook my head, smiling. "I guess Rodney gave them the nicknames. That's not altogether surprising. Rodney was a cockjuggler."

"So are you," Ramona teased.

"It's true, and I don't judge a fellow juggler of cocks for their extracurriculars," I said with a hand out. "He was always kind of shitty to them." My tone softened a little, the edge all gone as I thought back, wishing I'd seen Bodie back then, wishing he hadn't just disappeared into my periphery. "They were around a lot — hanging at practice, sometimes at the parties. I just don't know why they hung around when Rodney was such an asshole to them. He was always teasing them about something, but he was so slick about it, you know? Most of the time, I didn't know if he was complimenting or cutting me down. Bodie had so much more in common back then than I realized."

I hated Rodney for what he'd done to all of us and found myself scowling at the memory of him, but I brushed it off and bucked up, smiling again with a shrug.

"Anyway, his loss. And now I find out that Diddle grew up to be Bodie, the super-hot surfer hunk. I would have bet a million dildos that I'd never see him again and been wrong, and I've never been so glad to be wrong in my life. He was incredible. Life-changing. He's real smart too. I mean, he was always a brainiac in high school, and now he does … something in computers, I think."

I got a look from Veronica. "You don't know what he does for a living?"

I made a noise like an air leak. "You are such a judgy whore, Ronnie. One of these days, the tables are gonna be turned, but instead of being all *Oh, look at me. I'm so perfect and smart and do everything right,*" I mocked, "I'll be like, *Way to go, bitch!* and buy you a really big, whorey penis cake."

She laughed.

"I'm gonna tell the erotic baker to make it spurt vanilla icing. I'll have them make licorice pubes and everything. Dick cake. It's genius really — two of my favorite things. And *that's* what you have to look forward to — no judgment."

Veronica shook her head, though she looked entirely amused. "You are so bad, Penny."

"I am. And I'm just like a bad penny too. I always turn up. There's no getting rid of me."

"Wouldn't want it any other way." She slung an arm over my shoulder. "You're a good friend—"

"Thank you," I said sweetly.

"Even if you're disgusting."

I leaned into her as we walked up to Tonic's door. "Aw, I love you too."

Ramona pulled open the door, and Veronica and I walked in, still canoodling. "Precious" by The Pretenders played over the speakers.

"Look, Ronnie — it's your song!"

She laughed, slapping me on the ass when we parted.

Ramona beelined for the counter where Shep waited, smiling from behind his thick beard. I swear to God, he and his brother, Joel, had the most virile hair of any men I'd ever seen.

She practically jumped into his big, meaty arms. Ramona was a tiny blonde thing covered in tattoos, and he was a big, hairy beast with a smile only for her.

I found myself smiling too, watching how gross they were. They almost made me wish I wanted to fall in love.

The thought actually made me laugh out loud.

I made my way to my station in the back and stepped into my little cube to get myself situated.

Tonic was one of the premier tattoo parlors in Manhattan, so good that most of us were booked out for months. Joel and Shep had opened it forever ago and had curated some of the best talent in the city — so much talent that they got attention in the way of awards, magazine features, and even a deal with a TV studio.

About a year before, we'd started filming a reality show in the shop, which basically turned the place into a telenovela. Drama city. But man, was it fun, and everyone had seemed to get it all out of their systems in the first season. Season two would start filming soon, kicking off with Ramona and Shep's wedding.

I sat at my desk, humming along to Stone Temple Pilots, pulling out my sketchbook to work on a piece for that afternoon, and in a snap, the day was nearly gone. My thoughts had been on Bodie the whole time.

I wondered all sorts of things — what was he doing? Where had he been all those years? Where the fuck did he learn to bang like that? What had happened to the kid I knew so long ago?

I'd always liked Diddle. I remembered him making me laugh, even when I was sad, the snark in him appealing to the snark in me.

I never thought about him like I had been since running into him, and now it bothered me a little that I'd been so shallow back then. Of course, I was sixteen and had been obsessed with a complete and utter dickhole. I'd had no sense. None. If I had, I'd have dumped Rodney and found somebody who at least had a little respect for me and wouldn't give Anna Dorf *rides home from school*, which I'd later learned was code for *blow jobs.*

One time, we had all been at a bonfire on the beach for a kegger, and Rodney just left me there. One minute he was there, the next, *poof*, I had been stranded at the beach with no ride home.

I'd been sitting away from the crowd, drunk and crying and dejected, and Bodie had sat next to me with his drink. He hadn't asked me what was wrong or pointed out that I was crying. He hadn't mentioned Rodney at all. He'd just sat there with me until my tears ran dry, and then he'd asked me if I'd ever seen *Donnie Darko*. And for the next hour, we'd talked about a hundred other things — movies and music, our teachers and school gossip — and by the end of the night, I'd felt like I was going to be okay after all. He'd asked me if I needed a ride home and delivered me safely at my doorstep like a white knight.

It was maybe one of the nicest things a guy had ever done for me without expectation on how they'd be repaid. Bodie had given exactly what I needed in the moment without me having to ask. He'd just known.

And now … now Diddle had gone and grown up, and boy, had he grown up right.

I couldn't help but smile, my heart all flippy and fluttery and ooey and gooey. I thought about all the things he'd done to me and thought about how many more I wanted him to do. I imagined his body, so strong and hard, his smile, so bright and gorgeous, and then smiled even wider at the knowledge that those braces that had helped disguise him back then had granted me that smile.

I thought about his lips and how they were the exact same shade as the head of his cock, just like I'd figured. And then I was thinking about his cock and clenching the saddle stool between my thighs to relieve the pressure. Three shifts of my hips, and I probably would have had an orgasm. That was just how ridiculously hot I was for him.

I didn't even know why he was any different from the other dudes I'd dated. I'd been with plenty of guys — hot guys, funny guys, smart guys, dumb guys. Rich guys, poor guys, and more. But Bodie was like the best of all of them, rolled into one. If I could have hand picked a guy, with the brains, looks, attitude, and wang skills I wished for, it would be him.

And now I couldn't stop thinking about him, couldn't stop wondering when I'd see him again. And I wanted to see him again as soon as possible even if it was too soon.

Maybe it was just because I'd known him so long ago. Maybe it was because he'd nailed me into oblivion. Maybe I was just infatuated, which was my primary function.

All I knew was this: I was so very impressed, and it was so very hard to impress me.

Once, I'd heard Patrick, one of the other tattoo artists, joking about a chick being dicknotized. And the word hit me as my needle buzzed in my hand, working on an elaborate henna design on a girl's thigh.

I was dicknotized.

I laughed way louder than was appropriate, thankful for having the foresight to have moved my gun, since the girl in my chair jumped a mile.

"Sorry," I said through my giggling as I got back to work. "So, I have to warn you. I'm a verbal processor, and there's something I've gotta talk out. Can I ask you a question?"

"Sure."

"Have you ever had dick so good that you can't ever forget it? Like, you're obsessed with it?"

"I'm a lesbian."

I rolled my eyes and traced the purple lines of the transfer on her thigh. "Oh, come on, killjoy. Voodoo pussy. Ever have one?"

She sighed wistfully. "Yeah. Her name was Brandie."

"Ha! Mine's Bodie. Maybe they're gender twins. So, what's the story with Brandie? Did you get over her VP? Ever forget it?"

"Nope. Never."

I frowned. "Well, the problem for me is that my dick is temporary."

"How come? Is he, like, from Austria or something?"

One of my brows rose. "That's really specific, but no. He isn't leaving the country."

"So, what? Is he not into you?"

I laughed. "Oh, I'm pretty sure he's into me. Like, *all the way* in, if you catch my drift."

"Yeah, I think I get it," she deadpanned. "So, what's the problem? He married?"

"No, not married either. Just … I don't know. I'm not really the settle-down type. I've dated more guys than I have lipstick, and I have a metric fuck-ton of lipstick. As in like a grand total of twenty-thousand-Sephora-points fuck-ton."

She snickered.

"I wonder if a couple more hook-ups might get him out of my system?"

She shook her head at me like she felt sorry for me.

"What? That's a valid, reasonable question. And entirely possible. Maybe he'll be super stinky or gross next time. Or maybe he never flosses."

"No one flosses."

I gave her a look. "Seriously, do you even know how to have fun?"

She gave me a look back.

"I like you," I said with a smile. "And I predict that in two more meetings with his magnificent hammerhead, I will have had it all fucked out of my system."

"Why two more?"

"Because, by the end of date three, it always goes south. Usually it's about them turning into crazies or coming on too strong. It's just like on *The Golden Girls*. Dudes propose to Blanche like she's the last woman on earth, and within a week of meeting her. She always turns them down though, that sassy bitch. She's my guru. When I don't know what to do, I just ask myself, *What would Blanche do?*"

"So, what would Blanche do?"

I thought about it. "Well, she'd bang him until it got weird and then kiss him goodbye, wiggling out the door, twiddling her fingers at him."

"Why not do that?"

"Ugh, I hate the thought of it getting weird, that's why. It's easier to just bolt before it happens. I've gotten so good at dipping out of the third-date situation."

"Mmm," she said noncommittally. "When will you see him for date two?"

I frowned. "I don't know. Date one was last night, and I'm still recovering. Physically. You know, because he nailed me so hard."

"Naturally."

"I have two whole bangs left, so I've gotta make the most of it. I need to maximize my bang-to-date ratio. But, if I could do whatever I wanted, I'd see him tonight. Or now. You don't mind if I just go, do you?"

She laughed. "Sure, and this is free, right?"

"Obviously."

I sighed, gun buzzing up my arm as I kept working. "He's exactly what I need right now."

"So are you going to call him?"

I frowned. "It hasn't even been twenty-four hours."

"Hold up," Ramona said from the wall of my booth, startling me.

"Jesus," I said, heart jumping. "I've got a tattoo gun in my hand, asshole. Give a warning cough or something."

"Sorry. I was eavesdropping and have unsolicited thoughts to share."

"Well, by all means, do tell." I gestured for her to go ahead.

"Since when do you follow rules? If you want to bang, call him and bang."

I nodded my head as I considered it. "I approve of your logic."

"I mean, what are you afraid of? That he'll think you're coming on too strong?"

We both laughed real loud at that. As if I knew another way to come on.

"Seriously though," Ramona said, "if you want to call him, call him."

I really wanted to, but the rule had been so deeply ingrained in my brain that I struggled to override it.

"Penny, if he called you right now and asked you over, what would you do?"

"Pretend I got diarrhea so I could leave," I answered without hesitation.

Ramona nodded. "That's what I thought. Also, someday you're going to try that line and it's not going to work."

I waved her off with a laugh. "Please. No one questions diarrhea." I turned to the girl in my chair for the final word. "What do you think? Honest answer, no bullshit."

She smirked. "I say, go get that dick."

So I laughed and decided to do just that.

- BODIE -

was so deep in the code on my screen that afternoon that I almost
missed my phone buzzing on the desk. And that would have been
a goddamn shame because it was a one-worded text from Penny.

Question.

Insta-smile happened as I picked up my phone, sat back in my
chair, and typed.

Answer.

Little dots bounced.

Would you think I was needy if I wanted to see you again tonight?

It would be a little hypocritical of me to judge.

More dots as she typed, and I stared at my phone with a healthy
helping of disbelief.

It hadn't even been a day, and here she was, asking to see me
— the girl who didn't date. And maybe it was nothing. All I knew
was that I'd gone to bed with a smile on my lips and her face in my
thoughts, and I'd woken up exactly the same way. My mind had been
rolling her around like a fine wine, appreciating every second I'd had
with her over and over again. And if I had a chance to see her again,
I'd take it, and I'd use it.

So, sounds like we're both needy then. What to do, what to do?

I typed back, my smile stretching. *I could think of a thing or two.
Or three. If you come over later, I can show you. I'll have visual aids.*

Tell me there will be graphs. I love a good graph.

I laughed out loud, garnering looks from Phil and Jude, who
flanked me at their monitors.

Girl, I've got graphs like you've never seen. Big, long graphs, packed with data I compiled all by myself.

Fuck, I love it when you talk dirty to me. I'm off at 8. Be there around 8:30?

Good. And make sure you don't have panties on.

Too late.

I set my phone down and leaned back in my chair, sighing, knowing I looked like a sap. My saving grace was that I was thinking about all the places I'd fuck Penny in my apartment in a few hours.

"Was that her?" Jude asked, looking like a hyperactive puppy.

"Yeah. She's coming over tonight."

Jude shook his head. "Man, I cannot believe you bagged *Penny*. After all this time. I guess your high school voodoo shrine in your closet didn't completely go to waste."

My face went flat. "I didn't have a shrine."

Phil snorted. "You kept a gum wrapper from a stick of Wrigley's she gave you junior year."

"Fuck you. It had her number on it."

"Sure it did, buddy. What about that broken bracelet you kept of hers?"

I rolled my eyes and chuffed. "She asked me to fix it."

"But you didn't," Jude shot.

"Because it was too broken," I volleyed.

"Then why didn't you give it back to her?"

"Because it was fucking broken, and I didn't want to admit it to her, dick."

Jude gave me a look. "You wanted to keep it."

"Jesus, I'm not arguing with you about this, Jude." He was right. I'd never tell him. "She's coming over tonight at eight-thirty, so I need you guys to … you know. Leave."

Phil frowned. "Man, we were supposed to work tonight."

"Yep, and now you two are going to work at Angie's."

47

Phil pouted. "I won't get any work done, though. I can't be with Angie and not hang out with her."

"You'll find a way."

Jude perked up. "Philly, ask her to make those blondie things she makes. Or brownies. Or, like, she can bake anything because I want to eat her sweets."

Phil's face hardened. "You're not eating my girlfriend's sweets. Those sweets are *mine*."

Jude put his hands up. "Easy there. I'm talking about the baked goods, not the baker."

Phil was still pouting. "I can't believe we're getting kicked out so you can nail Penny. No," he said with a shake of his head, "I can't believe you're actually nailing Penny. Is she the same as she was in high school?"

I thought about it. "Yes and no. She's just … *more* now. People love to say they don't give a fuck, but Penny actually means it. She's got her own gravity, and it's so hard not to want to know her, want to orbit her, even if just for a minute. When she walks in a room, everyone turns to look. But she was always that way. It was why Rod picked her out to torture in high school; he wanted to rein the brightest star and treat her like his pet."

"Ugh, that dick." Jude folded his arms. "Penny was so gone for him, and he didn't give a single shit about her. While she was gushing over their six-month anniversary, he was bragging about the laundry list of girls he'd fucked behind the bleachers. And she had no idea, not for two full years. She was stupid for him."

I sighed. "Well, seems Penny has flipped. She *doesn't do* dating. Ever, apparently."

Phil pushed his glasses up his nose. "Do you think it's because of Roddy?"

"I don't know." I rubbed the back of my neck. "I guess it's possible.

I don't know how many times I found her abandoned at a party or crying after one of their fights. It was like I had a sixth sense for her. I'd just stumble onto her and know how to make her feel better." I sighed. "All I know is that she says she doesn't do feelings and wants no strings, which is fine. For now."

Jude jacked a brow at me. "For now?"

I shrugged. "If I make myself indispensable, maybe I can hang onto her. I've got a shot, and I'll be damned if I'm gonna waste it."

"You sure that's wise?" he asked. "I mean, aside from the fact that she told you she didn't want anything serious."

"I'm not saying I want anything serious. I'm saying I have a feeling what she means is she doesn't want anything *complicated*."

"So you think you're an exception to the rule."

"Maybe."

"You want to be."

I smirked. "Maybe."

Jude snorted. "Well, you've only been fantasizing about her for ten years."

Phil warily watched me. "So, what are you going to do?"

"Whatever I can, Philly. Whatever I can. Keep things easy and simple. I don't want to own her."

Jude opened his mouth to speak, but I cut him off, "I mean I want to own her with my dick—" he looked satisfied at that, "but I'm not trying to put her in a cage, ever. I want to show her that it doesn't have to be messy or hard. It can be easy and fun. I just have to respect her space."

Jude laughed. "Oh, man, you should tell her that while you're nailing her. *I just respect you so much, Penny,*" he teased in a girlie voice.

"You are such a dick, dude."

He kept laughing. "I know."

"I didn't think I'd hear from her so soon, but I'm not complaining. Last night wasn't enough. Tonight won't be either. Hopefully she's just as into me, and we can keep this going. Easy."

Phil still wasn't convinced. "Doesn't sound easy. Relationships need three things to be successful." He held up his fingers and ticked them off. "Respect, communication, and trust. If any one of those things breaks down, you're in deep shit."

"Thanks, Dr. Phil." Jude started laughing all over again.

Phil looked wounded. "Angie told me that, and it's fucking true. I'm just saying — if you're not communicating about where you're at, your shit's gonna fall apart. Kablooey."

I tried not to overthink it. "Don't worry, Philly. I'll talk to her about it when the time comes."

"And in the meantime?" he asked.

I smirked. "In the meantime, you leave so I can woo her."

"With your dick," Jude said.

The fucker popped out of his chair and ran off before I could deck him.

Dicknotized

-PENNY-

wet my smiling lips as I knocked on Bodie's door, trying to ignore my banging heart, hyperaware of the soft fabric of my skirt against my bare ass and the point where my thighs met, warm and naked and sizzling at the thought of him.

Dicknotized. I'd been completely and utterly dicknotized.

The door swung open, revealing Bodie, tall and blond and beautiful, smiling that megawatt smile at me.

"Hi," I said stupidly, smiling back like an idiot.

"Hey. Come on in."

He moved aside so I could pass, and I swayed my hips, hoping he'd catch the motion of my black skater skirt to remind him that I wasn't wearing panties.

When I looked over my shoulder at him, it was obvious my nefarious, self-serving plan to convince him to ravage me had worked.

His eyes were on my upper thighs, and his lips were pinned between his teeth.

I decided to prolong the inevitable, stretching out the tease for as long as I could with the desire to rip each other's clothes off crackling between us.

I set my bag next to the couch and looked around the apartment with my heart beating well above the normal resting rate. "I didn't really get a good look at your place last night. I love it." The loft was open, with exposed bricks and warehouse windows, simple, modern furniture, and tidy, considering three dudes lived there.

"Thanks. Phil and Jude have been here for a few years now."

I shook my head, still looking around. "Man, they must have great jobs."

"They did," he said as he approached from behind. "Phil is a software engineer, and Jude is in digital design. They quit so we could work on our video game together."

I started wandering just before he reached me, heading toward their office space. "Really? You're designing a video game?"

"Mmhmm." He was still behind me where I'd left him.

"Which desk is yours?" I asked, standing in front of the three, which were all side by side, facing the windows. Six monitors sat on top, two for each desk.

"This one," he said against my neck, surprising me.

I hadn't heard him approach. One hand slipped around my waist while the other pointed at the desk in the middle.

"And what do you do here?" I leaned back into him, my plan largely forgotten when he pressed himself against my ass.

"Mmm, lots of math."

His hands moved from my hips to the bend at my thighs, his fingers reaching between my legs, and I arched my back to shift my ass against the length of him.

"Not really up for conversation?" I asked breathlessly.

"I am," he whispered against my neck.

His hot, wet tongue for only the briefest of moments.

"But first, I want to fuck you like I've been daydreaming about all day."

I swear to God, my pussy flexed like he was speaking directly to it.

His fingers clenched, gathering my skirt up with them until his glorious hands were on me.

First, he found my piercing and stroked it, circling with no hurry at all, teasing me. Then lower, dragging the pad of his finger up the line at my center, so slow, so light that he had my hips shifting, my core aching.

I whimpered, and his finger clenched at the sound.

"Don't tease me," I begged. "Fuck me."

"Oh, don't worry, Penny," he said calmly and quietly and with authority I hadn't realized I'd granted. "I'm going to."

My brain had already exploded, and my awareness was focused on every place we touched, so when he disappeared for a second, the loss was a cold shock against my hot skin. But then he grabbed my hand, pulling me over to the couch. When he sat, he pulled me down to sit next to him, my heart pounding as I tried to kiss him. He had other plans, stopping me by cupping my cheek. His thumb slipped into my mouth, and I closed my lips over it, telling him with my eyes that I wished something else were in its place entirely.

"Lie down," he ordered gruffly, guiding me to stretch across his lap with my ass up and my knees and elbows on the couch.

His cock was rock hard against the space between my belly button and clit, and I found myself wriggling against him, shifting slowly, my pulse frantic. I felt crazy. He was actually driving me mad, and he'd barely even touched me.

Dicknotized. If I were a cartoon, my eyes would be pinwheels with dicks in the middle, spinning around and around.

I was already panting, partly because I had no idea what he was going to do to me.

Where are his hands? Why aren't they on me? Why aren't they in me? I need them to touch me.

Part of me just wanted him to flip me over and fuck me senseless. The rest of me wanted him to tease me forever.

I looked back at him, but he wasn't looking at me. His eyes were on my ass — my skirt didn't fully cover it, lying down like I was.

"Cross your ankles." His hand found my ass cheek and squeezed, kneading it as his thumb slid under the hem of my skirt.

I did as I had been told, my heart hammering.

His hands were reverent as they lifted up my skirt, flipping it so my entire backside was on display. His face was reverent too, as if he'd found some secret of the universe under my skirt.

Bodie grabbed my ass again, groaning softly, his cock flexing under me. His thumb slipped between my ass and gripped, spreading me open, and I arched, lifting it into the air.

"That's right," he breathed, voice deep. "Open up for me." His hands moved — one kept me exposed, the other explored.

First were his fingers running down the line and to my clit for a split second of glorious pressure before trailing back up. Then down they went with more pressure as he passed through the slickness of my core, wetting his fingers even more. The third time, his fingers nestled between the length of my lips, the tips capturing the ball of my piercing, and my hips bucked in answer. When he shifted them laterally, the sensation across the entire length of me coupled with my piercing circling my clit was too much.

I gasped, heart slamming, nails scrabbling for purchase against the leather couch cushion, my face buried between my clenching hands.

"Please," I groaned. "Fuck, Bodie. Please. *Please.*"

He said nothing, and I couldn't look, not with starbursts flashing behind my pinched lids.

I felt his wet fingers move up and then his thumb, now somehow wet too.

It was so slick, so smooth, that it didn't even give me pause when he circled the tight hole I rarely let anyone near.

His thumb gently ran across me, his fingers stroking my pussy at the same speed, same pace, the pressure increasing until he flexed his fingers and slid into me, both holes at once.

I raised off his lap, my mouth hanging open, my breath frozen in my lungs, but he didn't stop. He stroked me, played my body, pushed every button, even buttons I hadn't known I had. His fingers performed some exquisite gymnastics that I'd be thinking about for a decade, though in the moment I didn't care how he was doing it, only that he didn't stop. Ever. His pinkie rocked against my clit as the rest of his hand fucked me with tender determination.

The deeper he went, the harder he went, the less control I had. Part of me wondered if I'd ever had any at all.

I couldn't even move, just laid there on his lap with my ass in the air. My hands moved to his leg under me, gripping his jeans, bracing myself.

"Come on, Penny," he said roughly, begging. "Come, so I can fuck you."

His hand flexed again, and three pressure points that he pressed screamed.

"That's right. Come on. Come for me."

Another flex. My heart strained against my ribs.

"F-f-fuck," I groaned as my body orgasmed, not a single thing in my control. "Fuck, fuck, fuck," I whispered against the leather of the couch cushion with every pulse of my body, full in every possible way and nowhere near full enough.

"Thank God," he breathed. A flurry of motion, he moved my

limp body off his lap, put my knees on the ground, and moved behind me, kneeling between my legs.

I barely possessed any awareness of my surroundings, not until he grabbed my hips and slipped into me from behind, hitting my G-spot like he fucking had radar for it.

"*Fuck!*" I cried, sliding my hands into the back of the cushion to hang on as the orgasm I'd thought was gone got a second wind.

"Jesus fucking Christ, Penny," he growled as he pounded me.

His hand twisted in my hair and pulled. My orgasm thundered back to life with every pump of his hips. I didn't even know how — it just wouldn't stop, rolling through me like it would never end. My body was on fire, writhing and wriggling and flexing and contracting as he slammed into me over and over again, finally coming with a moan, a cry, a shudder, and jackhammering hips that hit the end of me so hard that I couldn't breathe.

I don't even know how we came down or how long it took or what happened after that — I blacked out from bliss.

When I regained a fraction of my senses, I found myself lying on the rug, tucked into Bodie's side, both of us still fully clothed other than his unbuckled pants, condom still on.

I didn't even remember him putting it on, and the fact that it hadn't even crossed my mind when he was nailing me from behind freaked me out. But only for a second. Lucky for me, he was a trustworthy guy, and he had been since high school. Maybe it hadn't crossed my mind because I *did* trust him.

That foreign thought freaked me out too.

I didn't have too long to contemplate it before Bodie seemed to reconnect his wires, turning to look down at me with a smile.

"So," I started, the word lazy, "if you tell me you earned your nickname by fucking girls like that in high school, I'm really going to be burned about missing that shot."

He chuckled and ran his hand down my arm. "Trust me — that was not the case. Roddy started it. First I was D, and Jude was Judie. Then D evolved into Diddle and Judie to Dee Dee. The nickname had nothing to do with anything other than him trying to humiliate me. I didn't see a vagina in real life until college."

"Really?" I asked wondrously, nestling into his side a little more.

"Yeah, really. I mean, you saw me. When it came to my friends, I had a mouth and confidence to beat their asses at literally anything, but I didn't have the courage to *really* talk to girls. You and I were around each other enough that I could have. I should have."

"We talked," I offered.

"Yeah, but not like that. I just didn't think I had a chance. Not then."

My heart sank. I wanted to tell him that he was wrong, but at sixteen, I had been looking for guys like Rodney — fast car, fast hands. Hell, I didn't know how different I was now. The thought made me feel even worse.

So instead of arguing, I curled deeper into his side.

His arm flexed in answer.

"College was … fun then?"

"You could say that." I could hear him smiling as he continued, "It probably wouldn't have been, if not for surfing."

"Yeah, what's the story with that? I don't remember you surfing in high school."

"That's because I didn't. My dad tried to get me and Jude to surf with him from the minute we could swim, and we did a little when we were kids, but once we hit junior high, we were more interested in playing D&D in the basement than sports. I blame the whole reject-what-your-parents-want idea. They're total hippies. I mean, they supplied weed to half the high school like it was fucking milk and cookies."

I laughed. "Your mom made a mean edible. She'd put her *vegan* cookies in those little sandwich baggies with a ribbon on it and smile and pat your cheek when she gave it to you. Half the time, she wouldn't even let us pay."

"It's funny now, but I was so embarrassed. How I didn't turn out to be a burnout is beyond me." He was still smiling, fingertips tracing circles on my back. "Anyway, before we left for college, Dad finally convinced us to surf with him for the summer, and Jude and I figured it was the old man's last chance to hang with us before we were gone. We fell in love with it and went at least once a day in college. We were those crazy fuckers, freezing our asses off at five a.m. so we could get a good session in before class."

"I love that," I said, imagining Bodie running into the ocean in slo-mo with a board under his arm. "And then came the girls?"

"If I'd realized just how many girls, I'd have picked up surfing way sooner. Maybe then I could have stolen you away from Rod — that dick."

"Ugh, he really was. Is?"

"Is. We're still friends on social media. His Snapchat makes me want to fucking vomit."

I felt squirmy at the mention of Rodney. We weren't friends anywhere, not after he'd stretched my heart out to the point that it lost its shape.

I changed the subject. "Hey, I hate to ask, but I was so antsy to get over here that I didn't eat after work. Do you have anything? I'm not picky. Popcorn will do. Cold cuts. Hot Pockets. Whatever you've got."

"Yeah. We've got some frozen pizzas, I think."

"Mmm. Totino's?" I asked as we got up.

"Red Baron."

"I'll take what I can get, I guess."

He laughed and headed back toward the bathroom, fooling around between his legs as he walked. "Gimme one second."

"Take your time," I said, my eyes on his ass, the top of which was exposed from his unfastened pants.

He disappeared into the bathroom, and I sat down at the island in the middle of the kitchen, leaning on the counter, musing.

My body purred like a kitten, thanks to him, and I found myself fluttery and smiley and absolutely happy. Bodie was good and he was fun and he was perfect. And I knew I was going to miss him when he was gone.

One more date, max.

I loathed the notion. I loathed it so deeply that I felt sick at the thought of not seeing him again.

He walked back in before I could think twice about it, smiling that goddamn smile that made my vagina spell his name in Morse code. I pushed my feelings away. I'd live in the moment. It was what I did best.

Bodie opened up the freezer and moved things around for a minute. "Bad news. No pizza."

I frowned. "What have you got?"

More shuffling.

"A bag of peas, a half a bag of crinkle fries, and some popsicles with freezer burn."

My frown deepened.

He closed the door and turned to lean on the other side of the island. "We could order one?"

"That'll take forever and I'm starving. What are the odds of a PB and J?"

He smirked. "Pretty good. Just depends on your jelly preference."

"Grape or strawberry?" I asked. This was a test.

He narrowed his eyes, recognizing the challenge. "Strawberry."

"Good. If you'd said grape, the whole deal would have been off."

He laughed and moved around the kitchen, gathering supplies.

"Wait, it's smooth peanut butter, right?"

He shot me a look over his shoulder from the pantry. "Of course.

We're not animals, Penny."

"Thank God. Proper PB and J has universal rules that must be honored."

He laid everything out on the island between us. "So, how did you get into the tattoo business?"

"Well, I was always into art, you remember?"

He nodded as he set four slices of bread out on a cutting board.

"After graduation and Rodney dumping me, I just had to get out of Santa Cruz. My aunt lived here in Manhattan, so I crashed with her. She was tatted up like crazy. I went with her to get a few at Joel's shop, and when I was waiting for her one time, sketching, Joel asked if he could take a look. I'd never considered the profession until he asked me if I'd be interested."

Bodie smiled. "Kismet."

I folded my hands on the countertop. "It kinda was. He gave me my first tattoo. This one." I turned to show him the piece on my shoulder and upper arm. "Joel … he's like a big brother to everyone at the shop, and he brought most of us in as apprentices and taught us everything he knows, which is a lot."

"Like a big brother … not a big boyfriend?" Bodie asked, still smiling.

I laughed. "Oh, definitely not. He's not my type, and plus, he's engaged to the producer of our reality show, Annika."

His hand stilled, peanut butter knife hanging midair. "Reality show?"

Another laugh. "I thought you might have known. Don't watch much TV?"

He shook his head. "You're on TV?"

"I am. It's a reality show — *Tonic,* named after the shop where we work. Real original, I know. We're about to start filming season two."

His head was still shaking. "That's crazy. What's that like?"

I shrugged. "It's fun. Kind of weird having cameras in your face all the time, but I don't mind. Last season was drama though — Annika was kind of a bitch. She lied to Joel before she made it up to him, and he ended up putting a ring on it. I wanted to rip her face off for doing him wrong, but she's like nine feet tall and Russian, so I'm pretty sure she'd beat my ass. I've got a real big bark though."

He slathered on the peanut butter and opened the jelly jar. "I remember that bark very well."

I laughed. "Yeah, I guess the Rodney breakup wasn't super private."

"I'm pretty sure every parent and student in the audience heard what you had to say about him dumping you at graduation."

I felt myself blush. "Well, he deserved every word."

"No arguments here. You guys used to fight like crazy."

"Because he drove me crazy. Like, on purpose. I swear, he kept me just close enough to keep me coming back for more and far enough away that I never felt like he was really mine."

Bodie didn't speak for a second as he spread strawberry jelly over the peanut butter, all the way to the edges, like a good boy.

"Think he's why you don't date?" he asked, his face still.

I chuffed. "I don't think. I know." I thought about it, feeling my willpower turn into steel at the thought of Rodney. "Here's the thing, Bodie. When I love, I don't do it halfway. I go all the way into the fire until it burns me up. It's obsessive. I lost myself once to someone else, and I'm not doing it again."

He nodded and closed one sandwich, then the other. "You sure it wasn't just Rod?"

I shrugged. "Not really interested in finding out."

"So you've never felt the urge to stick with a guy, even without commitment?" He sliced our dinner into triangles and plated them.

I squirmed, and he saw it.

"I'm not asking for myself, Penny. I'm just curious."

I sighed. "If I'm being honest? No. I used to, and I've tried to, which only reinforced my belief that relationships aren't for me. It's just fun, and I don't need any more commitment than that. I'm committed to my job. I have my girlfriends, and they wouldn't hurt me. I don't need a man to be happy. I just need a man for my vagina to be happy, but that bitch doesn't run my life."

He laughed at that and handed my plate over. "Want something to drink?"

"Just water, thanks."

"I've really only done flings too," he said as he made his way around the kitchen. "I mean, there were a few girls I dated for a while, but nothing serious. Just never turned into more. Know what I mean?"

"Yeah, I do. It's so hard when you're different people or you have different expectations. But sometimes there's just no connection. Like when they don't get your jokes — that's the worst. Or they just go straight to stage five clinger."

He chuckled and set our glasses in front of us. "It was so weird when I first started dating because I had no idea what I was doing. Like, I had no experience, so I thought I was supposed to woo, date, and fall in love with every woman I was interested in, so I tried. But then I realized that chicks were like guys sometimes too. That dating is not about wooing and love. It's all about expectations, you know? Like some girls really do want full commitment with a ring in the future, or it's nothing. But that's such a weird thing to expect when you're nineteen."

I picked up one triangle of my sandwich. "I mean, seriously. People don't know how to live in the now. Why do we all have to have some five-year plan that won't even be possible to follow? Life doesn't work that way. Everything is fluid."

I took a bite and moaned as my eyes rolled back in my head. "I don't know if it's because I haven't had one of these in forever or because I'm starving, but this is incredible."

He smiled at me as he chewed and swallowed. "It's the peanut-butter-to-jelly ratio."

"You and your math," I said with a shake of my head and a smile on my lips, wondering why he had to be so funny and smart and hot and amazing. It wasn't even fair. "The only time I love math is when it's coming out of your mouth."

His smile climbed on one side. "What's sixty-nine plus sixty-nine?"

I narrowed my eyes, trying to sort it out.

"Dinner for four."

I laughed and took another bite.

"I'm like pi — really long and I go on forever."

More laughing, lips closed, chasing it with a sip of water so I wouldn't choke.

He leaned on the counter, still smirking at me. "I'm not obtuse; you're acute chick."

"Okay, that one was bad." I kept stuffing my face now that the hunger switch had been flipped.

"What do math and my dick have in common?"

My brow rose as I swallowed.

"They're both hard for you."

That time, I laughed hard enough that I snorted.

Bodie set down his sandwich and dusted off his hands. The look in his eyes made me take one more bite, a big one that I chewed hastily, figuring dinner might be over.

"Can I plug my solution into your equation?" he asked, voice low and smile crooked as he rounded the island.

"I dunno. Can you?"

"Maybe I can be your math tutor for the night." He spun me around on the stool. "Add a bed." His hands slipped up my thighs, opening them. "Subtract your clothes." His hands moved higher until they rested in the bend of my hips. "Divide your legs." He nestled between my legs, angling for my lips. "And multiply."

I wanted to laugh, but when he kissed me, I forgot what was so funny.

- BODIE -

Obsessed— *that was what I was.*

Obsessed with her salty, sweet lips against mine.

Obsessed with her milky-white thighs around my waist.

Obsessed with her silky purple hair between my fingers.

Obsessed with *her*.

I'd been kissing her for long enough that she was panting, and my heart was thundering like a racehorse.

She was perfect — other than the fact that she didn't want to date me. Yet.

I broke away, leaving her sitting on the stool with her eyes still shut and her lips parted like they were waiting for me.

"I want you naked," I growled as I reached behind me to pull off my shirt.

When I looked down at her, her eyes were half open as she fumbled with the zipper on her skirt.

I dropped my pants and stepped out of them, grabbed her by the waist to lift her up and set her down hard enough that her ass slapped against the surface of the counter with a pop and a yelp.

My hands moved up her waist and under her Ramones shirt, pushing it up and over her head. Her lavender hair spilled out of the neck like a waterfall, and I tossed the shirt behind me. She reached for my face, pulling me to her for another kiss, and I lost myself in her hot mouth for a long moment — until she shifted, pressing her wet pussy against my shaft.

I groaned into her mouth with one hand clutching the back of her head to keep her mouth against mine while the other roamed to her breast, kneading and squeezing, my thumb playing with the barbell in her nipple until she whimpered.

That sound connected straight to my cock. I wanted to record it. I wanted to hear it on a loop. I wanted to touch her until she moaned and called my name.

I broke away. "Naked. Now."

She reached behind her back, panting, and she unhooked her bra as I swept an arm on the island behind her to clear it, sending utensils clattering to the floor. She was shimmying out of her skirt when I lost all patience and pulled it down her legs to toss it.

"Lie down," I ordered.

Penny rested back on her elbows, her body stretched out in offering, illuminated by the overhead lights.

She was a fucking dream, a fantasy, with her legs spread open and eyes hot, locked on mine, as I grabbed a condom from the pocket of my jeans. When I ripped open the packet, she shifted her gaze to watch my hands grip my cock and roll it on. Her lip slipped between her teeth, and I stroked.

"What do you want, Penny?"

"I want your cock," she breathed, opening her legs wider. "I've wanted it since I walked in the door. What do you want, Bodie?"

I stepped to her, one hand still pumping my shaft, the other grabbing her ankle to pull her to the edge of the counter.

"I want to bury myself in you until I can't get any deeper. I want to fill you up so much, you'll feel empty when I'm gone." I rested the tip of my cock against her piercing, pressing it into her with my thumb on my shaft. "I want to fuck you so hard, you'll never forget me."

She writhed and whispered, "I won't if you won't."

I ran my cock down the line, and when I hit the dip, I flexed my hips, filling her agonizingly slow, my eyes on the seam where I disappeared into her.

"*Fuck,*" she whispered.

When I glanced up, her head was hanging back, her neck stretched out, her long white fingers circling her taut, rosy nipple.

"Jesus," I breathed, my thighs trembling as I pulled out slow and eased back in.

My hands slipped under her thighs and brought them up parallel with my body, her calves tucked between my ribs and arms. I felt her feet stretch out to a point as I pulled out and slammed in.

She lay down flat, chest heaving as one hand worked her nipple and the other found the piercing between her legs, rubbing a circle in time with my hips.

She felt like heaven, soft and wet and tight, and as I watched her touching herself, I was too close, too soon. I wanted to fuck her all night, all day tomorrow, all week. For a year. For as long as she'd have me.

I slowed my pace and pulled out, eliciting another whimper from her — this time, in mourning — but I ignored it, grabbing her thighs to scoot her back until her hair hung over the edge, giving me room to crawl up with her. I pushed her thighs apart with my knees, and she lifted her legs, opening them up, hooking them around my hips as I positioned myself to slide into her again.

"Come on," she said hotly. "Fill me up."

So I did, not at all gently that time, not stopping until there was no space between us.

I caught sight of the jelly jar and smiled, slowing my hips so I could reach for it. She peeled her eyes open and looked over, wickedly smiling back.

"Still hungry?" I asked.

She nodded.

I dipped my thumb into the jelly and brought it to her lips, parted and so full, smearing it across the bottom one. Her pink tongue slid out to lick it clean, and I cupped her jaw, slipping my thumb into the heat of her mouth. She closed her lips and sucked, wrapping her wet tongue around it.

I hooked the digit and forced her mouth open so I could take it with my own, wanting her tongue against mine.

My hips took control, rocking and pumping and fucking her, unaware of anything before or after, only that moment, only her body.

She bent her legs wound around my hips to force me to get as deep as possible, holding me there as she twisted at the waist to guide me onto my back. I did, not caring that I was lying on a sandwich, not caring about anything outside of the feeling of being buried in Penny.

She sat up and rested her hands on my chest, her eyes down and lips parted, and when she moved, when she shifted her hips and moaned, my head kicked back, my hands gripping her tattooed thighs like she'd fly away if I didn't hang on to her.

"Bodie," she called.

I found myself enough to open my eyes and sit up, wrapping my arms around her to crush her against me, to bury my face in her neck, to twist her hair in my hands as she rocked against me making the sweetest noises I'd ever heard.

"I'm gonna come," she whispered, her hips moving faster with every rotation.

I let her go, leaning back enough that I could watch her with my hands on her hips, guiding her as she ground and bounced harder against me, the slap of her ass against my thighs speeding my pulse, speeding time. And when she came, breasts jostling, a cry on her lips, eyes pinched shut, I kept her hips going as I came so hard, I thought my chest was going to explode from the force.

The sight of her coming would be burned into the back of my eyelids for the rest of my life.

She collapsed on top of me, and I lay back, taking her with me. She pulsed around my cock, slowing with each heartbeat, and I pumped inside of her lazily in answer.

"Hey, Penny?" I asked, my voice low and rough.

"Hmm?" she hummed against my chest.

"Are you the square root of negative one? Because you can't be real."

She laughed, nestling a little deeper into my chest, and I tried to pretend like she wasn't already finding her way into my heart.

Fuck You, Brad

-BODIE-

enny had left that night with a long goodbye kiss and a smile full of promise, and since we'd seen each other twice in twenty-four hours, I figured I'd hear from her soon.

Wrong.

The first day hadn't been so bad although I ended up in the gym twice to try to get my mind off of her. The second day, I'd tried to satiate my thoughts by watching her show. I'd avoided it because I thought it might be creepy, and when I'd turned it on, it was with the intention of watching a single episode. Eight hours later, I'd made it almost through the season and had Cheetos dust all over my T-shirt. And I'd felt a zillion times worse. I'd even picked up my phone to text her enough times that I threw the fucking thing in my nightstand drawer so I'd stop thinking about it. That had lasted a solid hour before I'd caved and retrieved it and commenced staring.

I was on day three, and I wasn't happy about it.

Three days. Three agonizing days of pounding away at my keyboard instead of her ass. Three days without a single sexual pun that hadn't come from my brother. Three nights of my hand on my jock, thinking about her spread eagle on my counter. Three long days without my hands in places they tingled at the thought of. Places where my tongue should be, like deep in her—

"Dude, did you hear me?"

I turned to Jude, frowning. "Huh?"

He rolled his eyes. "God, you're so fucking sad. Just text her."

I scowled. "Don't you think I would if I could?"

"What's the matter? Fingers broken? Didn't pay your phone bill?"

"Fuck you, Jude."

"You act like she's some delicate fucking flower."

My eyes narrowed. "She's more delicate than you think. I can't just text her, man. That's not how this works."

He shook his head. "Your big plan to woo Penny is to not talk to her? It's to let her ghost you?"

"She hasn't ghosted me, asshole."

"Maybe she has, dickwad. You haven't heard anything in three days and have been walking around here like a goddamn rottweiler who had his bone stolen."

My scowl deepened.

"Get it? Your *bone*?"

"I hate you," I muttered as I turned back to my screen.

"Liar. You know I'm right."

I turned in my chair to face him again. "No, you're fucking not. My big plan is to leave the ball in her court so I don't come off as needy. The last thing a chick who wants no strings needs is a guy up her ass."

"Maybe she *does* need a guy up her ass," he joked with his

eyebrows waggling.

"Fucking cretin."

"I'm just saying, what rule states you can't even text her after three days?"

"Oh my God," I groaned with a roll of my eyes. "All of them, dipshit. You had a girlfriend way too long."

"And you might have cocked it all up by acting like you're not interested."

I huffed. "I've gotta play this smart, Jude. She's going to come back around. I know it."

"And if she doesn't?"

"Then I'll figure it out." My hope sank like the Titanic, slowly and with a chill. He wasn't wrong, but he wasn't right. There was no way of knowing, not until she texted me. I checked my phone, just like I had about four billion times in the last three days.

Nothing.

I ran a hand through my hair.

Jude watched me. "You should take a walk. Get out of the apartment. We've been cooped up here for three days, working and binge-watching TV, and I think you need some vitamin D, since you're not giving any."

I made a face. "Hilarious, jackhole. And I would have already *seen* her show if you'd fucking told me about it when you found out."

"I *did* tell you, bro."

"Dude, there's no way I would forget you telling me that *Penny* was on TV. Literally no fucking way."

"Well, there's no fucking way I *wouldn't* have told you because I knew you'd had a boner for her for a decade."

I chuffed, opening my mouth to argue, but he cut me off.

"I'm serious. Why don't you get us ice cream? It's, like, a thousand degrees out, and you're miserable. No one can be miserable after ice cream. It's scientifically impossible."

I sighed and stood, sticking a finger in his face. "Fine. But only if you promise to keep your fucking mouth shut about Penny. It's hard enough without your nagging."

"Yeah, I bet it is."

He tried to flick me in the nuts, but I jumped back and countered with a solid slap upside the back of his head.

"Get me some cherry chunk," he called after me.

I flipped him off over my shoulder as I walked to the door, opened it, and slammed it behind me.

Frustrated was a good word to use — sexually, emotionally, generally. I'd had a little taste of something that had consumed me like wildfire, and now that I was deprived of it, I felt wild. Feral. Like I'd crawl out of my skin if I couldn't see her, smell her, touch her.

Even the thought of touching her had my johnson reacting.

Maddening, that was what it was.

I stepped out into the blazing summer afternoon, and my mood spoiled like rotten milk in the heat. I mean, why hadn't she called? We'd spent an hour in the shower the last time I saw her and another hour in my room, in my bed, touching, talking, kissing. She'd made me feel so good, and I thought the feeling was mutual.

Maybe I was wrong. Maybe she was playing me.

Maybe I was just a fuck boy, someone whose body she could use.

The thought made me feel cheap. Cheaper still when I wondered how many guys out there had felt just like I did.

Maybe Jude was right and I needed a new plan. At what point should I stop waiting? At what point should I take action, and what could I do? Because one thing was perfectly clear.

I wanted to be with Penny in any context she would let me have her. But to be with her, I had to play by her rules even if I bent them to get my way. I wanted to win, and I wanted to win *her*.

There wasn't much I could do besides texting, not without crossing the line. Showing up at her work would *definitely* be crossing the line. I could send her flowers at the tattoo parlor, but that would be way too big, too serious. I imagined her getting flowers from me and her eyes bugging out like I was psycho. Or worse — I imagined her laughing.

No. Definitely no flowers.

I huffed, running my fingers through my hair again, annoyed with myself for being so annoying. But I felt like an addict with no dealer, cracked out and irrational and driven to the point of desperation.

At that thought, I took a breath and told myself to ease up. The plan was to wait, so I'd wait.

She'd come around. My hope glimmered, revived by the thought. And when she did, I'd take advantage of every single second I had with her.

- P E N N Y -

The bell over the shop's door rang, and Ramona laughed.

"Penny, delivery."

I glanced up from my desk in my booth to find a delivery guy looking around the room with a vase of flowers in his hand.

My heart shot into my throat.

Bodie!

Yeah, his name had an exclamation point in my head because I hadn't stopped thinking about him for three full days and nights, and I was mildly — extremely — annoyed that he hadn't texted me. Of course, I hadn't texted him either.

The third date loomed, and I wanted to stave it off for as long as possible. I mean, until I couldn't even stand it anymore. I was probably almost there because the thought of those flowers being from him made my vagina do stuff. Squeezy, clenchy stuff.

I hopped out of my seat and bounded to the delivery guy. "Are those for me?" I asked, grinning like a goddamn fool.

"If you're Penny, yes, they are."

I squealed and bounced on the balls of my feet. Every one of my co-workers watched me like I'd been possessed.

I had been. By Bodie's dick and math jokes.

The delivery guy had me sign his little doohickey and handed me the flowers, which I promptly skipped over to the desk with, and Ramona and Veronica appeared by my side, eyeballing me.

"This is literally the first time I've ever seen you excited about getting flowers," Ramona said incredulously.

Veronica watched me like my body had been snatched by an alien.

"They have to be from Bodie," I said, digging through the rose blooms for a card. "He hasn't even texted."

"We know. You've only mentioned it every hour, on the hour, for three days." Ramona patted my arm.

I found the card and plucked it out of the bouquet with an, *Aha!*, opening it with frantic fingers.

My stomach fell into my shoes with my smile.

"To Penny. Miss you. Consider my offer. Love, Brad," I read aloud.

Veronica groaned. "Ugh, fuck you, Brad!"

I read it again, sure there was some mistake. "Brad? I haven't even fucking seen that shithead in weeks, not since he asked me to move in with him. The curse of date three." I picked up the bouquet by the vase and dropped it in the tall trash can behind the desk.

Ramona eyed them, torn. "Do you have any idea how expensive those are?"

I pointed at her. "Don't you touch those. Those flowers are

tainted by freaknut *Brad* and his inability to take a hint. Those flowers are from the wrong guy."

I was whining, and I didn't even care. I was way too butthurt to care.

"It's not fair," I said, bobbling a little.

Joel frowned at me from his station in the front of the shop before glancing at Veronica. "What's the matter with her?"

She took my shoulders gently, angling me to him as I pouted. "Bodie hasn't called her."

"New fuckbuddy?" he asked.

"Doesn't he like me?" I asked, my voice squeaky.

"I'm sure he does, honey," Veronica cajoled. "Maybe you should just text him. You obviously want to see him again."

I groaned. "I know, but it's date three! And instead of turning into a pumpkin, he's gonna turn into *Brad*." I tossed a hand at the trashcan as if those flowers explained everything.

Joel sighed. "You like the guy, right?"

I nodded.

"Then fucking text him, you weirdo."

"But what if—"

"Who cares? You want to see him, so see him. If it falls apart, deal with it."

I was still pouting. "Why do you make everything seem so simple?"

"Because it is." He rested his meaty, tattooed forearms on his knees and leaned toward me. "Listen, your afternoon job canceled, right?"

"Yeah," I answered begrudgingly.

"It's too hot in here, and your booth is the hottest in the shop. Go cool off. Cold shower. Ice cream. Something."

"But what about the walk-ins?"

"Max is here for walk-ins. You just get outta here." He jabbed a finger at the door with authority.

I sighed. "Fine. But only because you said ice cream, and that's my weakness." I could already taste the cold salted caramel on my tongue. This also made me a little sad — it reminded me of Bodie.

Who even ARE you right now?

I walked back over to my station to grab my bag, stopping by Veronica's station next to Ramona, who leaned on the short wall.

"Just text him, Pen," Ramona said. "You'll feel better."

I nibbled my bottom lip. "Even if he gets clingy? Even if he bugs out?"

She laughed and kissed me on the cheek on my way out. "Better him than you."

I sighed and headed into the sweltering sun, slipping on my sunglasses.

My problem was this: I was obsessing.

I was so predictable, I could have been a fucking atomic clock. I'd always been this way, and it was one of the many reasons why I didn't date. I didn't like how I felt, which reaffirmed that the three-date rule was just as much for myself as it was for them. And here I was, after only *two* dates, already all itchy over Bodie. He was just so dreamy and funny and smart, and I couldn't stop thinking about him.

All of this was dangerous.

Of course, it was entirely possible that I'd gotten weird simply because I was holding out. Maybe if I just ripped off the Band-Aid and saw him again, it would take care of itself. Once he got all gooey on me, I'd probably lose interest anyway.

That placating and naive thought put a little spring in my Chucks and a smile on my lips.

We could have our last hurah and let the chips fall where they may. Let fate take its course. Which, in my experience, meant I'd be absolutely over him and ready for whatever was next.

My heart folded in on itself at the fleeting thought that it might be *me* who'd be gooey over *him*. But I waved my thoughts away like bumblebees after the honey pot and resolved to text him when I got home.

But when I pulled open the door of the ice cream parlor, I stopped dead in my tracks as a smile spread across my face like peanut butter on toast.

I didn't have to text him after all because he was standing right in front of me.

His broad back was to me as he waited in line, peering into the cooler at the flavors on display.

I swear to God, my heart did a roundoff back handspring and stuck the landing as I walked up to him.

"If I went binary, you'd be the one for me," I said as I brushed against his arm, my knuckles grazing his.

He whipped his head around, blue eyes bright. And when they connected with mine, his smile could have lit up midnight.

He let out a laugh. "That was a good one. I didn't know you spoke nerd."

I shrugged, smiling. "I don't. I speak Google."

"What are you doing here?" he asked, sounding surprised.

"Getting ice cream. Isn't it obvious?"

Another laugh as the attendant asked him what he wanted.

Bodie turned to me. "Want to join me?"

"I'd love to."

"Know what you want?"

"A scoop of salted caramel in a waffle cone, please."

The attendant nodded and looked to Bodie.

"Mint chocolate, one scoop in a waffle cone too. Thanks."

We stepped over to the register, and Bodie pulled out his wallet to pay.

"How've you been?" he asked, the question tight from hiding another — *Why haven't I heard from you?*

But I smiled. He was still interested, and that right there was proof.

"I've been good, just working a lot. You?"

"Same. Jude kicked me out since I hadn't seen daylight in days. It's too hot to go outside without the promise of the ocean or ice cream."

We were handed our ice cream cones and turned to find the inside of the shop packed.

I frowned. "Way too hot, but outside we go."

He followed me to a table for two on the patio, and we took seats across from each other.

I grinned. I couldn't help it. I swear he'd gotten hotter in three days — his eyes were bluer, his hair blonder, his smile brighter as he grinned right back and put on his sunglasses.

Either that or my imagination was a sad, sad substitute for the real thing.

"Highway to Hell" came on the overhead speakers as I took a long lick of my ice cream and moaned.

Pretty sure Bodie was staring at my mouth from behind his shades.

"I've been thinking about you," I started, sticking out my tongue to run my ice cream across it.

He wet his lips and smirked. "Me too."

When he licked his ice cream and flicked his tongue at the top, I felt warm all over, and it had nothing to do with the ninety-five degree weather.

I crossed my legs, my mouth undeterred as I licked that ice cream like my future depended on it.

"It was *so hard* not to text you." I closed my lips over the top of my scoop.

"How hard?" he teased me back.

I just kept watching that creamy ice cream on his tongue, squeezing my thighs together like a goddamn vise.

"It just kept getting harder and harder with no hope of release. Cruel really."

"So why didn't you text me?"

I shrugged, playing coy. "Didn't want you to think I was easy."

We both laughed for a minute.

"So how much did you think of me?" I asked innocently, fondling my cone.

"Oh, only about every minute of every day." His feet sandwiched my foot on the ground and squeezed, shifting his sneakers up and down in slow, opposite strokes, just an inch or two's distance.

Somehow, it drove me completely insane.

"You?" he asked.

"A time or two. Once when I was in the shower."

"Mmm," he hummed with his cone in his mouth.

"Another time when I was lying in bed, wishing you'd texted me. I thought about you a *lot* that night. Three times. Every time, I would think I'd gotten you out of my head and *whoops* — you'd pop up again."

"Well, I can't help popping up. Not when I remember you eat ice cream like that."

I smiled and dragged my tongue around the diameter of the scoop.

"All that thinking and no doing," he said. "I really feel like we should be *doing* a whole lot more than we have the last couple of days."

I nodded. "Why didn't you text me?" I tried to keep the uncertainty out of my voice.

If he'd heard it, he didn't react.

He shrugged and echoed my words, "Didn't want you to think I was easy."

I laughed. "Maybe I like easy."

"Well then, you're in luck. Because when it comes to you, I'm so easy."

Bodie's elbows were on the table and so were mine, the two of us leaning toward each other.

"What do you say we get out of here?" he asked.

And I smiled back. "I thought you'd never fucking ask."

Commando

- B O D I E -

We **hurried down the sidewalk**, still holding our ice cream, our free hands threaded together, fingers shifting and stroking each other's. Only Penny could make holding hands feel dirty.

She lived just around the corner — we didn't even have to stop for a light — and when we reached the building, we ran up the stairs, both of us laughing, bursting into her quiet apartment.

I closed the door, and our laughter faded to soft smiles as we watched each other, breathless, from across the room.

Penny took off her sunglasses and set them on the kitchen table, licking her ice cream as she kicked off her shoes.

I kicked mine off too, my eyes on her.

She wasn't wearing a bra — her nipples were hard, the barbells of her piercing straining against the fabric of her T-shirt as my cock fought the confines of my shorts.

Her fingers trailed down her sternum, and my eyes locked on them as they hooked under the hem of her shirt. And then she pulled, dragging it up until it rested just above her breasts, exposing her tattooed torso to me. Large etched and watercolor flowers climbed up her ribs, stopping under the curves of her breasts, meeting between them in a point, like a corset, and the artwork above framed them with perfect symmetry.

She stuck out her tongue and put it to the scoop, spinning the cone to coat it, but she didn't swallow. She left her tongue out, dripping creamy ice cream down her chin as she took her cone and dragged the scoop between her breasts and down to her belly button.

I tossed my ice cream toward the sink without looking, thankful to hear the thunk as it hit its target. There was no way in hell anything was going to stop me from getting to her.

I rushed her, closing my mouth over hers, sucking the sticky sweetness from her tongue as she moaned. It had been too long without her, too long since *this*. Her arms wrapped around my neck, and I stood, lifting her off the ground, her body pressed against mine like I'd been dreaming of.

"Bedroom?" I panted.

She jerked her head toward a room behind her. "That way," she breathed.

"Don't you dare leave that ice cream."

She smiled and kissed me, wrapping her legs around my waist as I blindly carried her through the apartment, bumping into furniture along the way.

I lowered her onto the bed and moved down her body, sucking on her skin where she'd left a trail to the promised land, cupping her breast in my hand.

I missed you, I thought, saying nothing with words and everything with the long caress of my tongue on her body.

When I reached her shorts, I looked up while I unfastened them — she lay there, head propped up by pillows, watching me as she ate the fucking ice cream cone that might be the death of me.

I pulled off her shorts and threw them before gripping her naked hips, my thumbs stroking that soft skin in the crease of her thighs.

"Do you ever wear panties?" I asked.

"Never. Can't stand them."

I laughed and pulled my shirt off, tossing it, and then my shorts, tossing them too.

One of her brows rose. "Do you?"

I smirked as I climbed up to meet her, nestling between her legs. "Nope, I never wear panties either."

A little laugh passed her lips before I kissed her silent.

Her shirt was still hitched up to her collarbone, giving me all the room to touch her that I wanted, so I did, my lips against hers as I squeezed and cupped, thumbed and twisted until her hips were rocking under me.

Her arms were around my neck, the ice cream dripping down my back from the cone still in her hand, and after a minute, she broke away and smiled.

"Roll over."

I smiled back and did what she'd asked, stretching out in her bed, vulnerable, waiting for her to do what she wanted.

Our eyes were locked as she straddled me, though she didn't lower her hips — she hovered above me, and I looked over every inch of her body that I could see.

She was a work of art — pale, pale skin covered in ink, purple hair and piercings, winged black liner that made her look like a cat, full, pouty lips that parted like she wanted to taste the world, starting with me.

Penny ran that ice cream across her collarbone — I touched her thighs: I had to touch her — and down her breast to circle her nipple. Then around the curve of her breast — God, I was so rock hard it hurt — down her ribs, and then lower still, dragging it over the hood of her clit.

I wanted to move, wanted to lick every part of her until she came, but before I could, she took that ice cream and dragged it up the length of my cock.

I hissed, the pleasure of touch and the icy-cold shock a mixture of sensations I hadn't been ready for.

She brought the cone up to her smiling lips and bit off a chunk before hinging at the waist, angling for my cock. And without any more pretense, she wrapped her hand around my base, lifted me up, and slid me into her mouth, dropping down until I hit the back of her throat.

I drew a shuddering breath with one hand on her shoulder and the other cupping the back of her head as her hot tongue dragged a lump of freezing cold ice cream up my shaft and down. And then, she bobbed her head again, sliding back down.

My fingers tightened in her hair — I wanted to slam into her mouth until I came, but I closed my eyes, trying to breathe.

Closing my eyes made it worse.

Over and over again she took the length of me, humming and sighing through her nose, eyes closed, long lashes against her cheeks, purple hair in my hands, her body rolling and shifting like its only mission was to make me come.

My cock flexed in her mouth, and I squeezed her shoulder in warning.

She let me go and crawled up my body — apparently she didn't want me to come yet either.

I sat up to meet her halfway, and my hands holding her jaw, tilting her head so I could get deep into her mouth, wanting to take her. I twisted to guide her onto her back, and when I broke away, her mouth hung open like it didn't know I was gone.

I reached off the edge of the bed for my jeans and growled, "Take your shirt off, Penny."

She opened her eyes lazily, ice cream cone somehow still in her hand, and half-reached for the nightstand. "Condom," she murmured.

"I've got it. Now take your fucking shirt off." I ripped the packet open and slipped that fucker on so fast it was a blur of hands and motion before she was shirtless, the ice cream had disappeared, and I was between her legs again, resting at the tip of her heat for a moment as we stared at each other.

"Oh God. Do it," she begged.

I flexed with a moan, and her head lolled to the side. I pulled out and flexed again, slipping in even easier as my lips found trails of ice cream on her body and licked her clean. Then again my hips pumped, and I hit the end with a jolt that ran up her thigh, jerking her leg. I grabbed that leg and pushed it open wider, spreading my own legs to get low, and when I slammed into her, her breasts jostled.

She gasped, head kicking back into the bed.

"God, Penny," I huffed. "I could fuck you all day. All night."

"Yes," she breathed. "Do that thing—" Another gasp as I ground against her piercing. "Oh, fuck. Yes, please. That. Oh God. That."

I didn't stop the motion once I knew what she wanted, only pressed harder, moved faster until her brows drew together, her lips parting, and she came all around me like thunder.

That face, her face. I couldn't stop myself, no matter how bad I wanted to. Three pumps of my hips and I came with her hands in my hair and my name on her lips like a prayer.

When I pressed my forehead to hers, when she trailed the tip of her small nose up the bridge of mine, I caught a glimpse of just how deep the deep end was.

And I had no idea how to swim.

-PENNY-

It took me all of about two minutes to come down from my orgasm with Bodie in my arms and the glorious weight of him pressing me into the bed before I freaked the fuck out.

I liked him.

I wasn't supposed to like him.

And now it had to end. All the fun. All the happy. All the Bodie. All that glorious D and laughing and excitement. Over. Poof. My three dates were up, and now my carriage was gonna turn into a pumpkin.

I had to walk away.

I didn't want to walk away.

Fuck.

My heart hammered, and I clawed my way through my thoughts. How could I tell him it was over? Did I even have to? Could I let him leave and just let the whole thing die?

I told myself I could. I also told myself I was a liar.

He propped himself up, holding my face in his hands as he smiled at me, and my insides trembled and fluttered in response. I was smiling back, betraying my freak-out so easily, I almost got whiplash. Or dicklash.

What is happening to me?

"I'm glad to see you, Penny," he said, his eyes on my lips.

"I can tell."

He kissed my nose and rolled away.

I sat up in bed and leaned against my pillows, pulling the covers over me as I watched him walk out of my room, stark naked. He turned the wrong way for the bathroom, and I forgot all about my anxiety, laughing when he passed the doorway again, pointing in the other direction.

God, I was in the deepest of shit. All the way up the creek of shit with no paddle.

Screwed.

Fucked.

And only partly in the literal sense.

I sat there, panicking over what to do. I should have been ready to tell him goodbye, but I wasn't. But I had to. It had to end.

Didn't it?

Maybe if he bugged out on me, everything would be easy. I would probably follow the old pattern, and I'd be turned off so fast, I could wave *sayonara* without question. There was still time — his dick was barely out of me, which was something I was really, really missing already.

But then again, maybe he won't bug out at all. Maybe he doesn't actually like you, a little voice in my head said.

I'd named the owner of that voice Peggy about eight years ago (thanks, Rodney!). My psychotic alter ego smoked Pall Malls and whispered around her cigarette, shuffling around me in her bathrobe with rollers in her hair, reminding me that I was a good lay and that was it. Because that was what I was good for — sex and tattoos. The good-time girl.

He's probably got another girl or two in his rotation, one who's less of a mess. Once he leaves, I doubt he'll ever speak to you again, she said, which was a point that should have given me a modicum of comfort but gave me absolutely none.

That sick feeling in my stomach was back. I fucking hated Peggy. She ashed on my soul and existed solely to make me miserable.

Peggy was why I wasn't allowed to have feelings.

I stole her imaginary cigarette and put it out, which shut her up long enough to light another one. It was the only thing that worked to keep her quiet — making sure she was stocked with beer and cigarettes and all the dick she could eat.

And when she was finally quiet, I wondered if *I* would be the one to bug out.

That thought sent my heart chugging so fast, it hurt.

He came back a second later with a cool, wet washcloth for me, which he handed over with a smile that panicked me even more.

Bodie made his way around the room, gathering his clothes — first his shorts, which I mourned as his ass disappeared into them, and then his shirt, another sorrowful moment of my day. And then he climbed back in bed with me, flopping down on his stomach at my side.

"I've got to get back to work."

"Okay," I said, waiting for him to profess his undying love or pledge to cherish me forever or admit that banging me was nice but he really thought we should call it.

But instead, he smirked. "Do me a favor and hit me up sooner rather than later next time, okay?"

I laughed, surprised and relieved and filled with traitorous hope. "That's it?"

His smile fell. "What do you mean?"

"I mean …" I paused, not sure what to say. "You don't want … *more*?"

His brow quirked. "You said no strings. This is what no strings looks like. Penny, you don't owe me anything."

I watched him, unsure if it was a trap. "You really mean that?"

He laughed at that. "Yeah, I really mean that." He crawled half into my lap, his arms on either side of my thighs as he looked up at me. "It doesn't have to be complicated. It doesn't have to be hard. It can be easy. And I'm around. Whenever."

As I sat there in my bed with the most beautiful man I'd ever known smiling up at me, I believed every word he'd said. I heard Veronica's voice in the back of my mind, telling me the three-date rule was stupid, and in that moment, it was.

Bodie had said it could be easy, and being with him was fun. Being with him made me happy. Being with him was like a balm to my blistering crazy.

But was that enough to throw my rule out the window and risk the consequences?

There were so many reasons to say yes, including:

1. That smile.

2. The warmth nestled in the middle of my ribcage.

3. That wonderful wang that had dicknotized me.

In fact, I'd been dicknotized so hard, that list was all it took to punt my rule into the end zone and do a victory dance. It was stupid and irresponsible and I didn't give a single shit. I wanted to be with him, and I foolishly believed I was safe and strong enough to know my limits.

So I answered him with a kiss full of relief and thanks and absolute pleasure.

When I broke away, he was smiling again.

"Hit me up, Penny."

"I will," I said.

And as he left, I reassured myself that I could have fun and keep seeing Bodie with no strings.

I couldn't even blame him for the fact that I was already falling for him, and I was so naive that I didn't even realize it.

Easy Peasy

- P E N N Y -

hit the bed with a thump and a bounce, naked and out of breath and grinning from ear to ear.

The bed jostled as Bodie flopped down next to me, smiling just as wide as I was, looking just as sated as I felt.

It had been four days of nothing but work and Bodie. Somehow I'd found myself at his place every night, plus once during my lunch break. Ramona had moved out, a tear-filled, horrible day that I ended in Bodie's bed. The void of her moving had been filled by Bodie and his smile and his jock and his big, muscly arms.

He was absolutely perfect.

There were no strings, not a single longing gaze, not one second where I felt the itch to ditch.

It was a goddamn miracle. I'd found the unicorn of men — a smart, snarky, magical sex creature who made me want to stay put for a minute — and I didn't think I'd been so happy in my whole life. I didn't feel crazy, and neither did he. It was easy, just like he'd said.

I hadn't laughed so much in ages. I hadn't felt so *good* in ages.

Bodie let me lead under the promise that I wouldn't wait too long between us seeing each other. As if I could stop. I was addicted. A-dick-ted.

I giggled stupidly to myself at the thought, and he somehow smiled wider, deepening his dimple.

We rolled to face each other at the same time, and I curled into his chest, his arms wrapping around me as our legs scissored.

"You sure are something else," I mused.

He chuckled, the sound rumbling through his chest and into me.

My smile falling as I thought about leaving. "Ugh. I wish I could stay for a while."

"Well, you can hang here as long as you want."

I frowned — in part because the thought of staying didn't bother me at all, which bothered me, and in part because I couldn't actually stay.

"I've got to head back to the shop to film an interview."

"I thought you weren't filming until the wedding?"

I snuggled deeper into his chest and smelled him shamelessly. "We aren't, but we have these interview things we have to do for a recap on what's been going on since the break. They're going to film a little for a montage at our dress fittings in a couple days."

"Is it weird being on TV?"

"Not really. I mean, every once in a while someone will know who I am, which is really strange. Like, they feel like they know you because they watch you on TV, and they know all this stuff about you, but you have zero context for who they are. Mostly I just smile and listen and take the occasional picture with them."

He laughed again. "You have fans."

"I do. So strange," I said with an echoing laugh. "Otherwise though, it's kind of fun. I like to show people what it's like in the shop, and our show is different from the other parlor reality shows — we don't focus too much on our personal lives. Sometimes it's unavoidable though. Like when Annika and Joel started banging on the sly. They had this huge blowup on film. Like, Joel ripped a camera out of a guy's hands and threw it across the shop."

He sucked in a breath through his teeth. "I saw that episode. I bet that wasn't cheap."

My mouth popped open. "You watched it?"

He nodded, smiling with his lips together. "I did. Is that weird?"

"Not at all. What'd you think?"

"Well, I binge-watched it in a day, so I guess you could say I liked it all right."

I chuckled as my cheeks warmed up.

"I liked seeing you work. And I liked your pink hair, too. But I think I like the purple better." He ran a strand through his fingers.

I sighed, smiling like a fool. But it was gone in a poof when I remembered I had to leave. "What time is it?"

He shifted to look, not letting me go. "Four thirty."

I groaned. "I've really got to go. I'm sorry."

He laughed, kissing my forehead before he let me go. "What are you sorry for?"

I peeled myself off the bed and moved around the room, putting on my clothes and gathering my things as I spoke. "Bailing so soon. I really do wish I could stay."

"Penny, you can come over for a quickie anytime you want."

He was propped up in bed, smiling back at me in a way that made me want to jump right back into bed with him.

In fact, once I was dressed — somehow in my mind, clothes could actually stop us from having sex again — I did climb back in bed to lie on my stomach next to him with a smile on my face and a secret in my hand.

"I got you something," I said mysteriously.

One of his brows rose with one corner of his lips. "Oh?"

I nodded and extended my hand, opening it to reveal a calculator watch.

He busted out laughing and took it, holding it up for inspection. "Where did you get this?"

"Chinatown. I was there buying hair dye and thought of you."

"I love it." He chuckled and leaned forward to kiss me. "What color hair dye did you get? Thinking about switching things up?"

"Oh, I think I'm happy where I'm at for now." I raised my feet into the air and crossed my ankles behind me. "I'm off tomorrow. Maybe we can see each other?" My eyes trailed over the tattoo on his arm and shoulder, which flickered as he put the watch on.

It capped his shoulder and ended mid-bicep, an octopus drawn to look like a Victorian-era etching, framed by swirling waves in the same style. He had a few other smaller pieces, but this one was my favorite.

"Yeah, I'll be around."

I touched his arm, tracing the artwork. "You got these done in LA, I'm guessing?"

"Venice Beach. Do you approve?"

"Mmhmm," I hummed, admiring it.

"Good. I'd hate to think I got ripped off."

I chuckled. "Does it mean anything in particular?"

He shifted to look at it. "I've always thought octopuses were interesting. They're the smartest creatures I've ever come in contact with. My dad caught one once and put it in our tank at home — he was always bringing home starfish and sea cucumbers and fish to add to the tank. I named him Stephen, and he was an escape artist. I'm pretty sure he was a whiz at game theory too."

I laughed, and he trailed a finger down my arm. "How about yours?"

"Mostly they have stories, but some are just pretty, like the flowers on my stomach. Ramona, Veronica, and I all have tiny tacos here." I pointed at the little line drawing of a taco about the size of a dime on the front of my shoulder. "Because what says friendship more than tacos?"

He let out a little laugh through his nose.

"This one is for my aunt." I ran my fingers over the two elephants that wound around my forearm, the smaller one holding the bigger one's tail. "She collected elephant things. After she died, I sketched this up, and Ronnie tattooed me. Now I can carry her around all the time. Elephants don't forget."

His smile fell. "I'm sorry, Pen."

"It's okay. Cancer fucking sucks," I said with a small smile, not wanting to get into it. "This one is self-explanatory." I held up my arm to expose the inside of my bicep where it said, *Oh yes I can.*

"What about this one?" He touched the Latin running down the back of my other arm.

"*Veni, vidi, amavi.* We came, we saw, we loved."

His smile was back, and it sent a slow burn through my chest — it was the smallest of things, a firing of a few muscles that shot a hint of understanding at me and hit me deep. So of course I changed the subject again.

"Thinking about getting more?" I asked.

"I actually had another one on the books, but then I lost my job and moved out here before I could get it done."

I perked up at that. "Really? What of?"

"A Japanese woodcut design of a wave, here." He gestured to his bicep and shoulder that wasn't inked.

"With the wave curling around your shoulder?"

He smirked. "Yeah."

"Still have the design?"

"I do. Why?"

"Because I can do it for you," I said, chipper and grinning. "Tomorrow. I'm off, remember?"

He laughed, and his cheeks flushed a little. "Yeah, but I can't ask you to do that for me, and not on your day off."

"You didn't ask. I want to." The thought of making my mark on his body sent a tingle through me I couldn't ignore. I silently did the math to see if I had time to jump him again before I had to go. I didn't.

He didn't look convinced, staring at me like I was a quantum physics equation.

"I mean it. And I want to see you tomorrow. Meet me at the shop, and we'll do your piece. Can I have it?"

"Are you sure, Penny?"

I shrugged. "Why not?"

He shook his head and swung his legs off the bed, making his way to his closet. I watched his butt like a creep without a single fuck to give. Then I watched his dick as he walked back.

What? It was a very pretty dick.

He handed the artwork over, his eyes twinkling.

"Thank you." I stood, stepping into him until I was pressed against his chest. "Let me know what time works for you tomorrow, and I'll be there."

I wrapped my arms around his neck, and his wound around my waist.

"I'll see you then." And with that little sentence, he kissed me like he was trying to make sure I never forgot him.

As if.

I was all warm and tingly again when he pulled away. He slapped my ass with a pop and stepped into Jersey pants before walking me to the door, leaving my body singing his name as it did every time we were together.

I felt like my feet were barely touching the ground as I walked the few blocks to the shop, daydreaming about Bodie's body and his smile and his dimple.

He was right; things didn't have to be complicated. I didn't have to answer to him, and I didn't expect him to answer to me. Although I did find myself telling him where I'd be or what I'd be doing, and he seemed to do the same. It was just so *easy*, just the two of us.

Of course, we'd spent every minute we could together, though it didn't feel unreasonable. We'd never spent the night together, but we'd spent late nights and full afternoons all tangled up with each other. I knew the amazing noises he made, knew what he liked, what he wanted from my body. I knew his laugh and his smile, knew his hands, knew every inch of his body. I'd spent over a week exploring it, and what a glorious week it had been.

I was struck for a moment that I hadn't even considered being with anyone besides him since I met him. But the thought didn't freak me out — how could I want something other than absolute perfection? What could possibly lure me away?

I was struck again when it crossed my mind that he could be seeing someone else, so struck that I nearly tripped over my own feet and hit the sidewalk.

Surely he felt like I did. I mean, we hadn't discussed our relationship or defined anything. He'd said I didn't owe him anything, including exclusivity.

The thought made me irrationally angry, so irrationally angry that I fantasized about hunting down an imaginary bitch who had tried to touch him and scratching her eyes out.

I frowned as I crossed the street.

It had been a very long time since I was jealous, particularly of a made-up thieving man-stealer.

This confused me on levels I wasn't ready to admit existed.

So instead of admitting anything, I reminded myself that he had been with me daily. We'd had so much sex that there was no physical way he'd be able to have *more*.

At least I had that. The thought cheered me up.

I bounced into the coffee shop to grab goodies for everyone before heading to Tonic. I made the rounds once I got there, passing out everyone's usual drinks along with a few lemon bars — they were the best in the city, I swear — stopping at Joel's booth last. The Clash was playing over the speakers, and I smiled, thinking about kissing Bodie as a hundred people sang along with "Rock the Casbah" all around us.

Joel eyed me, smirking a little from behind his dark beard. "You okay?"

I smiled and leaned on the wall around his booth. "Peachy keen, jelly bean. I'm here for my interview with Annika."

His eyes sparked at the mention of her name. "She's upstairs in the control room getting everything ready."

"You excited to start filming again?"

He shrugged. "You know how I feel about all that. But I'm glad Annika has something to do. Without an objective, she comes unglued. I think she reorganized every book I own, color-coded my closet, and rearranged my sock drawer twice. And that was just in the first week."

I laughed. "Well, I'm glad she has a sweater to knit now, something to keep her busy."

"Me too."

"Hey, I wanted to run something by you. I was going to do some work on a friend of mine tomorrow, if it's okay. You don't need my booth, right?"

He shook his head. "You're good. Who's the friend?"

I couldn't even play it cool; I found myself grinning. "Bodie."

One of his brows rose. "The guy who was supposed to send you flowers but didn't?"

I waved a hand, dismissing him. "No, I didn't want him to send flowers, but if I get flowers, yes, I'd like them to be from him."

He narrowed his eyes in concentration. "It's like you're trying to tell me something."

I laughed. "Yes, that's the guy."

"Hmm," he hummed, watching me.

"What?"

He shrugged and rearranged things on his desk. "Nothing. It's just you've never brought a flowers-not-flowers guy around."

"It's no big deal. He was supposed to have work done in LA and moved here before he could. I'm not even drawing it."

He chuckled. "Yeah, I mean, that makes it completely impersonal."

I rolled my eyes. "Ugh, Joel. You're such a drama queen."

He laughed extra loud at that.

I pushed off the counter and winked at him. "I'll tell Annika you said hi."

"You do that."

The bell dinged as I left and turned into the door right next to the shop, climbing two flights to get to the control room. Joel and Annika's apartment was on the second floor, and the third was rented out by the network to set up as an on-site base of operations. The door was unlocked, and I walked through the monitor room, which was usually bustling with PAs and producers, but it was relatively empty since we hadn't really started rolling yet.

Annika was back in the green screen room, waiting for me with a cameraman. She slipped off her director's chair and glided over to me, smiling.

I swear to God, she was the most beautiful woman I'd ever seen. If Joel were a dark, grumbly bear, Annika was like a porcelain doll —

all icy-blue eyes and ruby-red lips and long legs, her hair blonde and skin like milk.

"Penny," she said, cheerily — at least for her. She wasn't overly emotive.

"Hey, Annika," I answered. "Look at you, working that skirt."

I gestured to her black and white business clothes, which sounded nerdier than it was. Her clothes were immaculately cut, the lines clean and simple and modern and flattering. She looked straight off a runway.

She laughed. "I learned this summer that casual wear and free time don't suit me."

"I swear, I almost passed out when you came into the shop in leggings a couple of weeks ago."

"If a pipe hadn't burst, you'd never have seen it."

I chuckled and took my seat across from hers as a PA entered the room and miked me.

Annika sat and flipped through the sheets on her clipboard. "So, we're pretty basic today, just a little bit of catch-up. What have you been working on, how's the shop, how's life — that sort of stuff."

"Cool," I said, settling back into my seat as the camera started rolling.

Annika smiled. "All right, let's start easy. What's the weirdest tattoo you've done since we saw you last?"

"Well, weird's relative, right? Like, you'd think it was super crazy to get a tattoo of a gun, but I have two on my stomach, pointing down to my I-can't-say-that-on-network-television."

She laughed. "That's true. That's the whole point of a tattoo, right? That it means something to you. Lessons I learned from your boss."

"He's a smart dude. But to answer your question, I did a Care Bear tattoo on the back of a girl's calf that made me salute her bravery. Everybody has their thing," I said with a shrug.

"Okay, favorite piece you did?"

I thought about it and crossed my legs. "Damn, that's a hard one. But I did one on Veronica's arm that's two skeletons embracing, like one is clutching the other to its chest. I love being able to work with nothing but black ink, no color, just that ink and the negative space of skin to tell a story."

Annika was still smiling, her lips wide and red and perfect. "I love to hear you guys talk about your work. Sometimes I just listen to Joel geek out about art and tattoos with my head propped on my hand and my heart all fluttery." She sighed and glanced down at her clipboard. "So, what have you been up to this summer?"

"Nothing much. We've mostly been working on Ramona's wedding, but everything's been done for a few weeks, so now it's just a matter of waiting."

"What's left to come?"

I ticked everything off on my fingers. "Dress fittings tomorrow. Bachelorette party in a few days. Then it's time to get the lovebirds hitched."

"You make it sound so easy." She looked a little skeptical.

I chuckled. "Yep, and you're next. But you were built for wedding planning. I bet you have spreadsheets out the wang. Color-coded. With, like, fourteen tabs."

"At least I'm consistent enough to be predictable," she said on a laugh. "So tell me about the bachelorette party."

"Oh, that's not fit for censored television. Let's just say, there will be debauchery and plastic penis accoutrements."

She wrinkled her nose.

I pointed at her. "You're participating. No pussing out, dude."

Annika dodged the implication and smiled. "Have a date for the wedding?"

I waved a hand. "Nah, I'll just go stag."

Her smile fell. "You don't have anyone to bring? You always seem to have guys on your heel. Surely one of them looks good in a suit. Your taste in men is impeccable."

"Thank you," I said with a nod of my head, but I squirmed a little. "I dunno. Weddings are a big deal. Like, I'll have pictures from this wedding on my fridge until I've got tennis balls on the feet of my walker. Plus, there's love in the air at those things. I wouldn't want to catch something."

She laughed. "So you're not seeing anyone?"

I shrugged, still feeling squirmy. "I'm always seeing someone," I answered lightly.

"Who's the current guy?"

That stupid smile crept onto my face again. "Oh, just a guy," I lied, not wanting to talk about him on camera.

When things fell apart, I'd have to look back on any admissions without regrets. My stomach sank at the thought, but I put a lifejacket on that motherfucker, and it perked back up.

"Favorite thing about the guy?"

"His dick," I said without hesitation, knowing she'd have to cut the whole segment.

She burst out laughing, which was especially funny for her — she was a self-contained creature. But when she let loose, it was like a unicorn galloping across a rainbow.

"Well, I hope you change your mind about inviting Mr. Dick Guy to the wedding."

I laughed. "Oh my God. That's going to be my new name for him. Mr. Richard Guy."

"I'd love to meet the man who has you so into him that you won't kiss and tell." One of her brows was up, teasing me.

"Oh, come on. I don't always kiss and tell."

She gave me a look.

"Fine," I sighed, rolling my eyes. "I just want to keep this one to myself for a minute. Is that so wrong?"

"Not at all. I'm intrigued, that's all."

At that, I smiled. "You and me both."

Operation: Penny Jar

- B O D I E -

The next afternoon, **I walked** down the sidewalk toward the tattoo parlor where Penny worked, the sun shining on my skin, the birds chirping in my ears, and the same smile plastered on my face that had been there for a week.

Operation: Penny Jar had been a success. So far at least.

I'd seen her every day since we ran into each other at the ice cream shop. She'd knocked me out then, and just when I'd thought it couldn't get better with her, she'd proven me wrong.

I was right after all; Penny didn't want complicated. So I didn't complicate things. It wasn't hard — being with her was so easy and so fun that there wasn't a need to talk about more. Every second with her was perfect to the point of disbelief. A crush realized. A fantasy in physical form.

I'd shown her that I meant what I'd said, even if my heart betrayed it all. Because the pretense hung in the air between us — the pretense she'd asked for and I'd agreed to.

For her, this was temporary.

For me, it wasn't.

Not that I was looking for a commitment. I wasn't. But I knew I didn't want it to end until we'd run our course. Thing was, I didn't know how long the tracks were, and I had a feeling mine were longer than hers.

My plan was still in place: be so fucking awesome that I became essential, necessary to her. Of course, in doing that, I'd also found that she was indispensable to me.

Catch-22.

In any event, I was taking advantage of every second with her. Including today.

She'd surprised me when she'd offered to do my tattoo — it felt like a *relationshippy* thing to do. Personal. Intimate. She was going to mark me with ink that would stain my skin for my whole life. Of course, she'd marked hundreds of people, maybe even thousands over her career.

It was as small and impersonal as it was huge and meaningful. But I locked my focus on the end of the spectrum labeled *Not a Big Deal* just as I approached the parlor.

The word *Tonic* was printed in a font that looked like an old Victorian apothecary label with gold leaf and line work above and below, framing the word. When I pulled open the door, the sounds of Nirvana hit my ears as the sights the shop had to offer washed over me.

Everything looked vintage with a Victorian flair. Old velvet couches lined the full waiting area, and the walls were covered in macabre paintings in elaborate frames. Booths lined the long wall, all with counter-high walls to mark each space. Each booth contained a retro black tattoo chair, an antique desk, and cabinets for inks and supplies, I assumed. The electric buzz of tattoo guns hummed in an undercurrent to Kurt Cobain as he sang about heart-shaped boxes, and I scanned the room, looking for the flash of purple that would tell me where Penny was.

She bounded out from a hallway leading to the back, smiling and practically skipping to me as everyone in the shop watched her — her coworkers curious, the people in the waiting room practically salivating.

I had no idea the protocol for such a public greeting, so I stood there smiling, waiting for her to make a move that would tell me where the boundary was.

The thought was moot. She practically jumped into my arms, hooking hers around my neck as she kissed me hello with enough gusto that I felt it all the way down to my shoes.

She broke away, smiling at me with twinkling eyes. "Hey," she said, the sweet scent of bubble gum on her breath.

"Hey," I echoed, setting her feet on the ground.

She grabbed my hand and pulled. "Come on, let me introduce you to everybody."

I already knew who everyone was from watching the show, which was really weird. So I played dumb, following her into the shop a bit, walking up the line of booths to start at the front where a gigantic dude with an intense beard and the thickest head of hair I'd ever seen was tattooing a girl's back. She was stretched out on her stomach, back bare, and he moved his machine, stopping the buzzing by removing his foot from the pedal.

"This," Penny said, extending a hand toward him, "is Joel, the owner of the shop."

Joel smiled, but his eyes sized me up. "Good to meet you."

"You too." I tried to smile in a way that was amiable but also as masculine as possible, feeling the alpha roll off of him. He was most definitely the boss.

"And this," she said, guiding me to the next booth back, "is Tricky. Patrick if he's in trouble."

Patrick stood and extended a tattooed hand for a shake. The guy looked like a male model with a sharp jaw and deep, dark eyes, every inch of his skin tattooed, except for his face.

"Hey, man," he said with a sideways smile. "Heard a lot about you."

I took his hand and pumped it. "Thanks," I said lamely, wishing I had something to offer other than, *Cool tattoos, bro.*

Next down was a dark-haired, leggy brunette with lined eyes and red lips.

"So, you didn't officially meet the other night, but this is one of my roommates, Veronica."

Veronica smiled and waved. "Glad to finally meet you, Bodie."

"And this," she said as she dragged me across the room to the counter where a blonde stood, smiling, "is Ramona, my best friend and our piercer."

"Need your dick pierced?" she asked brazenly.

I couldn't help but laugh. "I'm good today, but thanks."

She shrugged. "Let me know if you change your mind. I've heard good things." She looked down and jerked a chin toward my waistline.

The girls cracked up laughing, and I shook my head, not even embarrassed. I took the fact that they had talked about my dick as a good sign.

A couple of guys were laughing in the booth behind Veronica's, which was our next stop.

"These knuckleheads are Eli and Max."

"Hey," they said at the same time. One punched the other in the arm.

I waved a hand, and she pulled me back to her booth.

It was very Penny. The artwork on her walls was everything from comic-style to detailed portraits. The largest heavy-framed painting was of a woman with a starburst crown, holding a flaming heart in one hand and a rosary in the other. And in the center of the smaller pieces on her wall was a gilded mirror, speckled and veined with age.

She smirked at me and patted the seat of her tattoo chair. "Come on. I don't bite."

"That's a lie, and I have the marks to prove it."

She giggled, her cheeks high and flushed and pretty.

I took a seat, and she moved to her desk to get the transfer she'd printed.

"Shirt off, please."

I waited until she turned around to face me before reaching back between my shoulder blades and grabbing a handful of T-shirt, pulling it over my head.

Her lip was between her teeth. She was wearing the same high-waisted shorts she'd had on that first night with the buttons on the front with a T-shirt that said, *Feed Me Tacos and Tell Me I'm Pretty,* in red iron-on letters that matched her lipstick. But the best part was that she had on tall black wedges, her legs long and knees together, toes pointed in. She looked like a goddamn calendar girl, and the way she was eye-fucking me had me wishing the booth had four walls and a door.

She blinked and walked over, hips swaying, lips smiling. "Is this too big?" she asked, holding up the transfer.

I opened my legs a little wider. "No such thing."

Penny laughed at that and held it over my arm, inspecting it. "I *do* like it when it's extra big."

She stood at the arm of the chair, and I slid my hand up the outside of her thigh.

"Oh, I know all about that."

She was unfazed other than shifting to lean into me as best she could with an armrest in the way. "I think it'll work. Let me put it on, and we can look at it."

She went to work, arranging the transfer before wetting it down with a paper towel. When she smiled down at me, a little jolt shot through me.

"You ready for this?"

"Always," I answered.

She peeled the transfer off and blotted my skin dry, inspecting it all the while. It was like she had flipped a switch and was all business and then flipped it again, all pleasure.

"Okay. Take a look."

I stood and checked out the placement. It started just above my elbow and moved up and around my bicep and the cap of my shoulder — it was bigger than I'd imagined but exactly what it should be.

"I like it," I said.

"Good. Me too." She nodded to her chair. "Go ahead and have a seat."

Her station seemed to already be set up, and she took a seat on a saddle stool with wheels, straddling it before rolling over to me, pulling on black rubber gloves.

Several reactions hit me. The sight of her rolling over to me with her legs open, snapping those rubber gloves, hit me below the belt. The realization that she was about to take a needle to me sent adrenaline shooting through my veins in a cold burst. And the look in her eyes got me right in the rib cage.

"All right," she said as she poured black ink into a little cup. "So here's the deal. This is way too big to do all at once if you want color. But I kinda think it'll look better all black, just the outline. We've got to do that first anyway, so if you want to have it filled in later, you totally can."

"How long until I can have more done?"

"A couple of months is usually wise." She loaded her gun, wrapping a rubber band around the base of it. When she hit the pedal to test it, she smiled. "But anybody can do it. The line work is the hard part. You don't have to come back to me to get it filled in."

My heart deflated just a bit, just enough. Penny was putting space between us, telling me we wouldn't be together in a few months, giving me permission to have it finished somewhere else.

She rolled her tray where she wanted it, scooting close to me with her eyes on my arm.

"Here we go." She pressed that buzzing needle into my skin.

The thing about tattoos is that when it starts, you think it's not so bad. Four hours in, and you feel like you've been carved like a turkey. So I enjoyed the burn before it consumed me.

Hearts worked the same way, I figured.

"You okay?" she asked after a moment, her eyes darting to mine for a solid second before looking back to my arm.

"I'm good."

I watched her work, admiring the sureness of her hand, competence radiating from her. She was confident, so certain, completely capable. Penny could take over the world if she wanted to. She could take me over.

She kind of already had.

I looked over the shop and realized I'd met all the important people in her life — her family. I was in her chair as a customer, but it was more than that. There was an intimacy to the act and intimacy to her bringing me to the place that meant so much to her. Not that she'd made a big deal about it, but I knew by how she talked about everyone I'd met that they were her *people*. And that filled me with hope and pleasure at the connection to her.

Of course, that connection scared me too. Because I knew deep down that I didn't have as much control as I'd thought I did over the situation. Every single day, she'd marked me in more ways than one, and I couldn't turn back any more from my heart than I could from the needle in her hand.

"So, Bodie," Ramona started from the wall of Penny's booth.

When I glanced over, she was leaning on the wall from the other side, next to Veronica. They were both smiling unabashedly, their eyes never quite reaching mine — they were too busy scanning my chest.

"What is it you do again?" Ramona asked.

"I'm a software engineer. My buddies and I are working on a video game."

They nodded their appreciation.

"What kind of game?" Veronica leaned in, shoulder to shoulder with Ramona.

"It's an open world role-playing game. Steampunk, story-driven."

Their faces were blank.

"Ah, like … think Victorian era, airships, like blimps. Treasure hunting, like Indiana Jones meets Han Solo but British."

They lit up at that, including Penny, and I found myself feeling pleased.

"What's it called?" Ramona asked.

"Nighthawk. It's the name of the ship."

Penny bounced a little in her seat. "Oh my God, that makes me want to draw stuff. This is seriously genius, Bodie. Who's doing your artwork?"

"Jude. He's a graphic artist and handles all of our 3D renderings. Phil and I are the code jockeys. Jude is the art."

Penny waggled her brows at Veronica, who rolled her eyes.

"So how does that work?" Ramona asked. "Like, what do you do with it when it's done?"

I took a breath and let it out as Penny carved a line in my skin and wiped it with a paper towel. "The first real step is to get a gameplay demo ready so we can pitch it to a big developer. The idea is that they pay us for the concept and bring us on as part of the development team. But we've been working on the demo for seven years," I said with a laugh.

"Man, that's intense," Penny said as she dipped her needle in the ink and got back to work.

"It's moving a lot faster now that we've been working on it full-time, but yeah. It's been a long time coming. I mean, we came up with the idea in junior high and have been working toward this ever since. Phil's focused on our outreach, networking through college and career buddies to see if we can get a meeting. There's this one development company that's at the top of the list. If we can get in with them, it's a guarantee that the game would be everything we could possibly dream of. They've got the chops and the cash to throw at it."

"What's the company called?" Veronica asked.

"Avalanche," I said, unable to keep the excitement out of my voice. "The games they produce are off the charts. But that's the pie-in-the-sky kind of dream. We'll probably get it picked up by a smaller company — I just hope they'll let us do the work to make it what we want."

Another gigantic hairy dude walked out of the hallway and into the shop, eyeing me in the chair, then he smirked at Ramona. He slapped her on the ass, and she yelped, laughing when she saw him.

"Hey, Shep," Penny chirped. "This is Bodie. Bodie, this is Shep, Ramona's fiancé and Joel's brother."

I jerked a chin at him in greeting. "How's it going?"

"Not too bad," Shep said, every word loaded, "other than the fact that my future wife is salivating over Penny's guy."

Everyone laughed but me. I was a hundred and ten percent sure that he could wreck my face without breaking a sweat.

"Come on, girls," Shep said. "Leave Penny alone so she can do her job without an audience."

They grumbled about it, but he effectively shooed them off, leaving Penny and me as alone as we could be in a tattoo parlor full of people.

Penny was engrossed in her work, and I watched her, smirking.

God, she was so beautiful, so talented, so strong and wild and free. A force of nature. I couldn't imagine ever changing her, couldn't imagine ever taking what made her *her* away. To lose those qualities would be tragic, a loss to everyone who knew and loved her. The thought that Rodney had tried to pin her down all those years ago, that he hadn't been happy until he'd stripped it all away, made me hate him all the more.

"Something about you with that gun in your hand is almost too much for me, Penny."

Her eyes caught mine and moved back to her work, though she was smiling. "You shirtless in my chair is almost too much for me, Bodie."

I chuckled. "Tell me you're free tonight."

Her smile fell at that. "I wish I were. I promised Ronnie and Ramona that we'd go out. You know, since last time we tried to go out, I bailed on them."

"Worth it."

She laughed. "So worth it." She shot up in her seat, eyes wide and smile big. "Oh my God, I have an idea. We should all go out together. Like, you should come with us and bring your brother. Make a group thing out of it. I want to hook Veronica up with Jude — she needs to get laid so bad. And then Ramona can bring Shep, and maybe Joel and Annika can come too."

"I doubt Veronica has trouble with that on her own."

"You'd be surprised."

"Well, I'm sure Jude would be down to help out," I joked.

She lit up like a floodlight, her red lips smiling wide. "It's perfect. This way I can see you, and Veronica can get the grump nailed out of her. Everybody wins."

I shook my head, smiling at her. "Schemer."

She shrugged and got back to work. "I get what I want."

"I'm sure you do."

As she worked, I considered the fact that she'd just asked me on a date. A group date, sure, but we would be going out with her friends, the important people in her life. In public. Not just getting together to hook up. No, we'd be hanging out all night, and *then* we'd hook up.

If that wasn't a date, I didn't know what was.

As she traced the lines of the ocean on my skin, I wondered if she realized it. I wondered if she knew. Or maybe things were just the same for her as they ever were. Maybe this was all just for fun, all for the thrill.

But I told myself not to overthink it. Because if I did, I might lose the glimmer of shine I'd found on Penny.

- PENNY -

My eyes scanned the thick crowd at Circus, looking for Bodie. We stood clustered next to a gigantic painting of Siamese twins in an ornate gilded frame. Ramona and Shep laughed with Joel and Annika, leaving Veronica and me on the edge of the circle, a little isolated. I considered canoodling with her, but she seemed as edgy as I was. Setups weren't her thing. Waiting wasn't mine.

Not that Veronica wasn't great company, but after having my hands on a half-naked Bodie all day and not doing anything about it, I was anxious to see him. And by anxious, I meant I felt like my insides were trying to get outside.

I should have gone home with him like he'd asked me to after his tattoo. But I wanted to see him tonight even more than just the afternoon, and I was afraid to overdo it with both. In hindsight, I should have just committed. God knew I couldn't get my fill of him, so it wasn't like I had to save myself.

I laughed to myself at the thought. The most he'd gotten out of me in a day was six orgasms. *Six.* The last one had taken him a full hour, but Christ almighty, was it a ringer.

My phone buzzed in my hand, since I was holding it like a needy girl in preparation of him getting there, and when I saw it was him, I fired off a response, navigating him to us.

I caught sight of him and hopped over, my heart doing all the warm and squeezy things in my chest. I slipped my hand into his much larger one and popped up onto my toes to kiss him for a brief, fluttering second.

"Come on!" I yelled over the music. "This way."

I led him, Jude, Phil, and Angie over to the group, standing between the tightrope walker in pasties with a sparkly thong and a platform for two hoop dancers who might have been naked — they were covered in body paint and glitter and sparkles.

Veronica perked up as we approached, and I smirked.

I doled out introductions where necessary, saving Veronica for last.

"Jude," I said, grabbing him by the arm and pushing him toward her with my free hand, "this is my friend Veronica."

She smiled. He smiled.

"I dunno. I'd say you were more of a Betty." One of his brows rose salaciously.

Her smile flattened faster than you could say *douchebag.* So did mine — that look meant he didn't have a chance in hell.

"Hey, Jude. Don't make it bad," Veronica snarked, throwing the *Never heard that before* back at him.

A girl in a top hat and red tails mercifully interrupted the awkwardness to take drink orders before disappearing into the ocean of people, and I leaned into Bodie, smelling him like a weirdo. I couldn't help it. The smell of his soap and whatever other products he used made me think of my face buried in his neck or his pillows or his chest. Other places too, places where I'd like to be buried in at that moment.

He wrapped his arm around me and pulled me closer, pressing a kiss to the top of my head.

"How's your arm?" I asked, sliding my hand around his middle.

"Still works," he answered with a flex.

I giggled like a dum-dum and leaned away, though I kept my arm around his waist, my fingers fiddling with the top of his pants.

"Thanks again for today," he said. "I wish you'd let me pay you."

"I'll tell you what — you can pay me back later."

He angled toward me, pressing his lips against my ear. "Oh, I plan to," he whispered straight to my vagina.

A shiver rolled down my back. "Can't we just leave now?"

"We could, but I'd rather tease you for the next couple of hours first."

I laughed as his hand slipped down to my ass and gave it a squeeze. "Ugh, I hate waiting."

"I know. That's why I love to make you wait."

Within a few minutes, everyone had moved around and mixed up, talking with each other, and I smiled to myself as I floated from group to group, happy that the odd collection of friends jelled. Joel and Phil were deep in a conversation about sci-fi that I understood zero of. Angie, who was the sweetest little bookish thing with big brown eyes and a giggle that instinctively made everyone in her radius giggle with her, had been talking with Ramona and Veronica about baking. Shep and Jude laughed together, swapping stories with Bodie, who smiled at me when I walked up.

Everything felt so *good*. All of us hanging out and talking and laughing. Bodie hanging his arm on my shoulder and kissing my temple and touching my hand, reminding me over and over again how much I enjoyed being around him. *He* made me feel good, and I wanted to make him feel good too.

The group shuffled around a few times, and a little while later, I found myself watching them all from the outside with Ramona, who bumped my arm.

"Have I told you that you've ruined my life?"

I frowned. "What? Why?"

"I went to the grocery store yesterday, and I couldn't stop thinking about the little old checkout lady's nipples when I noticed how pale her lips were."

I burst out laughing. Ramona looked pleased.

"Bodie's great, Pen."

I smiled. "He is, isn't he?"

She nodded, smirking. "I never thought I'd live to see you on a real date."

I frowned. "This isn't a date. This is a preamble to naked cartwheels and an attempt to get Ronnie laid."

That earned a laugh. "First, this is totally a date. And you guys have been all over each other in the cutest way."

My frowned deepened. "Yeah, because we're hot for each other."

"Oh my God, Penny. It's a date. Open your eyes."

I blinked, watching Bodie from across the room. "I mean, I guess *technically* it is, but that's not what we're doing. I'm not his *girlfriend*." I said it like it was a filthy word.

Ramona laughed, shaking her head at me. "You know that being a girlfriend doesn't mean you're chained up in somebody's basement, right?"

"If you say so." I took a sip of my tequila.

She let it go, thankfully. I was starting to feel itchy.

Ramona nodded to the group. "So Jude and Veronica went over about as well as lead frisbee."

I sighed. "Man, I'm so disappointed. They had to go and open their mouths and ruin my plans."

She chuckled. "They didn't even make it two sentences into a conversation. But look at them eyeballing each other."

"I think they're trying to explode each other."

They really were — the two of them were staring across the room with narrowed eyes, and I wondered what else had been said. It must have been seriously infuriating, and I wished I'd heard every word.

"Well," Ramona started, "even if the Ronnie trap failed, the Bodie trap is still fully in place and ready to blow."

I snickered. "Yeah, it is."

She smiled at me. "I'm happy for you, Penny. I really like him."

I sighed wistfully. "He's perfect for me right now. I had no idea that guys like him existed in the dating wild."

She opened her mouth like she had something to say but stopped herself, smiling instead. "Speak of the devil."

When I followed her eyeline, I found Bodie walking over, his eyes on mine in a way that made my knees go weak, though there was nothing lewd or suggestive about it. It was just *pervasive*, slipping into me, through me, spreading all over me in a way that set me on fire.

"Hey," he said with a smile.

"Hi." I smiled back like the fool that I was.

Ramona touched my arm. "I'm gonna go make sure Shep's not telling any stories he shouldn't. You know how chatty he gets."

I laughed. "Oh, man. Hopefully not the dick sock story again."

"Oh, he's well past that. We're into koala bear territory."

I waved her away. "Go. Run."

And with that, she headed back to the group, leaving me and Bodie alone.

"Having fun?" I asked.

"I am. I like your friends."

"I like yours too."

"Too bad about Veronica and Jude though."

I pouted. "I know. We were just talking about that. Honestly, I've met your brother, and I can't believe I thought it was a good idea. Pretty much the only thing they have in common is that they're single."

"Not true. They're both artists, and they have smart-ass mouths."

I laughed and stepped into him, resting my hand on his chest. "So, I was thinking about you surfing the other day."

"Oh, were you?" He pulled me closer.

"Mmhmm. And I was thinking about what a badass you are."

He laughed. "Said the badass."

"When you guys go, can I come with?"

One of his brows rose. "Any chance I might get you on a board? Because that would fulfill so many fantasies."

I drew a little circle on his chest with the pad of my finger. "Only if you promise to surf shirtless. I think it might be worth getting eaten by a shark to see that once before I die."

When he chuckled and kissed me, I thought I might melt right there in his arms.

"Have we waited long enough?" I asked when he broke the kiss like a tyrant.

"That was the question I came over here to ask. Are you ready to go?"

My heart thumped, and my lips smiled. "Only since you got here."

We said our goodbyes and headed out, hand in hand, then with our arms around each other as we walked to his apartment.

I thought about what Ramona had said, thought about Bodie and how easy it was to be with him. Even having been with him all night, he was never needy, always independent. In fact, I had been the needy one, seeking him out to touch him, kiss him.

I had no idea what had gotten into me, but when I actually

thought about it, it freaked me out.

Were we dating? Was I his *girlfriend*? I couldn't even say the word in my head without my insides shriveling up.

But when I thought about how I felt about Bodie, those shriveled up insides bloomed and filled up again. He'd told me it could be easy, and now … well, now I was on a date with him, one I'd set up without even realizing I was doing it.

If that wasn't going with the flow, I couldn't imagine what was.

He hadn't put any demands on me, hadn't pushed the boundaries of what I was comfortable with. He hadn't done anything but let me breathe, let me be, and somehow that was exactly what I needed. And he knew it.

We'd been on a date, and I hadn't felt trapped or uncomfortable or cagey at all. I felt good. I felt happy.

So I took that as a sign that I was on the right track. And if we could keep on being easy, then I could stay put — for a little while at least. Ride the wave. Enjoy the scenery. Get high off of Bodie.

I did my best not to think about what would happen when I came down.

Steak at Stake

- PENNY -

The next afternoon, I took a sip of my champagne, facing the mirrors in the bridal shop, but I turned as Ramona came out from the dressing room, cheeks pink and eyes shining.

She looked stunning and stunned and absolutely gorgeous.

She was a rustling of lace and silk chiffon as she spanned the room and stepped up onto the platform, pressing her palm to her stomach.

The dress itself was simple and beautiful with beadwork that looked Edwardian — structured and flowing all at once in draping designs. Her waist was waspish from the corset underneath the soft fabric, and the sweeping neckline cut the slightest V between her breasts, framing her chest and neck tattoos like they had been made for each other.

"It's happening. This is it," she whispered with a shaky breath. "I … for a long time, I didn't think it would. He never asked, you know?

STACI HART

He couldn't leave Joel, but Joel finding Annika changed everything. I should buy that woman an island."

Veronica and I laughed and moved to her side, turning to look at our trio in the wide-angled mirrors. But Ramona was looking down at us, smiling and crying.

"Thank you. Both of you. I couldn't do this without you, and I wouldn't want anyone else to share this with me the way you two have."

Tears filled my eyes too, and Veronica and I stepped up onto the platform to hug. The three of us hung onto each other for a long moment.

When we turned back to the mirror, I looked us over. "Damn, we look good."

We laughed. It was our final fitting, and everything was perfect. Our bridesmaid dresses were dove-gray chiffon, soft and flowing and long, each a little different. Mine tied around the waist with a deep V and flowing skirt that made me feel like a goddess. Veronica's was strapless, the top corseted and the skirt the same as mine.

I reached for the small table next to the platform where Ramona's champagne stood, bubbling and waiting for her, raising my glass as I placed hers in her hand.

"To your next beginning," I said simply.

And we touched our champagne flutes together with the sweetest of tings before taking a sip.

I'd barely noticed the camera crew until they began to pack up. One of the cameramen nodded to me with a smile as they disappeared.

Another thing to thank Annika for — she'd made sure we were bothered as little as possible. In fact, I bet she'd cut the emotional stuff altogether. After having her own personal life thrown all over network television last season, she'd made it her mission to preserve the privacy of our lives as much as she could.

The shop girls materialized to inspect Ramona's dress, and Veronica and I moved out of the way so they could work, still sipping our champagne. I felt a little bubbly in the head — I was on my third glass.

Ramona eyed me. "So, I hate to ask this."

"Uh-oh." My mood was instantly not so bubbly.

"Well, I put you down for a plus-one for the wedding, so I need to know if you're bringing someone."

I squirmed.

"I paid for an extra steak, Pen."

Veronica rolled her eyes lovingly, if that's a thing. "Just ask Bodie. You're seeing him. And I bet he looks good in a suit. I mean, unless he's a vegetarian because then what will Ramona do with his steak?"

I snorted. "Ugh, I don't know, guys."

Ramona and Veronica shared a look.

"She doesn't think last night was a date," Ramona said like I wasn't in the room.

"Ah," Veronica said back, equally traitorous.

"Listen, I realize it was a date."

Ramona perked up and cupped her ear. "What's that? You said I was right?"

I rolled my eyes. "Yes, you were right. He's just … I don't know. Easy. He's like a heart ninja." I made a karate chop with my hand.

"So why don't you ask him to the wedding?" Veronica asked.

"Hey, you don't have a date either."

Veronica's lips flattened. "We're not talking about me."

"You could always ask Jude," I offered.

She balked at that. "I wouldn't want to slit any throats at my best friend's wedding. There will be steak knives there."

I laughed. "Oh, come on. He's not that bad."

"He's the douchiest douche to ever douche, Pen. He is so into himself, and his jokes are fucking terrible. It doesn't even matter that he's hot and muscly."

"What? That's basically all that matters," I said. "Just tell him not to talk when he goes down on you, and you guys will be fine."

Ramona cackled and took a sip of champagne.

"I don't want to sleep with somebody I don't like," Veronica stated plainly as if I couldn't get her drift.

I shrugged. "Beggars can't be choosers, Ronnie."

She wrinkled her nose at me. "Anyway, we're not talking about me. We're talking about you. Just ask Bodie."

I wrinkled my nose back at her. "That's so much pressure. I mean, I can barely admit that we went on one pseudodate and you want me to ask him to a *wedding*? I don't even know if we could have dinner alone without me climbing out the bathroom window."

Ramona considered that. "I mean, a wedding is almost safer. You don't even have to be alone. He already knows Joel, Shep, and Annika. And us. It'll be fun, just like last night."

My face was still all pinched up.

Veronica smiled and cocked an eyebrow. "Just think of the after-wedding sex. You'll both be all dressed up. So many clothes to take off."

I bobbed my head in consideration. "Okay, now you're speaking my language."

"There will be dancing and drinking and eating," she added. "Bodie in a suit — just think about that. Those broad shoulders, his thick neck in that tie. Maybe he'll tie you up with it after."

I bit my bottom lip, imagining it. "Mmm," I hummed.

"It won't be a big deal," Veronica said.

And like the dumbass I was, I believed her.

"Okay, I'll do it."

They cheered, and we giggled and jumped up and down, careful of our champagne, which was what I blamed the giggle-bouncing on.

"Text him!" Ramona begged.

I rolled my eyes. "I'm not texting him to ask him to a wedding. I'll ask him tonight."

"What's tonight?" Veronica asked before taking a sip of her drink.

"Nothing, yet." I turned to the velvet chair where we'd set our purses and dug through mine for my phone.

"Did you see that lingerie shop across the street?" Ramona dropped the question like she was sneaky or something.

"Of course I did. Why? Think I should get a little something?" She shrugged. "Couldn't hurt."

I champagne-giggled some more and texted Bodie.

Busy tonight? I've got a little surprise for you.

He started typing before I even set my phone down, and I tried to pretend like that didn't make my heart skydive in my chest.

I'm free, and I've got news about the video game. Want to celebrate?

I shot off an answer as quick as I could. *Yes, please. My apartment okay? We'll have the place to ourselves.*

I'll be there. Text me when you're home.

I will. <3

I grinned. "He's in. Or he's not in yet, but he's about to be *so* in. All the way in."

Veronica laughed. "Yeah, yeah. We get it."

And just like that, I'd talked myself into asking Bodie to a wedding.

Heart ninja. I was helpless to fight him. He was just too sneaky.

- BODIE -

bolted out the door the second I got the text that Penny was home, barely waving goodbye to my brother and Phil. Her name cycled through my brain with every footfall.

I had news — big news — and there was only one person in the world I found myself wanting to tell.

Penny.

I should have been scared out of my mind at the fact that she'd already become the person I told everything, especially since we'd been dancing around what we meant to each other for two weeks. But I wasn't. I was too happy to be afraid, which was so beyond stupid that I thought I might have made it back around to smart again.

My heart banged from taking her stairs two at a time. Seconds after knocking, the door swung open, and there she was.

Just when I thought my heart couldn't beat any harder, it proved me wrong.

She stood there in the doorway in nothing but lingerie.

No, I couldn't even call it lingerie. It was like an elaborate necklace; from the collar hung dozens of silver chains that flowed around her naked breasts and torso, swaying with every breath, connected to a ring a few inches below her belly button. More chains hung down from there, draping over the perfect curve of her hips and upper thighs, and from the center of the ring was a chain tassel that brushed against her piercing.

Something about the swing and shine of it, the peekaboo of the tattoos covering her milky-white skin, the way the chains moved on either side of her breasts, her nipples pink and taut, framed by barbells — all of it overloaded my senses, and I found myself standing stupidly in the hallway, staring in wonder.

She laughed and reached out just enough to grab my shirt to pull me into the apartment, closing the door behind me.

I palmed her breast as she stepped into me, and I finally got a good look at the rest of her. Her hair was a brighter purple than it had been yesterday, and her lips were blood red and smiling at me. She wore a headband of some sort, but it ran across her forehead with hundreds of tiny chains hanging down, shielding her eyes just enough to drive me crazy.

"You like it?" she asked as she wrapped her arms around my neck.

All I could do was nod and kiss her.

God, she felt so good pressed up against me, her bare ass in my hands, her tongue against mine as I tasted her like it was the first time.

She broke away and smiled, taking my hand before turning for her bedroom.

The back of the contraption she had on was almost bare with another ring just over her ass where another little tassel swung with the sway of her hips, and more draping chains followed the curve of her backside.

"Where the fuck did you get this thing?" I breathed in appreciation.

She shot me a smile over her shoulder. "The store."

I shook my head as we stepped into her room. "I need to check out the stores where you shop."

She laughed at that and closed the door. The lights were low, just a few small lamps to bathe the room in a golden light, and her portable speaker played a slow, sexy sort of electronic music. Her hips moved to the beat just a little, sending the chains swinging and my cock straining.

I pulled off my shirt and dropped it by the door, kicking off my shoes as she closed her eyes, her body moving in a wave to the music like I wasn't in the room. I took the hint, dropping my pants and stepping out of them before moving in her direction.

She didn't want me to stop her — she would have looked at me if she had — so I climbed onto her bed and sat propped up against the pillows, watching her.

With every roll of her hips, my pulse ticked faster, and my eyes drank her in — her hair, her shrouded eyes, the light catching the metal hanging on her. Her lily-white hands moved down her body and across her breasts, her fingers grazing her nipples.

I gripped my cock — it was so hard it hurt — stroking myself to ease the ache, wishing it were her around me, but I wouldn't have stopped her if you'd paid me.

She spun around, sending the chains arching around her, her hips still shifting, her torso rolling, just like it did when she rode me. Her lips parted as she looked down, her neck and shoulders rocking opposite her hips, and when her hands moved down her body and between her legs, when her long white finger disappeared into herself, my cock throbbed in my fist.

I moaned a curse, and she looked up at me, slivers of her eyes burning hot through the curtain of chains, and I couldn't take it anymore. I moved to the end of the bed, rising up onto my knees to tower over her, slipping my hand into her silvery-purple hair so I could kiss her. Her mouth opened up, and her tongue slid past my lips as mine did the same, teasing each other. My hands were in her hair, our mouths open wide, our breath coming heavy, our bodies determined to find release, so determined that we were barely in control.

But I was never really in control. Not when it came to Penny.

She took my cock with both hands and pumped, and I groaned into her mouth, which did nothing but spur her on.

My control slipped even further away. I flexed into her fists, fucking her hands with my cock, fucking her mouth with my tongue. But it wasn't enough. I wanted more, and I always would. Anytime I said different, I was a fucking liar.

When I broke away, I sat on the end of the bed, setting my feet on the ground. I looked up at her, mesmerized by the shadows across her face as she looked down at me, her hands cupping my jaw.

She started dancing again.

Penny let me go and turned around — her ass was just under eye-level with that tassel swinging over places where I wanted my face. But before I could grab her and do just that, she rolled her hips in a figure eight and lowered her body until her ass was cradling my cock.

Up and down she went, stroking me with her body. My hands were on her hips, squeezing, but she didn't need me to guide her. She looked back over her shoulder and raised her hips, stopping when the tip of me rested against the center of her. And I wouldn't wait any longer, wouldn't be teased for another second — with a flex of my hips and a shift of my hands, I pulled her down onto me until I was so deep inside her, I never wanted to leave.

She sighed my name as I gently pushed her away by the hips to lift her, then pulled her down again, grinding against her every time I hit the end.

"Lie back," she breathed.

And I did with an aching chest and a racing pulse and the length of me buried in her.

Without separating us, she rolled her hips a few times, her hands on my knees, and I watched my cock disappear and reappear in the heat of her from the best possible angle, every part of her exposed and open and full of me.

She climbed backward onto the bed in a feat of skill, first one knee coming to rest outside of my matching thigh and then the other, leaving her straddling me with her feet tucked into my ribs and her ass in my hands.

Her body moved, needing no help from me as she rose and fell, and I was so focused on every inch of her that a nuclear bomb could have detonated and I'd never know — I'd have died a happy man. I cupped her ass low, so low that my thumbs grazed my cock with every up and down of her body until they were slick from her. And then I spread her open and ran my thumb around the rim of her tight ass. It clenched under my touch as I circled, and she sucked in a breath.

"Do it," she said, voice rough as she dropped down.

I smiled and pressed.

The warmth of her, the tightness of her around me in more than one place was almost too much. It was too much for her, her body working faster. Every moan and sigh out of her said she was close. And she wasn't alone.

One of her hands slid between my thighs, cupping my aching balls, and my eyes rolled back when her fingertips against the space just behind them.

My hand squeezed involuntarily, pressing my thumb deeper inside of her, and she gasped. The sound sent a shock through me, and my cock pulsed inside her.

"Fuck, Penny," I growled.

Her body moved faster, harder, her skin smacking against mine with every motion. "Say my name again," she breathed.

"Come on, Penny," I said, the words gruff and hard. My abs burned as I watched the lips of her pussy swallow me. "Come for me, Penny."

"Oh God. Fuck," she cried, her voice breaking as her body clenched around me like it wanted to keep me still.

But I knew better.

I sucked in a breath through my nose, pounding into her as I pulled her down onto me with a slap and a jolt. And when I came, it was with her name on my lips, her flesh in my hands, her body throbbing around me like a song I never wanted to end.

I lay back hard as our bodies slowed, our hips still connected, and I rocked her against me, savoring the feeling for a minute longer as we tried to catch our breaths unsuccessfully. My abs were on fire. So was the rest of me.

After a moment, she sighed and lifted herself off of me before stretching out with her back to the door, looking sated, smiling at me.

I ran my clean thumb across her bottom lip. "How come this never comes off?"

"I use a special lipstick that doesn't smudge if I think I might have a dick in my mouth."

I laughed. "Prepared for anything."

"A girl's gotta be."

I kissed her nose. "Be right back."

I climbed off the bed and made my way to her bathroom, unable to keep the smile off my face. It was the third time we'd gone bareback, having had the whole birth control/clean conversation after she practically begged me to fuck her bare. It'd been years since she had sex without a condom, and though I never asked, I wondered how it was possible that she hadn't been with anyone long enough to get to this point.

The thought made me feel like a king and a caretaker. It was a gift I had no intention of squandering. It showed her trust, told me she was letting me into more than her body.

I cleaned myself up and grabbed a washcloth for her, running it under the warm water before heading back to her bedroom. But I stopped mid stride at the sight of her.

She lay curled on her side with her back to me, purple hair spilling over the bed in waves, her head on her bicep as she toyed with her hair. My eyes followed the curve of her tattooed waist and hips, coming to rest at the center of her. My gaze hung on the silvery rivulets that streamed out of her, what I'd left inside her.

I was instantly ready to fuck her again. Needed to fuck her again. Wanted to fill her up with me, every part of me.

My eyes were still locked between her legs as I approached the bed and sat next to her, folding the washcloth before running it up the length of her, cleaning her tenderly, both hands fully occupied.

I never did anything halfway.

She sighed and rolled over onto her back, the chains flowing around her breasts and the curves of her stomach and hips, and I shifted until her legs were open and slung over my thighs. I kept cleaning, and she smiled up at me.

"Tell me your news," she said, her voice a little rough.

"We got a pitch meeting for the game." I was smiling, grinning even.

Penny popped up onto her elbows. "Oh my God! Bodie, that's … that's amazing! When?"

"Two weeks," I said as I went back to work on her pussy, which was as clean as it was going to get. I just didn't want to stop touching it. "There's a lot to do, so I might be busy until it's finished."

She frowned a little at that, spreading her legs wider. "Well, just don't forget about me."

I laughed. "That's funny, Pen."

Her frown disappeared, turning into a smile as she watched my hands. "God, I'm so happy for you. You gave up everything to follow your dreams. I'd never be brave enough to take a risk like that. It's impressive. You impress me."

"The feeling is entirely mutual, believe me."

She smiled, lying back with a sigh. "Tell me more about the game."

"Well, there's a madame of a pleasure ship, Gemma."

"Oh, I love this already."

I smirked. "She's a smuggler, and so are her girls."

"Naturally."

"Then there's Nate— he's the airship pirate and a smuggler too. They go on this treasure hunt together and have to team up — he has the map, and she has the key. Of course, the bad guy is after them with an army of goons called Ravens. Basically, they wear these leather masks they wear with beaks and top hats."

"Ugh, that is so cool," she said as I ran the cloth over her piercing softly. "I want to draw all the things — airships and girls in leather with knives and pistols and chakrams. What color is her hair?"

"Fire-engine red."

"A woman after my own heart."

I smiled. "So, how was the dress fitting?"

"Good. Everything was perfect, and we went home with dresses. Ramona cried, which made me and Ronnie cry. I blame the champagne though."

I chuckled and ran the cloth over her.

"So, I wanted to ask you something," she started, seeming nervous.

I kept my eyes on my task, hoping it would give her room to say what she needed to say. "Ask away."

"Well," she flexed her thighs, bringing her hips closer to me, "Ramona put me down for a plus-one, but I don't have a plus-one."

I tossed the washcloth toward her closet where her hamper was, trying not to smile. "Oh?" My focus was on my hands as I rested them on either side of her hood and ran my thumbs up and down the line of her center, soaking them.

"Mmhmm," she buzzed with her lip between her teeth and eyes on my hands. "Wanna go?"

My heart leaped. This was beyond a date. This was a wedding.

This was big.

I stroked her, opening her up, pressing against the warm pink hole that led to Shangri-la. "Sure," I said simply, hoping I sounded cool. Because inside, I wasn't cool at all. Inside, I was fist-pumping and whooping and jumping around like a maniac.

She smiled and sighed again as I ran my thumbs up to her piercing, slicking it, rubbing it, teasing it. I didn't want to say anything else about the wedding. If I did, I wouldn't be able to pretend like it wasn't a big deal.

"Good," was the last thing she said, a soft sound that left her lips on a breath as I worked her body with my thumbs.

Instead of speaking, I decided to use my tongue for other things.

I hinged at the waist and kissed her piercing with an open mouth and a sweep of my tongue, but she was a little too close for it to be comfortable, so I hooked her thighs over my shoulders, gripped her waist, and sat up, taking her with me.

Her shoulders were still on the bed, and her hands wrapped around my legs, nails digging into my skin as she gasped with surprise, then pleasure.

I buried my face in her, running my tongue up the hot slit I'd been touching. The metallic tang of what I'd left inside her sent a jolt through me, and I delved deeper into her, looking for more.

She rocked against my face, which I moved from side to side, nestling deeper into her still. Her fingers moved to her piercing, rubbing that bottom ball against her clit as her thighs squeezed, hips bucking. And when I hummed long and deep, she came against my tongue with a warm rush and a pulsing flex. With her thighs clamped around my ears, I couldn't hear anything but her distant moaning, and I slowed, kissing her swollen, tender clit gently.

Her body relaxed, and I lowered her back to the bed, my biceps on fire.

Worth it.

Her cheeks were pink as she pulled herself up to sit and got on her knees to climbed onto my lap, not stopping until our lips were a seam and her arms were around my neck.

When she broke the kiss, she smiled wickedly and backed away, ending up on all fours in front of me.

"Get up on your knees," she ordered.

I did, my heart banging, my cock throbbing when she licked her lips and crawled to me.

Her hand found my base, and her lips opened, tongue extending to guide my head into her hot, wet mouth.

I slipped my fingers into her hair, tugging off the headband so I could see her eyes as she looked up at me, her body a wave as she took the length of me into her mouth.

She moaned.

I hissed.

Her eyelashes fluttered closed, and she got to work, chains swaying from the curve of her waist and hips, and my eyes traced every line from the tip of her nose to her heart-shaped ass.

Heaven existed inside Penny's mouth.

My hips moved on their own, and she matched my rhythm, her hands on the bed, my eyes drinking in the sight of her on all fours with my cock in her mouth, and too soon, I was close.

I pulsed in her mouth, my hand in her hair clenching in warning, and she backed away, letting me go with a pop.

My heart beat so hard it hurt, my breath burning my lungs as she stretched out on the bed and motioned for me to follow, her hands reaching for my aching cock. I crawled up her body, and she took me in her hands.

"Get up," she whispered.

I straddled her waist, leaning over to brace myself on the wall. Her hair was fanned out all over the pillow, her eyes hot as she gripped me with both hands and stroked.

I was still so wet from her mouth. Her hands, gentle and firm, pumped and stroked, and my pulse raced. My hips sped. And when I came, my heart stopped from the act, from the sight of Penny, eyes closed and neck outstretched, hands around me, angling me to come in hot bursts all over her tattooed breasts, her collarbone, her neck, the chains.

"Jesus fucking Christ, Penny," I whispered, the words ragged, my brain on fire and body burning from her touch.

She opened her eyes and smiled, and I fought the urge to ask her if I could keep her forever.

Wait, What?

- PENNY -

Things *I would never in* my life forget: the sight of Ramona wearing a penis crown and a greasy, gyrating bohunk in her lap, who held onto his cowboy hat and humped her to the tune of "Save a Horse (Ride a Cowboy)."

I was possibly going to die from laughing, and I had *definitely* snuck a photo.

Veronica and I were chanting, *Mona, Mona,* as we threw money on the stage, which was ridiculous since we'd already paid to have her pulled onstage for public humiliation.

When the song ended, we all cheered, and the banana-hammocked stripper offered a hand to help her stand and guided her to the stage stairs with a kiss on the cheek. She curtsied as she walked toward our group.

The night had been a good one — heels were high, laughs were from the belly, and the drinks were cold and ample.

Ramona was tanked.

All was as it should be.

We took our seats at the edge of the men's stage, and I reached over to straighten Ramona's tiny veil with bobbling dicks on springs around the tiara.

She smiled at me, her eyes glossy and wet. "I love you, Penny."

"I love you too," I said on a laugh. "Need another drink?"

She nodded, grinning now. "Jameson on the rocks."

"I know what you drink, pumpkin." I booped her nose.

"You always take care of me, even when I'm a drunk bitch," she said, motioning to herself.

"Well, you take care of me literally all the rest of the time, so we're even. I'm the lucky one. And I pay you back in the form of humping cowboys and Jameson!"

Ramona giggled. "He was so hot. But not as hot as Shep." She sighed. "How the fuck did I get so lucky?"

"Well, for starters, you're a fucking catch."

"So are you. And now you got caught by Bodie the fisherman with his giant pole." She pretended to cast a fishing line from her crotch.

I cackled, only a little freaked out by the thought. "You are so drunk. Let me get you even more drunker."

"More drunker!" she crowed.

I flagged our waitress, who had on the most epic studded bra, thong, and garter set I'd ever seen. Like, so epic that I'd asked her where she got it and *maybe* bought it on my phone.

Once I was settled back in my seat, the music changed as a new stripper came out dressed like a B-Boy. The song was by Machinedrum and totally obscure, which caught my ear and my eye. It was a sexy dubstep song I had on one of my playlists, and he immediately won points for originality.

He was hot as fuck, gliding across the stage, popping and locking in the sexiest striptease known to woman.

I sat at the edge of my seat, hands in the air as I danced in place, excitedly singing the words.

B-Boy Johnny locked onto me with his lip between his teeth. He made his way across the stage to stop right in front of me and pulled off his shirt, rolling his body as he tossed it.

And just like that, he was planking on the edge of the stage with his feet in the air and his face inches from mine.

I laughed and sang the words to him, hoping he was harmless and/or gay. He spun away and danced some more, but he kept coming back to me like I was the center point of the universe, like the dance was for me.

I didn't even have any dollars for him; I'd given them all to Ramona. This fact did not deter him.

A few minutes in, I felt a little squirmy — he was definitely not harmless *or* gay — so I turned to Ramona to give her all my attention, hoping he would get the hint. Instead of ignoring me like I wanted, he flipped off the stage and landed right in front of me, dancing in my direction until he had me pushed all the way back in my seat and was straddling me. So I let the man give me a lap dance like a good girl, slipping a couple of bucks someone had shoved in my hand into the waist of his pants.

I mean, the guy had to eat, right?

He spent the final two minutes of the song in my lap, taking my hand to run it down his chiseled chest and abs, and we laughed at the brilliant awkwardness of it all.

A month ago, I probably would have gone home with him. But tonight? Tonight I wasn't interested at all, and I couldn't stop assessing him.

He was tall but not as tall as Bodie. And he had a great smile, but his bottom teeth were a little crooked where Bodie's were almost unnaturally straight, thanks to his orthodontist and those braces that had helped hide him from me years ago. Plus, B-Boy Johnny was missing that dimple that made me crazy. No way was he as funny as Bodie either. I knew almost without a doubt that Bodie ate better pussy.

So I endured that lap dance like a champ as well as a little kiss on the cheek he gave me before he gathered up his clothes and cash and disappeared behind the curtain.

Another guy came out, a gigantic, jacked motherfucker, who smirked and danced across the stage to R. Kelly, and I zoned out. Not my type. He was too … brunette.

I frowned.

He was too Not-Bodie.

I was instantly uncomfortable, which instantly surprised me.

Never in my life had I been with a man who no one could match up to. I'd never been with a man who was so easy to be with that I found myself on a date with him without even realizing it. I'd never been with a man so much over such a short period of time and not gone insane or driven someone else insane.

The whole thing was baffling and made me so uneasy that I needed to get up. To walk. To change the scenery.

So I leaned into Ramona and grabbed some of her singles. "I'm gonna go get a drink. Be back."

"Don't we have a waitress?" Her face quirked up like a cartoon character.

"Yes, but I forgot something. I'll be back. Just watch that." I pointed to the stage, and she smiled.

"Okay, hurry up!" she slurred, not taking her eyes off the stripper.

I nodded to Veronica to make sure she knew she was in charge before heading deeper into the club.

It was co-ed — really, most of the club was women with just a small stage for the wang. And as I walked through the club, I zeroed in on a girl with a superhuman bootie who was working her way up a side stage pole. When she did the splits with her crotch an inch from the ceiling and the pole wedged between her tits, my mouth hit the floor, and I cheered, hurrying over.

"Shut up and take my money!" I called, waving a stack of dollars as I took a seat on the edge of her stage.

The woman defied gravity. Her hair was long and curly, and she spun around that pole like it was easy, which I knew to be an absolute lie. I'd tried it once on a dare and had pole-burn for a week.

I had no idea how long I sat there, but let me tell you this; when she got down on her knees in front of me and booty-clapped to 2Pac's "Hail Mary," my life was forever changed. I swear to God, I found Jesus in her G-string.

Ramona materialized at my side. "What the fuck, Pen? What are you doing over here? You know I depend on you for supplementary entertainment at these things."

"Because, look." I grabbed her by the chin and turned it so she could see the Booty-Clap Queen speak the gospel.

Her eyes widened. "Oh my God. That is incredible," she said reverently.

"I know. Plus, those guys were just meh."

"Just meh?" she asked, turning to look back at me like I was nuts. "You're kidding, right? That breakdancer was hot enough to have made the cut for *Magic Mike*, and he wasn't even gay. I'm about ninety-six percent certain he wanted to impregnate you."

I laughed. "I mean, he was okay. But he wasn't like *this*." I gestured to my new hero as she spun down the pole like a goddamn sexual siren.

She giggled and grabbed my hand. "Come back over. It's almost time for Annika's lap dance, and you know the look on her face is going to be so fucking worth it."

I sighed and followed her back to the men's stage, but she'd let my hand go before we got close, so I hung back for a second, watching my friends from afar.

I felt so weird, so off. I was usually the one up at the edge of the stage, stuffing money in my bra so the only way the strippers would get paid was with their faces in my cleavage.

But tonight it seemed kind of boring.

In fact, I kept thinking about Bodie. I wondered if he could dance like any of these guys, and then I wondered if I could convince him to strip for me. I wondered if he would have liked my new mentor's galactic ass as much as I had. I wondered if he would have been jealous when B-Boy Johnny was all up in my grill.

I wondered if one of the ladystrippers had been on him, how I would have felt.

And then I imagined pulling a stripper out of Bodie's lap and shoving her, subsequently being escorted out of the club by security. It didn't make me feel better. I mean, shoving an imaginary stripper who had dared to touch Bodie made me feel better, but the reality was that I felt a little tingle in my chest that scared the shit out of me. Feelings. Real feelings.

Not-Bodie's Armani cologne hit me before I sensed someone standing next to me.

"Hey."

I turned to find B-Boy Johnny smirking at me, fully clothed, with his hat pulled down over his eyes.

I bet he's balding. Bodie's hair could stop traffic.

I smiled politely. "Hey. Good job out there."

"Thanks. I couldn't help but notice you."

I laughed patronizingly and pointed at my head. "Yeah, it's the hair. Kinda stands out."

"It's not just that," he said, slipping a hand around my waist.

"You're … I dunno. Different."

Johnny was apparently real wordy. And handsy.

I chuckled and put a hand on his chest as I twisted out of his grip, itching to get away. "You're sweet, but I have a boyfriend."

He was still smirking. "That's all right. It's just mind over matter, baby. If you don't mind, it don't matter."

I couldn't help but laugh again as I stored that one in my Come-On Lines folder. "I'm sorry. Have a good night," I said as I walked away.

My heart was banging. I had no idea what had gotten into me. In fact, I couldn't remember the last time I'd turned a guy down who was hot and could move his hips like a fucking snake.

But what nearly knocked me over was the fact that I'd called Bodie my boyfriend. I stopped dead in my tracks as that tingle in my chest worked down my spine.

Wait, what?

It wasn't like I'd never lied and said I had a boyfriend just to get away from a guy, but that wasn't what this was. When I'd said boyfriend, I'd meant *Bodie*. I had thought his name as clearly as if I'd spoken it. I had seen his dimple in my mind like my name was written in it. I'd felt his presence as if he were standing in the room with me.

I didn't want B-Boy Johnny because I wanted Bodie and no one but Bodie.

I was so freaked out that I barely got to enjoy Annika's lap dance by the hulkiest black man I'd ever seen outside of a Knicks game. He got so in her lap and in her face that I could barely see her around him. She was half-crying, half-laughing and wholly amused, though clearly uncomfortable. Her eyes were closed for a good portion of the show, which seemed to only egg him on.

I had a sneaking suspicion that it was her first encounter with a stripper, which made it that much better. And I was too busy wigging out to get any mileage out of the jokes I'd been saving up to embarrass her with.

Within an hour, we were stumbling out of the club, heading toward Shep and Ramona's new place, laughing and chatting along the way. We stopped on our way to get pizza from a window booth, which was the only reason Ramona wouldn't be puking her guts up all day the next day.

And all the while, my thoughts were on Bodie, just as they had been all night. I didn't think I'd said more than ten words since we left the strip club, and I used them all to order pizza.

Somehow, I'd found myself in some sort of relationship without even realizing it, and I had no idea what that meant.

Denial was a thing, and I was the queen of it.

For weeks I'd been seeing him, and I'd had no desire to look anywhere else. He was smart and hot. He knew how to work my body almost better than I did, knew how to make me laugh and make me swoon and make me *happy*.

Peggy was quiet. Probably too quiet.

But from the jump, I'd said no commitment. From the start, I'd said we should talk if we caught feelings.

Clearly, I'd caught feelings, and no amount of antibiotics would save me.

I wondered if that meant I had to tell him, and my stomach dropped at the thought. I couldn't — not yet. I mean, *yet* was such a dumb word to use because I didn't know if I could *ever*. If I admitted it, it would be real. If I admitted it, things would change. And I didn't want things to change.

The pizza was like cardboard in my mouth as I walked in the back of the laughing pack.

The real issue was that I didn't know for certain that he had feelings for me too. I didn't know if I made him feel as good as he made me feel. Whatever he felt — if anything — he kept on lock. He was totally blasé, super chill, reminding me over and over again that this was all for fun. Implying that it meant nothing.

Me calling him my boyfriend definitely wasn't nothing.

I wondered just how he felt, if he'd call me his girlfriend if a stripper hit on him. The thought of asking him made me gag, and I tossed my pizza in the next trash can I came across. I didn't want to know if he didn't feel the same. I didn't want whatever we had to end, not until it was inevitable. And the only way it would be inevitable was if I opened my big fucking mouth.

Things were too good to blow it all up. So I'd keep it to myself for now, maybe forever. Because I didn't want to lose him. Not yet, and definitely not tonight. Tonight I wanted to see him more than ever.

I grabbed my phone from my clutch and texted him.

Still up?

My heart skipped when I saw him typing. *I am. Working late. How was the strip club?*

Good. I had my mind blown by a stripper's ass. I mean it. My whole universe was shaken.

Learn any new tricks?

I smiled. *I don't have nearly enough junk in my trunk to do what she did. I don't have enough core strength either.*

Hahaha. What are you doing now?

Well, now that I know you're up, I'd like to be doing you.

What do you know? My schedule just cleared.

God, I was so into him, and I couldn't even be mad about it.

Be there in thirty.

And as I put my phone away, I felt lighter. Because denial was a sweet, sweet place to be, and I'd stay there until I was dragged out, kicking and screaming.

- BODIE -

thought I'd be able to finish what I was working on before Penny came over, but there was no way. Instead, I bugged Jude and Phil while they worked, antsy out of nowhere.

Penny did that to me. Made me crazy. Made me want things I couldn't have. Every day it got harder to play it cool, harder to pretend. But until she was ready to talk about it, I'd keep it to myself.

She knocked on the door, and I walked over, trying not to hurry, throwing my chill on at the last possible second.

Penny looked incredible, as she always did. Tonight she was in the tightest black jeans I'd ever seen in my life, the waist high and her crop top short, exposing a slice of the flowers tattooed on her stomach and ribs. She wasn't wearing a bra again, and I tried not to think about how many men noticed the curve of her breasts, the peaks of her nipple, the bars on each side.

It wouldn't have bothered me so bad if I'd known she was mine.

She smiled and stepped into me, and I pushed the thought away as I pulled her into my chest and kissed her.

I closed the door, and we walked through the living room.

"Hey, guys," Penny said, wiggling her fingers at them.

They waved over the backs of their chairs, not turning around.

"Working hard?" she asked as we walked into my room.

I closed the door and reached for my phone to turn on music. "Always. We're in DEFCON One now that we have a meeting."

She smiled and sat down on my bed, reaching down to unbuckle her shoes. "It's so amazing, Bodie. I have a good feeling about this."

"Me too," I said as I stretched out in bed, propped up by my pillows. "So tell me about this stripper's ass."

She laughed and climbed up the bed, sitting next to me on her knees. "It was magnificent. It made me want to do a thousand squats because if I could badonk my donk like that, I could die knowing I'd accomplished something that made the universe a better place." She perked up and popped off the bed. "Oh! I brought you something."

When she bounded back over from her purse, she hopped up on the bed and bounced a little, holding something behind her.

"How'd you know you'd see me tonight?" I asked, smirking in an attempt to keep my eagerness hidden.

She shrugged. "I couldn't be around all that gyrating and not come see you after. Okay, now — you ready?"

"I dunno. Am I?"

She chuckled. "You are. *Voilà!*"

When Penny brought her hand out from behind her back, it held a small painting, about five-by-seven — an illustration of a girl in a leather bustier and leather garters with knives strapped to one thigh, red hair blowing in the wind, and an airship behind her. The word *Nighthawk* arched over the top of the watercolor drawing, framed by gears.

I took it reverently, my eyes raking over it in wonder. "Penny, this is gorgeous."

Her smile could have been a thousand watts. "You like it?"

"I love it," was all I could say.

"I told you it made me want to draw. Bodie, I'm just so happy for you. And I want you to know that I believe you can do this. I believe you can do just about anything."

I rested my hand on her thigh, and her face softened as she leaned into me, pressing a sweet kiss to my lips. When she backed away, I saw something new in her eyes, something different. Something good. Something more.

I felt the warmth of it spread through my chest.

I wanted to speak, but if I did, I'd admit things, and if I admitted what I wanted to admit, the feeling could be gone just as soon as I'd earned it. So instead, I cupped her cheek and slipped my fingers into her hair, bringing her closer to kiss her with more intention.

Penny communicated through sex and through ink, and maybe I could do the same. Maybe I could telegraph how I felt through my lips alone. Maybe she could feel my heart through the tips of my fingers.

I hoped she could. Because the game we'd been running was long, and I felt the end coming too soon. There would be a moment when we couldn't avoid it anymore, when the words wouldn't stay inside me any longer.

The chances of her feeling the same were slim, and I knew it. I'd known my odds when I stepped into the lion's cage and started this dance with her.

But that didn't stop me from hoping.

Wild Horses

-PENNY-

"**So when's your boyfriend coming?**" Ramona asked my reflection in the massive mirrors of the bridal suite.

"Hopefully the second I can get my dress hitched up," I answered without missing a beat before sipping the champagne in my hand to punctuate the joke.

Ramona and Veronica laughed, and I shimmied my rack in my bridesmaid dress with one hand.

"Seriously, my boobs look amazing in this. Maybe he'll come before I can even get it pulled up." I turned to inspect my ass, which was on point. "Anyway, I'm not calling him that. I don't like that word."

Veronica raised one brow. "And what are you calling him?"

"My slam piece. 'Cause he's Sexy Like A Motherfucker, and he can slam me all night. Like, literally all night. My vagina has never been slammed on the Bodie level."

She snickered. "Slam piece? I mean, whatever helps you sleep at night."

"No wonder he somehow tricked you into being his *girlfriend*."

Ramona was baiting me. I was no dummy even if I was a sucker.

Oddly, the moniker didn't make me want to puke up my champagne and donuts like it had a couple of days ago.

"*Slam piece*," I said flatly. "You act like I've pledged my undying devotion to him. God, a girl can't even get steady dick anymore without everyone starting a pool on when she's going to get engaged."

Ramona laughed — she was cool as a cucumber, which was beyond all reason, considering she was an hour away from getting married. We stood in the middle of a regal room with a chandelier the size of Delaware and more French antiques than I'd ever seen in one place outside of a museum. She looked beautiful, blissfully happy, and without a single indicator of nervousness, which was impressive seeing as how she was about to walk down the aisle.

She touched my arm, her eyes and smile full of love. "I'm happy for you."

I smiled back, my heart so furry and warm and full that I didn't know if all the happiness would stay in my chest. "You too. Are you ready for this?"

She shrugged. "I've been waiting for this day forever, but I'm just … I don't know. Zen as fuck. I don't even care how things go — in an hour, I'll be his wife. And then we'll eat and drink and dance and fuck like rockstars in the Kennedy suite."

"Yeah, you will," I said, gyrating my hips.

"Everything is done and taken care of." She hooked her arm in mine and hung her other around Veronica's shoulders. "I have you two. I have Shep waiting for me at the end of an aisle to promise me forever. There's nothing else I could possibly wish for."

I misted up. "Ugh, you're so happy it's disgusting."

Ramona laughed. "I know. Isn't it amazing?"

I rested my head on her shoulder and took in the sight of the three of us in the mirror. "It's kinda the best thing in the whole world."

My phone buzzed in my pocket — my dress had pockets, guys; winning hard. — and I pulled away, reaching for it.

The photo displayed behind Bodie's name lit up my phone and my insides; I was nuzzled into his neck laughing, and he was laughing too, his dimple flashing.

Veronica laughed and pointed at my screen. "Oh my God. *Boyfriend.*"

I rolled my eyes and answered the phone, smiling. "Hey," I said as I stepped off the platform, passing the tornado that was Ramona's mom on my way out. I swear, I think she was shouldering all the nerves for both of them.

"Hey," he echoed, his voice rumbly and low and velvety.

My body reacted immediately to that one mundane syllable like it was a secret password.

I hadn't seen him in two days, since after the strip club. We'd been too busy with wedding stuff to have a free millisecond.

"Are you here?" I asked.

I could hear him smiling. "I am. Just got here."

"Meet me by the bar."

"Already there."

My grin stretched wide as I rushed to the door, calling over my shoulder that I'd be right back.

I hurried through the garden where people were milling around, waiting for the ceremony to start. The venue was gorgeous, an outdoor garden with a big tent for the reception and a gazebo in a hedge alcove that felt like a fairy land. There was a rope swing and a massive bar that had been imported from a pub in France, all brass and mahogany and gorgeous and elegant.

But not as gorgeous as the man standing in front of it.

His dirty-blond hair had been cut short on the sides, kept longer on a top, combed back and to the side in a gentle swoop, and I nearly stopped in my tracks at the transformation. The laid-back surfer in a muscle shirt and sneakers had been replaced by a clean-cut masterpiece of power. The gravity of the vision of him pulled me toward him like a tractor beam. He looked like he'd stepped off a magazine cover with tan skin and eyes shining a shade of sky blue that felt infinite. The suit he wore fit him perfectly — charcoal gray swathing every angle of his broad shoulders and chest, one button of his coat fastened, his shirt crisp and white, and tie thin and black. One hand rested in his pocket, his coat bunched up at the seam where his hand and hip were, and the other held a scotch.

I was nine hundred percent sure my uterus whispered his name when he smiled at me, popping that dimple and my ovaries with a simple flicker of cheek muscles.

I might have floated into his arms, slipping mine around his neck as I kissed him. There was quite literally nothing else I could have done when I saw him standing there, dressed like that.

His lips were so warm and familiar and soft and sweet. The two measly days we'd been apart felt like a month.

I pulled away, humming, but I didn't give him his neck back, just fiddled with the short hair at the nape, marveling over the soft bristling against my fingertips.

"Your hair," I whispered, smiling as my eyes scanned him in wonder.

"You like it?"

"I love it. If it wasn't combed, my fingers would be buried deep, deep in it."

He laughed softly, the sound rumbling through his chest and into me. "Later we'll bury all kinds of things in all kinds of places."

I answered with a laugh of my own. "What in the world possessed you to do it?"

Bodie shrugged. "I went in for a trim and decided to cut it. It matched the suit."

"True. But do you think you might grow it back out?"

"Why? Miss it already?" he asked with a smile, holding me tighter.

"Maybe. I do love your long hair, but this is so soft." I ran my fingers over it. "And I swear, somehow, your jaw looks a hundred times sharper. You've got a good looking head, boy. You could be a part-time model."

He laughed at that and kissed me again.

I smiled up at him feeling dreamy and light and unbelievably happy. "I missed you," I said without thinking.

His face held its shape, but something behind his eyes shifted, sending a jolt of uncertainty through me, cooling my mood. "I missed you too."

I swallowed and looked at his tie, running my hand down his chest. "Where the hell did you get this suit?"

His smile shifted sideways into a smirk. "Same place as you get your lingerie."

I laughed. "Oh, I very much doubt that."

Bodie chuckled, his hand on my hip, thumb shifting against the soft silk before he twisted the tie around his finger and held it up. "So tell me, what happens if I pull this?"

I pressed the length of my body against his and smiled, stretching on my tiptoes to get to his ear. "Boom, I'm naked."

His lips were at my ear too. "Good to know."

The man was magic. He could whisper anything in my ear — *My grandma makes a mean scone. I'm all out of peanut butter. I wish I had more time to climb trees* — and I'd forget that there was ever or would ever be anything to do besides him.

I sighed into his ear, and he held me a little closer. I found myself pouting because I couldn't stay right there like I wanted.

I pulled away and stepped back, though I slid my hand down his arm and to his hand to hold it. "You gonna be okay out here? It's about to start, so it shouldn't be long before I'm back to entertain you."

He held up his scotch, smiling. "I'll keep myself company." He paused, his eyes on mine in a way that I felt in the tips of my fingers and toes. "You look beautiful, Penny."

My cheeks flushed, and I smiled back. How could I not? Adonis in a suit was smiling at me with a scotch in his hand and a suit that made my vagina do an involuntary Kegel.

"You're not so bad yourself, handsome. I'll see you in a little bit."

"I'll be waiting," he said.

And the words worked their way through me like I'd been the one drinking scotch.

- BODIE -

watched Penny walk away as I took a sip of my drink, my eyes running over all the places I wished my hands were. The deep V of the back of her dress, framing her tattoos. The small circle of her waist, tied by that little sash that would strip her with a tug. The swing of her hips as she hurried away in the direction she'd come from.

A sigh rose and fell from the bottom of my lungs.

I hadn't seen her in two days, not since she came over after the bachelorette party. Things had been the same that night as they had always been — we'd spent an hour or so wrapped up in each other, an hour or so talking and laughing, and then she'd left. But something had shifted, something I didn't know how to place or what to do with. All I knew was that I could feel the depth of it in me and in her. And she hadn't run away.

We hadn't spoken about the status of our relationship since the ice cream parlor, and her shock that day — when I'd reaffirmed that I wouldn't ask for more than she was willing to give — was still fresh in my mind.

How could she have gone for so long without knowing this feeling? Without wanting more than just a fuck boy?

I wanted to know. But the last thing I wanted to do was ask.

Because the last thing I wanted was to lose her.

So as far as I knew — as far as she'd said — things were the same. But what she *did* didn't match up with what she *said*. She'd tattooed my arm. She'd spent almost every day with me for weeks. We'd been on a date, and tonight I was her date at a *wedding*.

It didn't feel like no strings, no commitment, no rules. It felt like she was mine, and I was hers. It felt like we were together. And that felt good — so good that I wasn't likely to rock the boat out of fear I'd sink it.

I drained my drink and set it on the surface of the bar, checking my calculator watch before following the signs to the gazebo.

Annika and I merged paths as we entered an arched tunnel covered in vines. In heels, she was almost as tall as me, her blonde hair in a loose bun at her nape and black dress sleek and simple.

She smiled, transforming her aloof runway model vibe, warming her up. "Hey, Bodie."

"Good to see you, Annika."

"You too. You're here with Penny?"

I didn't miss the mild surprise in her voice. I couldn't say I blamed her. I was probably more shocked than anyone.

"I am."

Her smiled widened. "Lucky you. Want to sit with me?"

I relaxed a little. "That'd be great. I don't know anyone who isn't in the wedding party but you."

She chuckled. "I only know the crew who were invited, but I'm just about the only one who's part of the production of the show who's here as a guest. The rest are filming."

I looked around once we exited the tunnel for the camera crew, finding them in little hidden alcoves, blending in like chameleons. I'd signed a waiver, and I still hadn't realized they were here.

"Huh. How about that?" I said half to myself, guiding her into a row of white wooden chairs.

"We want to film in the most unobtrusive way possible. It's not always easy, but thankfully, my boss is sympathetic to the cause." She wiggled the fingers of her left hand at me, flashing her engagement ring. When we were seated, she turned a little in her chair to face me, crossing her long legs in my direction. "So, how'd you land her?"

I wished I'd gotten another drink. "Well, I'm not sure I've landed her just yet."

"Oh, I am," Annika said on a chuckle.

I glanced at her, intrigued. "That so?"

She nodded. "As long as I've known her, she's never had a steady guy. She'll date one for a little bit and then flit off to the next, never getting attached, and I've *never* seen one of the guys, only heard the stories. She won't bring them around us like she has with you. And I've seen the way she looks at you, the way she talks to you. It's my job to read people, and I've been reading Penny for a year now. She likes you, and she's happy, happier than I've seen her. So I'm curious as to how you did it."

"I haven't done much but let her be who she is."

Annika's face softened. "Penny's like a wild pony; she's beautiful and untamed and completely free. Free from the tethers of judgment, free from being controlled, contained. She lives one day at a time, doing exactly what she wants, accepting her consequences without a single care for what anyone else thinks." Annika sighed at that. "She's the freest woman I've ever known or seen, and I have more respect for that than anything. I'm even a little envious."

I nodded, smiling at the truth of her words. "I know what you mean."

"But she loves to run. That's the trick, the catch I haven't seen anyone overcome." She shook her head. "None of this — you and her, I mean — is any of my business, and I don't mean to pry. I'm just so interested in how you snagged her. You're like the pony whisperer."

I laughed at that. If she'd replaced pony with pussy it might have been spot-on. "Honestly? I don't even know. She asked for no strings, so that's what I've given her. I let her lead. I respect her too, respect what she wants even if it's not what I want."

"And what do you want?" she asked. But before I could answer, she waved her hand as the color rose in her cheeks. "I'm sorry. My job has me trained to ask personal questions that I shouldn't. Please, don't answer that."

"No, it's okay," I said as the music started.

We turned in our seats.

From the green archway, Penny appeared on Patrick's arm, that dress sweeping the green grass at her feet like she was floating, and her eyes found mine and held them.

"I just want her," was my answer to Annika, to the universe. To myself.

The ceremony was simple and perfect. Ramona and Shep were married under the gazebo, staring into each other's eyes like no one else was there. When they said their vows, when they kissed, a lump formed in my throat, and Annika pressed her fingertips to her lips. We all stood and clapped and cheered and smiled as they walked down the aisle — this time, as husband and wife. And when Penny passed me and her eyes found mine, they were shining, her cheeks flushed. She told me a million things I somehow couldn't decipher; I could only feel them all and try to understand.

I offered my arm to Annika, and we made our way into the reception tent and to the head table where our dates would be joining us. We sat next to each other, chatting as everyone found their seats.

The DJ kicked off "I Believe in a Thing Called Love" by The Darkness, and Penny blew onto the dance floor with Patrick, inflatable guitars in hand, air-strumming. Penny actually hitched up her skirt and slid across the parquet, red bottom lip in her teeth and head banging in time to the beat.

The rest of the wedding party came out, and once they were present, they made an archway with their black guitars, and then Ramona and Shep ran through to finish the song to a standing ovation.

After the song, they headed over to us — Penny practically jumped into my arms, sending me off balance, and I swung us to keep us upright.

The sound of her laughter in my ears was the sweetest song.

I set her feet on the ground, sliding her down my body, and she cupped my cheek and kissed me gently, smiling softly. She looked at me like I was a king, and I felt like every bit of one with her on my arm.

We took our seats and ate our steaks, laughing and talking and high off the night, the moment. Toasts were given. Speeches were made. Tears were shed. And all the while, Penny's hand was in my lap, our fingers threaded together.

And then the party started.

The sun had gone down, and the dance floor was illuminated by naked bulbs strung in arcs from one end of the tent to the other. Shep and Ramona's first song was a spinning, swaying, brilliantly choreographed dance to "Never Tear Us Apart" by INXS. After that, Ramona, Penny, and Veronica did their own choreography to "Scream & Shout," and the guys surprised them by jumping in halfway through with their own moves.

Joel, Shep, and Patrick — aka two tattooed Sasquatches and a male model — throwing lassos and yelling *Britney, bitch* was the most hysterical thing I'd ever seen in my life.

And then Penny was in my arms for the rest of the night. First, we were bouncing around to New Order and Lady Gaga. Then, The Clash came on, and I kissed her in the middle of a sea of people jumping and singing to "Rock the Casbah," just like the first kiss, the kiss that I thought of so often.

I pulled her outside to get a drink and spotted a swing on a gargantuan old tree.

I tugged her in that direction, stopping just next to it. "Remember the park by the beach where we used to party in high school?"

My hand rested on her waist, and she smiled up at me, reaching for the rope of the swing.

"How could I forget?"

"You're just the same as you were, except now you're more *you* than you ever were. You're just as beautiful. You're just as brash and brilliant. But now, you're free."

She fiddled with my lapel with her free hand, and her eyes watched her fingers. "Oh, I don't know about that. I want to be. I try to be. But sometimes, my freedom is a cage." She seemed to shake the thought away and smiled, meeting my eyes again. "Your outsides have changed, but your insides are exactly the same. I wish … I wish I'd seen you then like I see you now. If I had, maybe things would have been different. Maybe I'd be different." Her words were soft, her eyes bright and shining.

"I wouldn't want you to be any different than you are right now, Pen." The words were quiet, solemn.

And for a moment, we stood in silence until I couldn't take it anymore. I couldn't let her say anymore, because if she did, the thin façade I'd built would crumble and blow away, exposing me, exposing her.

So I kissed her instead. She tasted of bourbon and cake, smelled of jasmine, felt like silk against my fingertips, against my lips.

When I let her go, I guided her to sit on the wide wooden plank, her long fingers wrapping around the ropes to hang on. And when I pulled her back by her waist and released her, the gray silk of her dress billow and her silvery hair fly with the sound of her laughter in my ears.

Too soon after, the night was nearly over. The DJ had brought the tempo down, and I found myself in the middle of the dance floor with Penny against my chest, The Cure singing "Pictures of You" as the two of us moved in small circles on the parquet.

It was strange, how I felt. Like I was dreaming. Like my heart had opened up and so had hers. That we were open to *each other*. I could feel the connection like a tether between us. That everything that I felt, she felt. That everything I wanted, she wanted.

I kissed the top of her head, and she shifted her face against my beating heart.

I had to tell her. I needed her to know that I wanted her, wanted more, felt more. I wanted to soothe her, ease her fears, promise her anything she asked for. Because I'd give her anything even if it meant giving her nothing. Even if it meant we kept going just how we were.

But if I told her, things wouldn't go on like this. Things would change. I could lose her.

My heart skipped a beat against her cheek.

The war between trusting her with my feelings and giving her the space I knew she needed battled in my ribcage. When did the sacrifice of what I wanted become too much? How would I know she was ready, that I wouldn't scare her off?

I'd coaxed the wild pony out to eat from my hand, but putting a bridle on her was another thing altogether.

I couldn't tell her, not yet. I only hoped I had the resolve to hold on.

- PENNY -

I **could have stood there on** the dance floor in Bodie's arms with The Cure on repeat for the rest of my life.

The night had been full of magic.

Every moment between us deepened my feelings, and I knew he felt what I felt. I didn't know how I knew, but I did. It was as if every second that ticked by whispered, *Yes,* as if we were caught in something we couldn't turn back from, swept away in each other. I didn't even want out. I could drown in him, and I should have been afraid.

But I wasn't.

I felt safe. Safe and warm and cared for. This was what trust felt like, *real* trust between someone who valued you as much as themselves — I realized it distantly, as if I were floating above the two of us swaying in each other's arms. I trusted him because he'd proven that his words were truth. He'd agreed to everything I'd asked for. He'd made me promises and held them, and I had no reason to doubt him.

But when I really held his actions and words up next to each other, they weren't quite the same. He'd said it was all copacetic, sure, but he felt more just as much as I did. He wanted more. I'd denied my feelings, but he'd known all along.

I knew it as suddenly and clearly as if I'd looked in a mirror for the first time.

He'd just been giving me what he knew I needed, just like he always had. He'd sacrificed what he'd wanted to make me happy.

I thought I'd want to cut and run at the realization, but I didn't.

I couldn't, not only because he had done everything for me without asking for a single thing in return, even my heart, but I wanted to stay because he'd shown me how to trust again. He treated me with care and respect. He honored me without thought to himself.

I wanted to stay because I'd never been with anyone who didn't play games. And with Bodie, there was no power play, no control, no upper hand.

We were equals. And I'd had no idea something like this could even be real.

I had two gears — full-blown obsession and apathy. This gear that I was on was unknown, a lurch in my life that left me reeling, without any context or boundaries or rules.

That unknown brought a flicker of fear. But in the circle of his arms, with his heart beating under my cheek and his breath warm on my skin, I was safe. He was exactly what I needed, and he was everything right.

There was nowhere else I could have imagined being.

The DJ came on when the song ended, directing us to the front of the gardens so we could send Ramona and Shep off, and Bodie and I hurried over to the stairs. We each grabbed sparklers and lit them when we were told, holding them up so my best friend and her husband could run through. I'd sworn I wasn't going to cry, but there was no stopping it — the sight of them golden and beautiful and smiling and crying as they waved goodbye to all of us was too much.

When the door to the limo closed, I turned to Bodie, who smiled down at me as he captured my chin, and then he kissed me, stealing my breath, stealing my heart.

I was beginning to realize that I'd never stood a chance.

Worry sprang like a broken fire hydrant — I didn't know if I could keep my heart together. If I let myself go, if I opened that door, would I be able to maintain what we were?

The more I felt for him, the less rational I'd be. I'd scare him. I'd lose him.

I needed more time.

So I turned the giant wrench on that spewing fire hydrant and shut the motherfucker down.

Tonight, I wasn't crazy. Tonight, I had Bodie.

Tonight, he was mine.

When the limo was gone and the guests dispersed, Veronica and I dashed off to gather our things from the bridal suite. She took all of Ramona's things, citing a trip by Ramona and Shep's new place to drop it all off. Something in her eyes said she was a goddamn liar about her plans, and I should have pressed her. But I was too anxious to get back to Bodie to care. She could go be a sneaky liar on her own time.

The cab ride was too long, but I spent the duration tucked into Bodie's side, the two of us recounting the night like we hadn't been together for all of it. And then we were walking down my silent hallway together, smiling at our shoes. And then we were inside, and I was closing my door.

I took him by the hand, and he followed without question into my bedroom and leaned against the door as I turned on one of my smaller lamps just so I could see him. Just so he could see me.

My heart thumped at the sight of him, so tall and easy, hands in his pockets, the line of his shoulders and arms and long legs speaking to the artist in me. Because he was art with a heartbeat. But what hit me, what nearly stopped me in my tracks was the expression on his face.

The playfulness and charm were gone, replaced by something deeper, something *more*. It was the tightness at the corners of his eyes, the depth of his irises, so blue. It was the shape of his lips, the crease of his lips where something waited for me, words he didn't want to speak. Words I wasn't ready to hear, and he knew it.

But that was what Bodie did. He anticipated what I required

and gave it to me, even when the gift was his silence. He cared about me more than he'd said. But he still cared for me without demand, without expectation.

He was air and sun and soil, just existing around me to give me all I needed to grow. And all the while, I'd grown and blossomed and bloomed, not realizing that I needed him to keep me breathing.

I crossed the room, overwhelmed and overcome by the revelation, trying not to think of what it meant or what it would mean. Instead, I looked into his eyes and told him without a word what I felt for him. I told him with my fingers slipping under his coat that I wanted him. I told him with my lips pressed to his that he'd changed me and there would be no going back.

His body was hard against my palms as they roamed up his chest, and I leaned into him, the two of us angled against the door, me standing between his legs so I could reach his lips.

And that was the thing that struck me the most; he felt what I felt. He knew what my body told him just as much as I knew what his told me.

Never in my life had I felt this before. I'd had power sex. I'd had flirty sex. I'd had fun sex and serious sex. But in that moment, I became aware of a fact that that changed me, there in my room, kissing Bodie.

I had never been intimate.

I wasn't just hungry for his body. I was hungry for his heart and soul.

I wanted all of him. I just hoped I could hold onto him without it breaking me.

My tongue swept his lip, and he opened his mouth, turning my face with his hand, and I opened up in kind, leaning into his palm. He pulled me into him with his free hand — the length of him pressing against my belly sent a shock up my spine, to my lungs, springing them open as I sucked in a small breath.

He hooked his arm around my waist, keeping me flush against

him as he pushed away from the door, leaving my feet dangling off the ground, even as I wished they were wound around his middle but my dress wouldn't allow it. And then gravity shifted as he lay me down in bed gently. But he didn't lower his body onto mine like I wanted, and I hung onto his neck like it could convince him to.

His hand ran up my arm and to my face, and he broke the kiss with a smile, his eyes laden with something that betrayed the levity of his lips.

"I'm not going anywhere, Penny," he whispered, coaxing me to let him go.

But the words meant more than that to me.

I relaxed my arms, and he stood, his eyes sliding up and down my body as he unbuttoned his coat and grabbed his lapels, pulling it open, exposing his broad chest, then shoulders, then arms. His big hands tugged the knot of his tie, slipping one piece from the other with a whisper of silk. And it seemed to take an hour for him to unbutton his shirt. I could have watched that in slow motion on a loop — the sliver of skin on his chest that grew wider with every button, his hands gripping both sides as he opened it just like he had his jacket. Except when that crisp white shirt was gone, all that was left was his beautiful naked chest, all shadows and angles and planes and the tattoo on his arm where I'd put it.

He could have undressed and redressed and undressed again and again, and I would have laid there and watched, content and unhurried and perfectly satisfied.

His pants were next, his leather belt in his fist sending a burst of images through my head — his cock in his hand, the pop and sting of that leather belt against my ass. He snapped open his button with a flick of his fingers, lowering his zipper just as quickly, kicking off his shoes and dropping his pants in movement that felt deliberate and restrained.

And then he was naked before me, the man who'd snuck his way in without me even realizing.

I moved to sit, but he stopped me, laying me back with his hand on my cheek and thumb shifting against my skin. I turned my head to press a kiss into his palm, and he bent to kiss my lips, a kiss without demand but one that burned with smoke and fire and want and need.

He still wasn't in bed with me, and I reached for him, wanting him on me, around me, in me. Just wanting him. He was too far away, but he didn't give me what I was asking for, not this time. This time, he would do what he wanted.

Bodie walked to the end of the bed and slipped his hand over the bridge of my heeled foot and up my leg, pushing the hem of my dress up with it. I opened my legs, and one of his knees slid between my calves and then the other, his hand still on a track up my leg as he climbed onto the bed and knelt before me.

His hand moved from my thigh to the tie of my dress, a simple bow, and he slid the silk between his fingers, meeting my eyes as he pulled. The bow came undone and fell away, and my dress opened just enough to expose a slice of skin down to my belly.

He sighed, his eyes on his hands as he ran his fingers down my sternum, down my stomach, hooking under one side to expose my breast, leaving the chiffon pooling around the bend of my hip. But that sliver of me was naked, from my neck to the center of me, and his eyes drank me in like he was parched.

I spread my thighs, opening myself up to him. And he lowered his lips to my offering, closing his eyes as he kissed the hot line between my legs like he was confessing a secret.

My hands slipped into his hair, my hips rocking and breath shuddering, my pulse climbing as my body neared the edge, the blissful edge.

I called his name — a plea— my hands on his shoulders to tell him I needed more, that I wanted it all, I wanted everything, and he climbed up my body, his hand on my jaw, his fingertips in my hair, the tip of his crown at the slick center of me. And then he looked into my eyes and shifted his hips, filling me up, claiming me as his, giving himself to me, all in a breath.

His body moved, rolling and flexing, his eyes on mine, his lips parted and brows together, and he said my name. And that whisper on his lips was all it took to push me over that edge in a rush of heat and a burst of electricity down my spine, sending my back arching and lungs gasping and body pulsing. And at my release, he found his own, my name in a loop that followed every thrust of his hips as they slowed.

Our eyes were closed, his forehead against mine, his body pinning me down and our breaths mingling. And for some reason, I felt tears pricking the corners of my lids, my nose burning and a lump heavy in my throat.

I wrapped my arms around his neck and pulled him down to bury his face in my neck so I could hide from him. Because in that moment, for the first time, I'd found something real, something beyond me, even if I didn't know what to make of it. I only knew how it felt, and I felt it all the way through me, through every atom. And I made a vow never to forget it.

If I hadn't been addicted to him before, now there would be no hope. No amount of rehab would cure me.

We held each other like that for a long time before he rolled onto his side, pulling me with him and pulling out of me in one motion. He kissed me sweetly before rolling out of bed and heading to the bathroom, leaving me alone.

I lay there on my side with my back to the door and my heart full of shrapnel. It burned — my chest was shredded and smoldering and elated and aching. I didn't know what it meant. I didn't want to think about what it meant. I just wanted him back in bed with me. I wanted my name riding his breath and his arms around me and his lips against mine.

I wanted simple and easy. But we were past that.

He came back a minute later with a warm washcloth and cleaned me up like he always did but without the intention of more. Something in him was reserved, contained, like he was trying to separate from me.

The thought made me want to hang onto him more.

He stood and began to collect his clothes, and I felt my heart break.

"Stay," I said simply, holding my breath in the hopes that he would say yes, the word hanging in the air as he turned to me.

I had never intentionally spent the night with anyone — I'd never wanted to. But the last thing in the whole world I wanted was for Bodie to walk out that door.

His face was soft and cautious as he asked, "Are you sure?"

And when I smiled and nodded, relief washed over him, and he slipped into bed next to me, holding me in his arms, whispering my name as we drifted off to sleep.

Bear Trap

- BODIE -

I **poured a ladle of pancake** batter into the pan with a sizzle, smiling as it spread into a perfect circle.

It was a little late for me — I had to get home to work, the impending meeting looming over me like a dark cloud — but still I'd crawled out of Penny's bed, wishing I could stay there all day.

There were a lot of things from the last eighteen hours I'd never forget, but Penny curled up in bed, swathed in fluffy white bedding in the morning sunshine, her tattoos and purple hair bright against the crispness of her sheets — that was almost at the top of the list. Dancing with her to The Cure and pushing her on the swing were up there too. But the very top? The number one?

Her eyes locked on mine when she'd given herself to me.

A jolt of happiness and pleasure and anxiety shot from my stomach to my throat at the thought. As much as I wanted to talk to her, that moment had been enough for me. She didn't need to say anything.

I just knew. I knew how she felt and what she wanted. That line of communication was so much deeper than words could ever express.

At the same time, I had to let her lead. So I'd tried to tell myself to go like I knew she always needed me too. And when she'd asked me to stay, it was all I could do not to confess my feelings on the spot. Instead, I'd slipped into bed with her and told her in all the other ways I could that I needed her.

I slid the spatula under the flapjack and flipped it just as her door opened.

She shuffled out, yawning, her hair in a purple bun on top of her head. And she was wearing my dress shirt, the hem cutting her mid thigh and only the tips of her fingers visible past the sleeve cuffs.

I could have died a happy man.

She smiled at me, her eyes blinking slowly as she sidled up next to me and wrapped her arms around my bare waist.

"You cook," she said in wonder.

I laughed and picked up the box of Bisquick. "No, I follow directions."

She laughed. "If I'd known I'd wake up to you making pancakes in dress pants and no shirt, I would have asked you to stay over a long time ago."

I wrapped an arm around her back. "If I'd have known you'd wear my button-down like a nightgown, I would have begged you to let me stay."

She nuzzled into me, but I felt the wall crumble a little, felt her uncertainty behind it in the small sigh that left her.

So I kissed her crown and changed the subject. "There's coffee."

She kissed my chest and slipped away. "You are just too good to be true."

The words held double meaning, and I knew it. But I kept my

eyes on the task at hand, moving the pancake onto the stack I'd been building and poured another.

She poured her coffee in silence and took a seat at the table. When I snuck a glance at her, she was cradling her mug with both hands, bottom lip between her teeth and her brows together, sending my heart off a bridge.

I set down the spatula and strode over to the table. The worry in her eyes was so clear when she met mine, and I knelt next to her chair, grabbing the seat to turn her to me.

"Get out of your head, Pen."

She didn't say anything, only watched me with the question *Why?* shifting in her irises.

"Hey." I cupped her face with my heart hammering a warning. "It's okay. This can be easy," I soothed, smoothing my face, smiling gently with a handful of oats and Penny stamping her hooves in front of me. "Nothing has to change, okay? I … I feel it too, but we don't have to name it or label it. Let's just do what we feel like doing, just like we have been. Call me when you want. I'll do the same. It can be easy, Penny."

She took a breath and touched my cheek. "Promise?"

And I sighed, the easy smile on my face now one hundred percent genuine from relief. "I promise." And I sealed the lie with a kiss.

She melted into me, winding her arms around my neck and squeezing to bring our bodies flush, her legs parting to make room for my waist. My hands traveled from her cheeks to her breasts to her ribs to her hips, and then I grabbed her ass and held her to me, using every muscle in my core and thighs to stand.

She wrapped her legs around me and hummed into my mouth as I turned for the bedroom.

Penny broke away, lips swollen. "What about the pancakes?"

"Fuck the pancakes," I whispered before pressing my lips to hers again.

- P E N N Y -

I **watched Bodie washing dishes in** his white button-down and dress slacks as I sat at my kitchen table with my chin propped on my hand and a dippy smile on my face.

I didn't even know who I was anymore.

Bodie had spent the night, and I'd slept better than I had in my whole life. He'd made me pancakes and fucked me senseless and danced with me and made me laugh and made me *happy*. And as freaked out as I was, I kept telling myself that it was going to be okay, just like he'd said.

He'd promised. And I believed him, which was probably naive. In the moment, I couldn't have cared less.

He turned with a smile, drying his hands on a dishtowel before striding over to kiss me gently.

My eyes were still closed for a second when he broke away, and he chuckled.

I sighed and pried my lids open, chin still on my hand. "I hate that you have to go. How much work do you have?"

His smile fell, and he looked a little tired at the thought. "A lot. Too much. I'm not even sure how we're going to get it done in time."

"You will. You're a mathmagician."

"Ha. If only I had a magic wand."

I waggled my brows. "Oh, but you do."

He leaned down to kiss me again before backing away, his blue eyes searching mine. "Hit me up, Pen." The words were soft and edgeless but with a hidden request in the shadows.

So I smiled, having heard him and understood, and said, "I will."

He pressed another small kiss to my temple and walked away, and I watched him until the door was closed.

The second it clicked shut, Veronica threw open her door with her eyes like a couple of fried eggs and her hair a mess, striding into the room.

She pointed at the door. "Oh my fucking God. Did Bodie spend the night?"

I smiled with my lips closed and nodded, making the bun on top of my head bob.

She squealed and did a little *Flashdance* before swooping into the chair next to me. "I thought I heard him, but I was afraid it was someone else. And if it was someone else, I was prepared to brain you with a frying pan."

I frowned, offended. "You thought I might have come home from the wedding with someone besides Bodie?"

She huffed and rolled her eyes. "You've done it before."

"Not true. I always go home with my dates, asshole. But yes, that was definitely Bodie. And he definitely spent the night. And he *definitely* made me pancakes this morning."

Her cheeks flushed, and she giggled. "God, he's such a fucking catch, Pen."

I eyed her. "Why are you so happy?" I scanned her face and body and lit up. "You got laid!"

Her blush deepened. "No, I didn't."

This time, I pointed. "Oh my God, you did! You got nailed! *Finally.* I was worried your junk was gonna dry up. All dust bunnies and mothballs and shit," I said, wagging my hand at her nethers.

Another eye roll. "You are such a drama queen. We're talking about you and Mr. Math. Penny, he spent the night. Like, what the fuck does that even mean?"

I shrugged and drew a little circle on the table with my finger. "It means I got pancakes and morning sex."

"Don't do that. I'm serious. This is a big deal."

"I know, but we're not … I dunno. Calling it anything. We're just letting it be what it is," I said simply.

"And how long do you think that'll last?"

I chuffed, my emotions bubbling and steaming and hissing with uncertainty and anxiety. "God, why are you being such a dick about it? I don't know what it is. I just know that I like him. I like him a lot. I want to be around him all the time, and I want to tell him stuff and let him sleep in my bed. And the whole thing freaks me the fuck out *without* you on my ass, so maybe just lay off a little."

Her face softened. "I'm sorry. You're right. I just … I want you to be happy and okay, and I'm a little scared for you."

I sighed and sagged in my chair. "Me too. Ronnie, I don't know how to do this. Like, I have no chill when I really like a guy."

"In fairness, the last guy you really, *really* liked was in high school."

"And he made me crazy. Courtney Love, rip-down-the-curtains, where-the-fuck-is-my-man crazy. For two years. And through the whole thing, he treated me like shit, and when I lost my mind, he'd just press his finger to my forehead, and I'd calm down and give him whatever the fuck he wanted." My chest ached at the memory.

She sighed. "But he was manipulating you."

"Fuck yeah, he was. You know, one time, he called me at two thirty in the morning just to say hi. I thought it was so cute and sweet that he was thinking about me, and I asked him where he was. And you know what he told me? That he was at Anna Dorf's house — that skank. Motherfucker *knew* I hated her — she had the biggest thing for Rodney and didn't even pretend to hide it — and he straight-up told me that was where he was. He told me to stop being crazy. So of course, I'm upset trying to figure out if he was fucking with me, and we're going back and forth, and he's getting meaner, and I'm getting more and more pissed. And then I heard him ask someone for syrup."

"Syrup?"

"Yeah, because he wasn't at Anna's house. He was somewhere getting breakfast food. So I hung up on him. I got dressed and got in my car. There were two places he could get pancakes at that time in Santa Cruz." I held up two fingers for dramatic effect. "IHOP, where he wasn't, and House of Pie, where he was. I marched into that motherfucker, stomped over to his table, stuck my finger in his face, and told him never to lie to me about where he was because I'd fucking find him. He looked at me like he was scared to death of me, and he was probably wise to be afraid because I was in a full-blown psychotic break. And just like that, he pulled me onto his lap and laughed and told me he was only joking and that he loved me. The worst part is that by the time he got to the apology or diversion or whatever it was, I wasn't even mad anymore."

Veronica blinked, surprised, and I felt ashamed.

"I told you. Crazy. Psycho. I don't want to go psycho on Bodie. I don't want to wig out and scare him off, but all of this is … it's *happening,* and I don't know if I can even stop it. I don't want to stop whatever's going on between us, but I'm scared."

The admission spilled out of me, and the truth of it dragged my high down to the bottom of the ocean.

But Veronica reached for my hand and squeezed it. "Pen, listen, that's Peggy talking."

"Ugh, fucking Peggy!" I groaned.

"Exactly. She's trying to sabotage you, but don't let her. Fuck that bitch."

I didn't respond — I was too busy feeling sorry for myself — so she kept going with more determination.

"You are the toughest chick I know, and the very last thing I expect from you is to let fear stop you from doing anything. Jump out of the plane, Pen. Because Bodie isn't Rodney — he's not going to manipulate you or hurt you, not on purpose. Plus, you aren't sixteen; you're twenty-six. You've lived and learned, and you can do this. Bodie's worth the risk even if you fail."

I dropped my eyes to the table.

"You *aren't* going to fail."

I still didn't say anything.

"Okay, how about this? Let's come up with a … safe word of sorts. If you feel the psycho coming on, you just text me the safe word, and I'll save you. I'll be your shot of whiskey. I'll be your fucking life jacket."

I perked up a little. "Maybe that'll work. Can I pick the safe word?"

She laughed. "Of course."

I smiled as filthy words rolled through my head, but it didn't feel like a Dirty Sanchez sort of a safe-word situation. "Hmm," I hummed, thinking. Then I snapped my fingers. "Bear trap."

Her eyebrows shifted; one went up, and one went down. "Bear trap?"

I sat up a little straighter in my seat. "Yeah, like I'm skipping through the forest, minding my own shit, and then — *wham*. Bear trap. Totally derailed, chew-my-own-foot-off crazy."

Veronica chuckled. "I like it. So you just say the word, and I'll spring the trap so you won't have to eat off an appendage."

I sighed, feeling relieved. "I like this plan. Plans are good."

"Plans are great. And you know what?"

"What?" I asked hopefully.

She smiled with knowledge and understanding, and I felt a zillion times better.

"You're going to be okay."

And I was dumb and desperate enough to actually believe her.

#ThingsThatAreLies

- B O D I E -

Phil **shook his head and** pushed away from his desk. "I can't fucking figure this out, man."

I rubbed my bleary eyes with the pads of my fingers and rolled over so I could see his monitor, scanning the code, looking for errors.

"Here." I tapped the screen. "You divided by zero, and it's terminating."

Phil groaned. "I'm so tired. We can't keep going on like this."

I nodded. "Look, we'll get caught up tonight if we can keep our shit together. And tomorrow, you can sleep all day."

Angie appeared behind him with a plate of brownies, her big brown eyes shining. "Sounds like it's time for a break."

"Oh, sweet," Jude said, leaning over to swipe one. "Man, I'm starving," he said with his mouth full.

"Maybe we could order another pizza," Phil offered.

I glanced around at our desks — a graveyard of plates, coffee cups, napkins, and empty cans of Red Bull. "We had pizza yesterday."

"And the day before," Jude added.

Angie lit up. "Let me make you guys dinner."

Phil rested a hand on her hip. "You don't have to do that, babe."

She shrugged and smiled. "Oh, I don't mind. I'll make something easy. How does spaghetti sound? I'll run down and grab a salad and some French bread too, and make it extra fancy with sausage instead of beef."

My mouth watered at the thought. "So much better than pizza. You're an angel, Angie."

She blushed and waved a hand, giggling; the sound was like tinkling bells. All three of us smiled back at her.

Jude jerked a chin at Phil. "You picked a good one, Philly."

Phil just smiled.

I ran a hand over my face as I yawned, hoping I could stay up for another eight to twelve hours so we could get back on schedule. We were less than a week from the meeting, and the demo was so close to being ready. We just needed to spend the next week spit-shining it and working out the kinks.

And honestly, Jude had the most work cut out for him, getting the graphics where we wanted them. Because graphics would be the first thing that would sell it. Then story, then usability. And we were ambitious enough to want all three to be of such quality, there would be no way they could tell us no.

My phone rang from my desk, and I picked it up, smiling at a photo of Penny and me, a selfie we had taken at the wedding.

I hadn't seen her since I burned her pancakes two days before. And I hated the eight to twelve hours that stood between us.

I answered and sat back in my chair. "Hey."

"Hey yourself," she said on a laugh. "How's it going in the cave?"

"None of us have showered in days, we've had pizza for the last three meals, including breakfast, and our coffeepot has had hot to warm coffee in it for forty-eight hours straight."

"So, productive?"

"Very. We're almost caught up."

"Thank God. I miss you."

"I miss you too," I said, warmth spreading through my chest.

Jude flapped his hands and made kissy faces at me. I turned my chair so he was behind me.

"What are you up to?" I asked.

"The usual — just working a lot, thinking about you. You know, normal stuff. Can I see you tonight?" She was nervous and hopeful and a little cagey, and it broke my heart.

"I wish I could. We're right on the edge of the deadline, and it'll take us until the middle of the night, I'm sure."

"Oh. Okay. I figured, just had to ask."

Her disappointment was almost too much — I nearly caved.

"Pen, I want to see you. Are you around tomorrow? All I need is a nap and a shower and I'll be as hot and ready as a Little Caesars pizza."

She laughed, the tension dissipating just a little. "Sounds good. Just let me know when you're free."

"How about you tell me when you're off, and I'll make time."

Angie walked through the living room, digging through her purse. "Any special requests?"

I held up an empty can of Red Bull and shook it, and she nodded.

"Angie's over?" Penny asked, something tinging her words with anxiety again. Jealousy? My brows dropped.

"Uh, yeah. She's feeding us so we don't overdose on caffeine and junk food."

"Cool. That's cool."

I frowned. It didn't sound like she thought it was cool. "You okay?"

"Yeah, no, for sure. I just figured you guys were all No Girls Allowed, like the *The Little Rascals*." She attempted to joke, but it fell flat.

I tried to save it. "Just call me Spanky."

She laughed, but it sounded fake, and I got up and walked to the kitchen for a modicum of privacy.

"You sure you're okay?"

She sighed, a defeated noise and the first sign of honesty. "Yeah, I'm okay. I just really want to see you, that's all."

"I know. Me too. Tomorrow, okay? Anytime, you name it, and I'm all yours."

"All right, *Spanky*. I expect you to hold good on the nickname though."

"Deal. Text me later and let me know how your day is."

"I will," she said, and I could hear her smiling. That at least was a win. "Bye, Bodie."

"Bye," I echoed and hung up with a sigh of my own.

Penny was bugging out, and I wasn't sure what had happened or what I could do to ease her mind.

For two days, we'd barely talked — two days after a night that changed me, changed us. And now that the brazen, unapologetic, confident woman I'd come to care for had been exposed, her insecurities and uncertainties were apparent.

I didn't care past wanting to make it all right, make it better. Though part of me wondered if there was more to the shift in her.

I knew she cared, but maybe she didn't trust me after all. I sensed she felt I'd penned her in, and if I couldn't prove that I would take care of her heart, she could bust out of the fence and run for freedom. Maybe keeping her would drive her crazy. Maybe she just didn't know what to do with herself.

I shook my head and ran my hand through my hair, which still felt too short, as I stared at my phone, imagining her somewhere in the city staring at hers too.

Angie was still in the kitchen, jotting on a piece of paper. She smiled up at me. "Jude had a list."

I chuckled and leaned on the island. "Of course he did."

"Everything okay?" she asked, glancing at my phone.

"Yeah. I think so at least."

"How's it going with Penny?"

"I can't really tell. Things are getting a little … complicated."

Angie raised a brow. "Oh?"

"I dunno. Maybe complicated isn't the right word. Like, everything between us is fine, great even. But I think we're both having feelings, and only one of us knows what to do with them."

"Hmm. What's going on?"

"She's just acting cagey, uncertain."

Angie frowned. "How come?"

I sighed and raked a hand through my hair again. "She doesn't want commitment, and we've sort of outgrown the idea that it's casual."

"Have you guys talked about whatever feelings you're having?"

I shook my head. "I'm afraid I'll scare her off. She gets all in her head, and it's like I can just see her snowballing away from me."

"Do you know why she's so …"

"Skittish? She dated this guy in high school, and he was horrible to her. He was fucking half the school and somehow kept it a secret from her until they broke up. Not only that, but he had her so under his thumb, and I don't know if she ever escaped. Asshole," I hissed to myself, hot anger churning in my chest at the thought. "He had no idea what he had. And when she got hurt, she decided not to let herself ever get hurt again. Which meant she won't get into anything serious."

Angie watched me for a second. "I think you need to talk to her."

I squirmed.

"I mean it. You know, I always say that a relationship needs three things—"

"Trust, communication, and respect?"

She smiled. "That's right. How many of those do you have?"

"Two out of three. I think the trust and respect are there, it's just the communication part that's not happening."

"I know you don't want to lose her, but you might anyway if you keep your mouth shut. If she doesn't know how you feel, how can she be okay? And if you don't know how she feels, how can you be okay? You should be honest, communicate. Then it'll be easier to make decisions on what comes next."

"And if she tells me she doesn't feel the same and bolts?"

Angie's big brown eyes softened. "Well, then you'll know you weren't in the same place."

I scrubbed a hand over my mouth. "I dunno, Ang. That's not how dating works. It's all about this game, this power struggle. And Penny doesn't just play the game. She practically invented it. I'm an anomaly for her, and I know she cares, but I don't know if she knows how to play it straight."

"You don't have to play the game, you know? You don't have to participate. Just tell her what you want and how you feel and see if she feels the same way."

"Maybe I will. I've just got to be careful."

"I know," she said gently. "But you're not going to break her."

I only wished I could have believed that were true.

– PENNY –

t's cool.

We're cool.

Everything's cool.

It was my mantra for the rest of the afternoon at work, like a goddamn record skipping in an anxiety loop in my brain. It wasn't like I hadn't known he was going to be busy. I had. He'd told me. I knew. I swear.

It wasn't me. He just had work to do, that was all. Which meant nothing was wrong and everything was cool and fine and perfect.

My guts twisted up at the lie.

The last two days had been nothing like the two days before the wedding. Those days had been busy with wedding stuff and happy lovey-dovey feelings about Bodie. And then, shit had to go and get all serious.

My mood had vacillated a thousand times in forty-eight hours, going from perfectly content to doomsday in a five-minute span. We'd texted and talked a few times, but he was working, and I was trying to respect that. It was just that my psycho brain wouldn't comply.

I tried to visualize the wedding. I thought about the sweetness of Bodie's arms around me, his lips against mine. Pictured him holding my face in my kitchen, telling me it was okay.

Of course, then I thought about what he was doing. I mean, Angie was over there, but I wasn't allowed to be. I told myself that I'd be a distraction, but then I thought maybe he could use a break. He'd been working so hard, and I missed him. I considered swinging by with donuts or ice cream or some offering. I imagined him being so happy to see me, imagined him ditching work for a bit for kissing and laughing and talking, just so we could be in each other's arms for a minute, so I could hold onto the feeling of him, to reassure myself that things were fine.

I could just stop by for a minute or two or whatever — I had an hour before my next job — and I smiled to myself, grabbing my bag and blowing out of the shop without a word to anyone, daydreaming about him being so happy to see me that he'd kiss me and ask me to stay.

I wanted to see him. I could make it happen. I would make it happen.

Even though he doesn't want you to come over.

I nearly skidded to a stop on the sidewalk at the thought.

Fucking Peggy.

With a smile that would make the Grinch cringe, she told me that he didn't want me there, that he didn't want to see me. He wanted me to wait until tomorrow because he didn't care to see me, or maybe he wanted to dump me. Either that or he was seeing someone else. Or just didn't really like me all that much. He wanted my body, wanted my flesh, not my heart, not my soul.

I took a deep breath as cold panic set in. In the span of five minutes, I'd disregarded what he needed, what he'd asked of me, for my own wants and needs. I'd pushed up against that line, and the shock of the realization hit me with a jolt.

This was everything I'd been trying to avoid, everything I didn't want.

I'd broken the three-date rule for what had become my favorite dick in the whole world, and this was the price I'd pay. I'd turn into a hot, steaming mess and ruin everything, self-destruct, sabotage my happiness, burn it all down.

But it was too late to go back. The floodgates were open, and the current was too strong to close them again.

Although maybe, just maybe, there was a way to slow things down.

The curse of him giving me what I wanted was that he still wasn't being honest with me. I had no idea how he really felt, and that fact had me betraying myself and his wishes too. So I'd take a little space to buy a little perspective. It was time to take back an iota of control over myself — the helplessness I felt was overwhelming. It wasn't fun anymore. It wasn't good and happy and easy. It was sticky like flypaper, and I was stuck in it, trapped, immobilized.

I couldn't deny I cared about Bodie. But maybe, if I took a minute to get myself right, I could come back to him fresh and ready and happy again.

Peggy whispered that I'd never go back because I was afraid. So I kicked her down the stairs and shut the cellar door. And then I picked up my phone, pulled up my messages, and texted Veronica two words.

BEAR TRAP.

Savage

-BODIE-

The *worst four words in* the English language: *Hit me up, Penny.* When she blew me off the next day, I told myself she was just busy.

When she didn't call me for two days after that, I realized we had a much bigger problem.

My texts had been answered with single words and emojis. My calls had been sent to voice mail, followed by a one-off text that she was working, or out with Veronica or whatever the excuse *du jour* was. And the result was my absolute frustration.

So I kept busy with work and tried not to think about her. Which was, frankly, impossible.

That connection I'd come to depend on had been severed, and though I wanted to believe that she was just occupied, I knew she was putting space between us, separating from me. Leaving me. And

I was alone and isolated and driving myself mad at the thought of losing her.

I tried to problem-solve, picking apart every interaction since the wedding to look for clues. If I'd done something wrong, I could fix it. If there was a way to salvage what we'd had, I would find it. Because I needed her, and I wasn't ready to walk away. I didn't think I'd ever be able to.

Three days in, I realized I might not have a choice.

My options were few.

I could try to reach out while attempting not to pressure her, but what with her lack of reciprocation over the last few days, I'd already exhausted that avenue.

I could wait her out, give her space, try not to worry, and hope she came back — this was where I found myself.

Or I could let her go. I could write her off. Close the door. Move on.

But being an honest man, there was no way I could pretend like that was even a remote possibility.

Bring a Friend

-PENNY-

The shop hummed that afternoon from the dozens of people waiting with *Siamese Dream* playing over the speakers and the buzzing of tattoo guns in the air.

I should have been happy. I should have been content and smiling and wonderful since I'd gotten everything I asked for in the form of sweet, quiet solitude.

I didn't know who the fuck I thought I was kidding. I was miserable. I hated being alone I'd realized, which shouldn't have surprised me, but there it was. I was never alone. Alone was when my crazy blossomed into full-blown insanity — the curse of being a talker. If I couldn't talk, I couldn't figure it out. Half the time I didn't even know how I felt until I said it out loud, and right now, I had no one. Ramona was on her honeymoon getting banged senseless. Veronica was busy doing God knew what.

Trust me, I knew I should have answered Bodie's texts, called him back, and it was exactly what I wanted to do. But I was working hard to spare us both from having to deal with my psychosis. My solitary confinement was an attempt to decontaminate, an attempt to get my bearings so I could find my way back to him.

Problem was, my grand plan had backfired — the distance had made the crazy worse.

I'd made up an excuse not to see him that next day, once I'd gathered my wits and stopped trying to force my way into his apartment. I'd decided to take one day to think and separate and unscramble my brain. So I'd stripped and dyed my hair — this time, a pastel blue. I'd painted my nails. I'd taken a bubble bath and read an *entire* book. I'd cleaned my room. And the whole time, the whole fucking time, I had thought about Bodie and how much I'd rather be with him than at home.

I'd been certain I'd wake up the next morning feeling right as rain. No such luck.

And I'd found myself at a loss.

He'd texted me the day after, and I'd blown him off again, citing work, which wasn't a complete lie. He'd called me too, which I'd sent to voicemail like a coward. And then … then he quit messaging me altogether.

So I hadn't gotten in touch with him. But he hadn't gotten in touch with me either.

I tried to pretend like that didn't break my heart.

I didn't even know if we were good anymore. Maybe he didn't want to talk to me. Maybe I'd made him mad — I'd pushed him away, and if the tables were turned, I'd be pissed too. Or maybe he was just playing defense on whatever he thought I was playing with him.

What if I never heard from him again?

Part of me — a big part of me — almost called him at that

question alone. But what would I say about the last few days? Should I say I'd been busy? Should I tell him I'd been feeling things and risk his reaction?

What if he didn't want me like I wanted him? And what if he did? Could I be with him in the real way? Could I give him what he wanted, what he deserved?

I didn't even know anymore, but I'd had a lot of time to think about it.

If it were any other guy at any other time in my life, I'd have called on my little black book for comfort, but I'd rather have shaved with a rusty razor and risked tetanus. The thought of being with anyone else, even *calling* anyone else, made me feel sticky and gross.

That was its own bad sign.

Of course, the problem wasn't even really a problem. I wanted to be Bodie's girlfriend, but (A) I was crazy, and (B) I couldn't seem to find a way to admit that out loud to him.

Space was supposed to make me feel better.

Wrong.

And now it was all topped by anxiety that I'd fucked up.

I'd blown my dream guy off. And why?

Peggy. That's why.

Ramona floated into the shop, tanned and glowing and smiling as she said hello to everyone. I practically shot across the room and scooped her into a hug.

"You're back!" I cheered, nuzzling her like a puppy. "I missed you."

She laughed. "I missed you too. Look at your hair!" she said when she leaned back.

I smoothed it, smiling. "You like it?"

"I do. Does that mean …"

My brow quirked. "It means it felt like it was time for a change."

"Right." Ramona didn't stop assessing me, but she changed the subject. I thought at least. "How's everything going?"

"Fine, who cares, whatever! Tell me about your honeymoon!"

She laughed. "You act like we haven't talked every day since I left."

"I can't help it; I'm codependent." I hooked my arm in hers to walk back to my station. "Did you let him stick it in your butt?"

That one got a cackle out of her. "It's like the one time I can't refuse."

"That, and his birthday."

"Fortunately, he's a gentle lover when it comes to ringing at the back door. Like maybe the *only* time he's gentle."

"Psh, lucky."

She squeezed me. "I missed you."

I squeezed her back. "You already said that."

"Well, it deserved saying twice. Now tell me what's been going on around here. You know all about Tahiti and honeymoon anal, so spill the deal."

"So," I said as we passed Veronica's station, "Ronnie is acting super weird. She's had *plans*."

Ramona's face quirked, and she looked around me to Veronica, who waved excitedly but was in the middle of a piece and couldn't get up.

"Weird," Ramona said quietly. "Maybe she's seeing someone."

"Maybe. I can't exactly blame her for not telling me either. I'd charbroil her for information. Fricasseed."

Ramona giggled, and we rounded my wall. She took a seat in my chair, and I sat on my saddle stool, so relieved to see her.

"So," Ramona started, "how's Bodie?"

My nose wrinkled. "We haven't really talked much since the wedding."

Her brows dropped. "Why not?"

I shifted to lean on my desk. "Because I'm a mess, and I ruin things."

She didn't answer, which forced me to keep talking. That asshole.

"I dunno, Ramona. I don't know what I'm doing. He got busy with work, so I didn't see him for a couple of days, and I bugged out. Like butthurt and needy and demented. I just figured a little space would do me good."

"Has it?"

I groaned. "No. I mean, yes. But no."

She sighed and gave me a loving look. "Just call him, Penny."

"But I'm unhinged! I don't do alone. I'm co-dependent and psychotic, and this is why I don't have boyfriends. *You know this!*"

"I know this. You've just got to get over it."

I laughed. "That's cute, Mona."

"I'm serious. You can't go dying your hair and then find a new guy every time things get hard."

I made a face at her. "That's not why I—"

"Liar! You wigged out, so you *wigged* out." She motioned to my hair. "Your hair is like a mood ring. Do you know how he feels?"

I inspected my cuticles. "Not really. I mean, I think I do, but I'm not sure."

"So talk to him, Pen. Be a grown up and call him and *talk to him.*"

"Maybe I've already screwed it up."

"Or maybe you'll call him and everything will be fine. Because he's into you. I have a feeling he's wigging out too. Hopefully he didn't shave his head or something."

I laughed and ran a hand over my hair, feeling insecure about it now that I'd been called out. "Do you really think it's that easy?"

"I really do. I mean, even if he doesn't want to be with you, that would be better than this, right? Because then you could just try to get over it."

I sighed. "Yeah." And then I thought about calling him. I thought about seeing him smile. I thought about just *being* with him, like it had been before Peggy came around, blowing cigarette smoke in my face. "I don't know how to get back to the happy place, Ramona."

"Tell him how you feel, and let him tell you how he feels. Once you talk about that, you'll both feel better. And instead of having to text Ronnie *BEAR TRAP*, you can talk to *him* about it."

"Traitor!" I shouted at Veronica, who shrugged.

Ramona leaned forward, resting her elbows on her thighs. "Just call him. It's the only way to stop the crazy. I know you're afraid, but not talking to him is what made you crazy in the first place. The only power anyone has over you is what you give them."

I took a long, deep breath and let it out slowly. "Okay."

She watched me for a second. "Okay?"

I nodded and smiled, reaching for my phone. "Okay." But before I could even unlock the screen, it rang in my hand.

The number was from Santa Cruz. It was a number I recognized. It was the first number I programmed into my Razr when I was sixteen and the number I'd dialed from my mom's cordless phone.

Rodney fucking Parker was calling me.

I stared at my phone stupidly for a second before snapping out of it to answer. "Hello?"

"Pen?" His voice was familiar and velvety and full of swagger and ease.

My eyes were big and round, and my mouth was sticky and dry. "Rodney?"

Ramona's mouth popped open

He laughed. "Holy shit. I can't believe you kept the same number."

"What the hell, man?" I said lightly, shooting for breezy, which wasn't easy considering every nerve in my body fired in warning. "How are you?"

"Good, good. Damn, it's good to hear your voice."

I mouthed *Oh my God* at Ramona, who blinked at me. "You too. What's up?"

"You're in New York, right? I caught your show on TV. Couldn't believe it. You're just as hot as you always were."

I stood and paced out of the shop and into the steaming hot afternoon. "Uh, thanks."

"So I called my agent, and she called your agent to get your number. If I'd known it was the same, I would have called you yesterday," he said, smiling on the other end of the line. "Listen, I'm in town with the band — we're playing at Lucky's tonight, and I've got a couple of tickets for you. Tell me you'll come see me."

I felt sweaty and a little nauseous. "Yeah, okay," I said a little sarcastically. I had literally no intention of going to see that asshole anywhere.

"Good. I was prepared to beg."

Rodney. Begging me. For anything.

It was the stuff of my wildest dreams and my worst nightmares.

I laughed. I couldn't help it. I had to be dreaming or having a full psychotic break or a stroke or something.

"You okay?" he asked as I laughed like a hyena.

I pressed my fingers to my lips and tried to stop, succeeding after a second and a few heavy breaths. "Yeah. Yep. I'm good."

He chuckled, and I remembered all the nights with him, all the kisses at my locker, all the hours listening to the band practice. All the good. All the bad. All of it rushed back over me like a tsunami.

"All right," he said. "The tickets will be at Will Call under your name. And bring a friend."

"Sure, sure," I answered as I swallowed my laughter.

"Doors open at seven. Man, I can't wait to see you. It's been too long, babe."

"Oh, yeah. Cool. For sure."

I hung up without waiting for him to respond. And then I sat down on the dirty fucking curb and burst into hysterical laughter.

Rodney had called me. And invited me to a show. And asked me to bring a friend. And called me *babe*.

The universe had to be fucking with me.

The last time we'd actually spoken, he'd dumped me after graduation, and I'd unloaded two years of feelings on him with my volume level at twelve and an audience of at least two fifty. I'd seen him at a few parties after that, and both times, we'd ended up fucking in a bathroom and his car, respectively. There was no talking either time.

After that summer, I'd moved to New York, and I hadn't really thought about him much. I had thrown myself into my life, my goals, which in part included not ever getting serious with anyone. Which insured they always wanted to get serious with me.

And I know what you're thinking — *God, Penny, you're such a liar. You thought about him all the time.*

But I really hadn't. He'd affected me, but I'd closed the door and tried not to let it bother me otherwise. It was simply a sticking point, a reason why, devoid of general emotions on the matter.

I was an excellent suppressor of emotion on that particular matter.

Things I could thank Rodney for.

My abs hurt a little from laughing, and I wiped a stray tear from the corner of my eye.

Rodney had done so much to shape who I was, and Bodie had undone it all just by existing, just by caring for me.

I thought about Diddle, the boy I used to know. I thought about the man he'd grown up to be and how brilliant and determined and wonderful he was. I thought about how good he made me feel, how he cared for me, how I cared for him. I thought about how different Rodney was from Bodie, how one could be so cruel and one so kind. How one could seek to tear me down while the other lifted me up.

I thought about how Bodie was everything I wanted, and I thought about how wrong I'd done him.

I thought about how I could possibly make it right again.

And then I unlocked my phone, navigated to my favorites, and touched his name, hoping I still had a chance.

- BODIE -

When my phone rang and I saw our picture on the screen, my heart stopped and started again with a jolt I felt down to my toes. I'd imagined the moment for days and had lost hope that it would happen, that I would hear from her. And now that my phone buzzed in my hand, I had no fucking clue what to say or do or feel.

So I went default.

"Hey, Penny," I answered, hoping I sounded cool.

She laughed nervously. "Bodie, oh my God. You won't believe who just called me."

A slow tingle climbed my neck. *Not what I thought she'd say.* "Who?"

"Rodney."

My insides liquified at that single word. "Really?"

She laughed, the nervousness slipping away until it edged on hysteria, her tone giddy and rushed. "Seriously! Get this: he had *his* agent call *my* agent." She laughed again, a burst of feverish giggling that made my blood boil.

I tried to chuckle, but it sounded a little like I was choking. "No shit. What did he want?"

"He's in town and has tickets to his show tonight at Lucky's."

More laughter — my pulse ticked up.

"He told me to *bring a friend.*"

"Great. I'm your friend. I'm coming with you."

Another round of giggling, this one hitting me in the heart, reminding me how much I wanted her for my own. It was a sound meant for me this time, a sound that said she wanted me with her.

All that was gleaned from a simple series of bursts of air from her lips.

"I didn't think you'd be interested," she said, half-joking.

If there was one thing I didn't joke about, it was Penny and Rodney in the same room together.

"Penny, I'm interested in all things related to you."

She paused for a second. "Listen, I don't really think—"

"I'm coming with you. What time's the show?"

Another pause.

"The doors open at seven, but I don't want to—"

"Pen," I said with finality, "I want to see you. I *need* to see you. And you're not going to Lucky's without me. So it's settled — I'm coming with you. I'll meet you there at seven."

"All right," she said quietly, tentatively. "How've you been?"

"Busy with work but good," I lied, suppressing a sigh, the pressure in my chest mounting. "You?"

"Oh, I've been okay. Just working a lot."

She lulled, and I grappled with what to say.

"I … I missed you."

My anxiety softened by the smallest degree. "Me too, Pen."

"Bodie, there's so much to say. I've been thinking about everything, about you and me, and—"

I heard someone call her name in the background, and she hissed a swear.

"I've got to go. Let's talk tonight, okay?"

"Okay," I answered with my heart drumming, and we said goodbye, disconnecting.

My palms were swampy as I slipped my phone into my back pocket and paced into the living room where Jude and Phil sat at their desks working.

I ran a hand through my hair as they turned to eye me.

"This is the worst possible thing that could fucking happen."

Jude's brow quirked. "What is?"

"Penny called." I turned to pace in the other direction.

"Wait, that's bad?" Phil asked.

I sighed. "Penny called to tell me that *Rod* fucking called her to ask her to go to his show tonight."

Jude's mouth popped open. "No shit."

"No shit," I echoed.

"Fuck," he said, running his hand over his lips. "This is bad."

"I'm so fucked. *Fucked.* Eight years later, and that asshole is coming back to throw a wrench in everything, and the timing sucks. We haven't talked, she's wigging out, and he's the one person who has the power to ruin everything. Nobody gets under her skin like he does."

Phil looked confused. "Why the hell would she agree to go?"

"Because," I huffed, walking back toward the door, "he's a fucking rock star, and he had her under his thumb for half of high school. Because she's *Penny*, and of course she wants to go. But I told her I'm going with her."

Jude laughed at that. "You *told* her?"

"Yeah, I fucking told her. You think I'd let her go without me? I mean, at least if I'm there, he can't get to her. Plus, there's too much unsaid that needs to be said once and for all."

"And you think Rod's concert is the right time? With him up on a stage, licking the microphone in a leather jacket?" Jude asked, shaking his head. "Bro."

I groaned and paced the room again, hand in my hair. "Fuck.

Fuck! What the fuck am I gonna do?"

Phil sighed. "Cross your fingers and pray."

"Go to Lucky's and deck Roddy as a show of manhood and territorial superiority," Jude said helpfully.

I shook my head. "I've just got to survive. Show up. And hope to God I don't lose her for good."

You Can't Actually Be Serious

-PENNY-

My emotions were jumbled up like Scrabble tiles as I worked through my day, trying to keep busy, which wasn't too hard. From the second I'd hung up the phone with Bodie, I'd had somebody in my chair, affording me plenty of time alone with my thoughts.

The last thing I wanted to do was go to the concert, and somehow I'd gotten roped into it. And Bodie had sounded hard and a little angry on the phone, and when he'd insisted we go to the show, I couldn't find a way to say no. I needed to see him as much as he'd said he needed to see me, and the prospect of seeing him, talking to him, was too much to argue. That on top of not wanting to make him any angrier.

The conversation had taken a hard left, and I'd found myself agreeing to go to my ex-boyfriend's rock concert with my current boyfriend-slash-slam-piece who I hadn't spoken to in days.

Basically, the whole thing was a fucking hot-ass mess.

The sound of Bodie's voice had made my insides squishy and warm. The thought of seeing him made it hard to breathe. I'd missed him so much that in hindsight, staying away seemed ridiculous and futile. I wanted to be with him; that hadn't changed. I was still scared; that hadn't changed either. All that had changed was my resolve to go after what I wanted instead of running away.

The problem was that I didn't know what to expect, and I dreaded meeting him at Lucky's.

I should have called it off. I should have told him to just meet me somewhere else, anywhere else. But the afternoon got away from me, and one thing after another went wrong. My last job, a massive back piece, ended up running over. Like, an hour over.

I texted Bodie the first chance I got, but by that point, he was already there. And the second I was finished, I blew out the door and caught a cab with my pulse speeding. I hadn't even had time to go home and change. I fussed over my clothes — my Misfits tee with the oversize neck, black miniskirt, shredded up tights and combats. And as I touched up my makeup, nerves overwhelmed me, stoked by the anxiety of being late and not knowing what to expect from the night.

When the cab pulled up to the curb in front of Lucky's, I spotted Bodie leaning against the wall next to the box office, his eyes dark and brows low, hands in his pockets and ankles crossed.

He looked gorgeous.

Gorgeous and pissed.

I paid the cabbie and slipped out of the car into the sweltering heat, trotting across the sidewalk to him as he pushed away from the wall.

I found myself breathless, probably from jogging. Or from Bodie — broody and tense and pumping out testosterone and pheromones at me like tear gas.

"Hey," I breathed, wishing I could wrap myself around him like a boa constrictor. As much as I'd thought I'd missed him, it was nothing compared to standing there in front of him without permission to touch him. "I'm so sorry I'm late."

He attempted to relax with a deep breath that lowered his square shoulders just a touch. "It's all right, but can we get inside? I could use a drink."

I smiled, hoping it looked like I wasn't nervous as shit. "Yeah. Of course."

We headed over to the box office in heavy silence, and I picked up our tickets. And within a few minutes, we were stepping under the blasting air-conditioning and making our way to the bar.

It was already packed and loud, and within ten feet, the air-conditioning was a distant memory — the heat from the hundreds of bodies packed into the space had turned it into a sauna. We waited in line at the bar, trying to shout at each other over the noise with a thousand things we wanted to say pressing on us like the oppressive heat.

Lucky's was general admission only, and we wormed our way through the masses to get as close to the stage as we could. Every second, the crowd closed in a little tighter around us, and I slammed my double tequila almost as fast as he slammed his double whiskey.

Bodie leaned down to my ear. "I'm gonna get us another round."

I nodded and yelled, "I'll be here," which sounded way less cute in scream-speak.

He disappeared into the crowd, and I took a breath and let it out. As excited as I had been to see Bodie, he was angry and tense, and it was my fault. The combination of me going radio silent, him having to wait an hour for me in the hundred degree heat, and the fact that we hadn't talked about anything we wanted to — it was almost too much to bear in the span of a few minutes.

It all of a sudden felt like a kamikaze mission, and I clambered for a way to salvage the night.

A few minutes after he left, he was back with a fresh drink, looking a little more relaxed. He smiled and brought his lips to my ear. "I found another bar upstairs, it was empty."

I reached up on my tiptoes to get to his ear in return. "Good. Thank you."

He repeated the ridiculous motion to get to my ear, the frustrating lag in conversation pissing me off.

"You're welcome." He ran a strand of my blue hair through his fingers. "You changed your hair."

I nodded, our lips had found places, our cheeks almost pressed together so we didn't have to move. "You like it?"

"It's different," he answered enigmatically just as the crowd began to cheer.

I turned to find the opening band making their way onto the stage, raising their hands to the crowd as they picked up their instruments. And just like that, any shot we'd had to talk was blown.

We bounced around to the opening band, pounding drinks. By the time their set was finished, Bodie and I hadn't spoken, and we'd each had three doubles. This could have been a good thing, except for the fact that we were both drinking to ease our nerves. Or at least I was. Bodie seemed to be drinking so he could tolerate me.

He went to get us our fourth drink during the set change. And by the time he got back, the lights were dimming, and the crowd screamed and clapped as Rodney walked out from backstage.

It was then that I realized something very important — far too late for it to matter.

I'd had a lot of bad ideas in my life, but agreeing to meet Bodie at Lucky's that night was hands down the worst.

My breath was still, my eyes blinking as Rodney fucking Parker — my albatross and cross to bear — took the microphone in a leather jacket and skinny jeans, looking like a goddamn motherfucking god.

He wasn't a boy anymore. He was a man with a guitar and a voice and that hair and those hands. I was like a bug in a spiderweb with my eyes locked onto Rodney as I struggled to break free. For two years, I'd been obsessed with him even though he hurt me, and there he was, in the flesh, a grown man, resurrected. My past stood there before me, and my future stood next to me whole I stood in the middle, completely frozen from the unanticipated shock of it all.

If I'd been able to form a cognizant thought, I would have grabbed Bodie's hand and run out of that stuffy, steamy, loud room like it was on fire. But since my brain had ceased primary functions, I found myself stuck to the spot with my mouth open and my drink warming in my hand.

It was bad. So, so bad.

I found my wits somewhere near the end of the set, stiff drink in my hand and stiff Bodie next to me. I snuck a glance at him and found him somehow looking even more pissed than he had when I walked up an hour late.

Disaster. Complete fucking disaster.

I slammed my drink, teetering a little under the burn as the no-longer-chilled tequila made its way through my esophagus, and then there was only one thing to do — get the fuck out of there as quickly as possible.

I grabbed Bodie's hand and lifted my chin, tilting my head to indicate I wanted to talk to him, and he lowered his face so I could reach his ear.

"Let's go," I said hastily and with a little bit of a slur.

He nodded, everything about him softening with relief, but before we could even take a step, Rodney was on the mic, and I heard my name.

"Penny! Hey, guys," Rodney said, his voice rumbling at a

trillion decibels from forty-eight-million speakers. "Check it out. See that girl there with the blue hair and the hips that could knock a motherfucker out?"

He pointed straight at me, and everyone turned around to gawk, except Bodie. Bodie stared at Rodney like he wanted to separate his head from his body.

"Come on up here, Pen."

I shook my head.

"Come on! Help me out, guys. *Pen-ny. Pen-ny. Pen-ny.*"

The entire fucking joint was chanting my name, and the next thing I knew, I was being pulled toward the stage by strangers, looking back over my shoulder at Bodie, begging for him to save me, begging for him to forgive whatever was about to happen.

I was lifted up and put on the stage, and before I could even protest, I was in Rodney's arms, pressed up against his chest as I angled away, scanning his crowd for Bodie, but I couldn't see shit. I didn't even know how Rodney had picked me out.

Stupid fucking hair. Dead giveaway.

"So, you might know Penny from her TV show, *Tonic*."

The crowd cheered.

"Well, wouldn't you know it? Penny used to be my girlfriend a long, long time ago, but I was a stupid little prick back then." His tone was self-deprecating, and I didn't buy it at all. "I wrote some of your favorite songs for her because, let me tell you something — you don't forget a girl like Penny."

He turned to me, all smiles as he let me go and stepped back, slinging his guitar from back to front, calling the song to the guys, and the drummer kicked off the beat.

And I stood there on the fucking stage with a hundred lights on me, a screaming crowd — minus one pissed off Bodie — singing along as Rodney serenaded me with their biggest hit. The song was a drug-and-addiction metaphor for love, all about this muse who had ruined him, left him hanging to dry, spent and tired and needing more.

I felt like he'd gotten his wires crossed about what had gone down between us.

I was shocked and stunned, locked to the spot to the side of the stage by the expectations of several hundred people. I couldn't walk off without causing a scene, and there were all those faces and eyes and lights — *so* many lights, blinding and sharp — pinning me down as a zillion thoughts zinged through my head.

I legitimately want to die.

Where did Bodie go?

God, there are so many people staring at me right now.

I should get an award for being so fucking dumb.

Fuck, it's so loud. This is ridiculous.

I should walk. But what if he stops the song? Then everyone is going to boo.

Do I even care?

Yes, yes, I care if three hundred people boo me.

Bodie's watching. He's got to be so pissed. I would be a raging psycho.

Why didn't we leave? We should have left.

What the fuck do I do with my hands?

I should have fucking called this off. Stupid, Penny. Stupid, stupid, stupid.

Am I supposed to smile? Dance? Sing along? I don't even know the damn words.

Seriously, death would be a welcome release. Any second now, I'll get struck by lightning and be put out of my misery.

And so on for approximately four minutes, while I stood there like a fucking idiot, wishing I could run like hell.

The song ended, mercifully, and Rodney made his way over, reaching for me for what I thought would be a kiss on the cheek.

Wrong again. So, so wrong.

His lips hit mine, soft and familiar, sending a rush of memories back to me, and I immediately turned my head, smiling awkwardly as I attempted to push him away. Discomfort covered me like a bucket of slime, and I pushed harder.

He finally stopped, but before he let me go, he nuzzled into my ear. "Come see me backstage after the show." His hand snaked down to my ass, and he squeezed it. "Fuck, you look good."

I pushed away from him hard, furious on the inside, laughing uncomfortably on the outside, with my cheeks flaming and all those people staring at me. When I turned, a security guy waited behind me with a hand extended to guide me down the stairs, and as I made my way down, I searched for Bodie in the crowd.

All I caught was a glimpse of the back of his head and the set of his shoulders as he wound his way through the crowd toward the door.

"*Fuck, shit, fuck,*" I hissed, a little wobbly from the tequila as I hurried as best as I could after him through the throng of people to the deafening sound of the band's final song.

I burst through the door and onto the sidewalk to find Bodie storming away.

"Bodie, wait!" I called after him.

He didn't stop.

My heart broke, and I trotted to catch up, laying a hand on his arm.

"Bodie, please," I said.

He whirled around so fast, I almost fell backward.

His eyes were hard, his jaw set and lips a thin line. I barely recognized him. "*What?*" he shot.

And the accusation in that single syllable cut through me.

"I … I—" I stammered with my mouth open like a trout, completely stunned by the shift in him, though not at all surprised. I deserved every bit of his anger and braced myself.

"Jesus, Penny. What the fuck am I supposed to do with you?"

I blinked, angling away from him a little. "What the fuck does that mean?"

He took a controlled breath, his eyes boring into me like icy blue drills. "I've done everything I know to do to try to make you happy, and the second things got real, you dropped me like a bad fucking habit. You didn't speak to me for days — *days*, after everything — and when you did call, you called to tell me *he* called you." He jabbed a single finger at the venue. "And then? Then we came here together—"

"Hang on, that was *your* idea! I didn't even want—" I tried to say over him, but he was a steamroller.

"—And the whole fucking time you were staring at him like he was God's fucking gift. He treated you like garbage, Penny. Fucking trash. And then you went up on that stage and you fucking kissed him and *I just can't with you, Penny.* I can't."

I fumed and stuck my own skinny finger in his broad chest. "I didn't kiss him, you asshole. He kissed me, and I *tried* to get away from him!"

He laughed, a sound as dry and hot as the desert. "Please. You laughed and smiled and *stood there* instead of walking away."

My heart stopped and started again with a painful kick. "What the hell was I supposed to do? Make a huge scene on the stage? Bodie, for fuck's sake, I came here with *you*."

"You haven't spoken to me in days!" he raged, the muscles in his neck taut and red. "You left me hanging, blew me off, and I'm supposed to feel good about you kissing that prick in front of three hundred people? I mean, what the actual fuck, Pen?"

"Hey, Penny," Rodney said from behind me.

I looked back in horror to find him jogging up with a smile on his face.

"I thought you were coming backstage?"

One second, Bodie was standing there with his fists clenched, looking like a coil about to spring, and the next, his arm was pulled back, and he coldcocked Rodney in the face.

I watched the whole thing happen in slow motion, accompanied by a series of noises — the smack of knuckles against flesh, my gasp, Rodney yelling *Son of a bitch!,* and Bodie's heavy breathing as he shook out his hand.

Rodney crumpled to the ground, and out of sheer, shocked instinct, I reached for him to help him sit up as he held his bleeding nose.

"What the fuck, man?" Rodney yelled but narrowed his eyes as he really got a good look at Bodie. "Wait … Diddle?"

But Bodie just shook his head and looked at me with eyes as cold and sharp as a switchblade. "You two deserve each other," he said. And then he turned and walked away.

Tears burned my eyes, my throat in a vise, my gaze on Bodie as he stormed down the sidewalk, taking all my hopes and wishes with him.

Ruined. I was ruined. My heart was ruined. And it had been ruined long before I let him in.

Rodney tried to make sense of what was going on, inspecting me. "You're dating Diddle?"

I sniffed, blinking to keep my tears at bay as I pulled Rodney to stand. "It's complicated."

Rodney wiped the blood from his nose and inspected his hand. "Well, he's gone now. Come on backstage."

He smiled around the gore on his face, the effect gruesome and sickening. Or maybe it was the tequila. Or the fact that Bodie had just dropkicked my heart.

I shook my head. "I just really want to go home."

His smile widened as he tried to put his arm around me. "I'll take you."

I turned to avoid his grip. "I can make it on my own. Thanks for the tickets, Rodney."

That smile of his fell, slipping into anger. "Hang on. You're not actually ditching me for *Diddle*, are you? That fucking loser never had a shot with you, not then and not now. He always had a thing for you. So fucking embarrassing."

I clenched my teeth, hot anger boiling in my ribs as the flip switched, illuminating everything I'd avoided, lighting up all the things that had been right in front of me the whole time, if only I hadn't been too blind to see.

"Fuck you, asshole," I fired. "He's fucking *incredible*. *You're* the loser. How dare you. How dare you call me up on that stage and embarrass me and kiss me without my permission in front of all those people. You son of a bitch — you *ruined* me, and now you think you can call me up and bring me to a show and fuck me like you used to?"

He shrugged and ran his tongue over his teeth, his hands slipping into his pockets and his body shifting into a position that was intended to dominate, intimidate. "Listen, Pen. You're a thing — you're on TV — and I'm in a band. We've got status, and we make sense, more now than ever. Why wouldn't I try to get back in with you? I mean, look at you. You and me on camera? On tour? I could fuck you like a rock star, just like before."

"Fuck you, Rodney," I said with a shaky breath.

I turned to go, but he grabbed my arm and said my name. And when I turned, it was with my tiny fist balled up and flying toward his eyeball.

The pop was the most satisfying sound I'd ever heard in my life.

Rodney yelled and doubled over, hands over his eye and ruined nose. "What the fuck, Penny? God, you always were such a fucking psycho," he said to his shoes.

So I did the only thing I could.

I put my hands on his shoulders and kneed him as hard as I could in the balls. And then I left that motherfucker next to the gutter where he belonged.

Hair of the Dog

- PENNY -

When I cracked my eyelids the next morning, the very first in my list of regrets was the tequila.

I felt like I'd been hit by a smelly, greasy garbage truck driven by Macho Man, who happened to be high on cocaine.

My stomach rolled, and I shifted to lie on my back, hoping to calm the raging bile down as it crept up my esophagus. A long drag of air through my nose helped, and I swallowed, reaching for the glass of water on my nightstand.

Bad, wrong. Bad, wrong, was the song my heart screamed, my brain expanding and contracting in my skull with every masochistic beat.

Yeah, tequila was the mistake that demanded all my attention. But Bodie was the regret that had broken me in the first place.

The night came back to me, not in flashes but like a creeping fog, spreading over me in tendrils. Bodie, distant and hot and angry, so different from the sunshine I'd found in him before. Rodney calling me onstage. The cold dread I'd felt as I chased Bodie out. The hurt when he'd thrown my heart on the steaming pavement. The satisfying pain from punching Rodney in his stupid fucking eyeball.

I flexed my aching right hand at the memory, and pain shot across the bones up to my wrist.

"Fuck," I croaked, opening my bleary eyes just enough to inspect my swollen phalanges.

My knuckles were split and swollen, fingers bruised, especially where one of my rings had been. Thankfully I'd taken it off or I probably would have had to cut it off. On top of that, I'd broken a nail over that fucker.

Worth it.

Of course, in a few hours, I'd have to use that hand to tattoo people all day. And as I closed my fist, I realized just how bad that was going to suck.

Still wouldn't suck as badly as the fact that Bodie and I were through.

He was right, and he was wrong. I was right, and I was wrong. I should have gone after him. I should have called him or texted him. I should have known better than to go to that show at all, especially with Bodie.

I shouldn't have waited so long.

I should have talked to him about how I felt.

And now it was probably too late.

Tears pricked my eyes, and I took a deep, shaky breath again. I'd come home to an empty apartment, drunk and hurt and defeated. A long shower couldn't wash away my guilt or sadness or loss. It couldn't erase all the things Bodie had said. It couldn't wash the dirt off my heart after I picked it up and carried it home. So I dried off, threw on the first thing I could grab from my drawer — panties and an inside-out New Order T-shirt — and slipped into my sheets in the dark.

And then I cried.

I cried until my pillow was damp and the burning in my chest had died down to a smolder. I cried until my eyes were swollen and my nose was red. And when I finally caught my breath and the tears ran dry, I slipped into a fitful sleep.

My muddled dreams ran in circles, waking intermittently to open my eyes to find my room spinning, tequila metabolizing out of my mouth and back into my nose. I hadn't been smart enough to eat anything or take anything, and I felt that mistake too.

I reached for my phone to check the time, and a shot of adrenaline sent my tender stomach on a turn when I wondered if he'd called or texted.

He hadn't.

And I was about to be late for work.

"Shit," I hissed and sat up too fast, dimming my vision and sending me back into the spins, heart banging its warning as I pressed the heels of my palms into my eye sockets until it passed.

I expended a healthy amount of caution as I slipped out of bed and shuffled around my room, pulling on jeans and Chucks, taking my shirt off to put it on right side out. At that point, I stumbled back to my bed and sat, wondering if I was still drunk. But no. I was dehydrated and brokenhearted, but I wasn't drunk. So I drank the glass of water on my nightstand, took four ibuprofen to guarantee success, and got out of bed, praying to the Mexican devil Agave that I would survive the day.

No makeup happened, and I pulled my hair up into a messy bun to match my messy life, tying a red rolled up bandana around my thumping skull, knotting it at the top. I didn't even look in the mirror. That was how you know shit was real.

I put on my biggest, darkest shades and hurried as best I could out the door and into the humid, sticky summer day to head to Tonic. The walk felt forever long, and I felt beyond dead.

By the time I opened the door and stepped into the air conditioning, I was practically dragging myself. The shop was loud and buzzing, and I didn't take my sunglasses off as I headed straight for my station with the singular goal to sit the fuck down.

If the music had been a record, it would have screeched to a halt at my entrance. The entire crew stared at me like I might bite them, and I might have if they'd stopped me from getting into my chair.

I dropped my bag and climbed into my tattoo chair, sighing as the cold leather touched my overheated skin, and I closed my eyes, leaning the chair back without a single fuck to give about anything but trying not to puke.

"Rough night?" Ramona said from my elbow.

I cracked my eyes to see the dark shape of her through my glasses.

"You could say that." My voice was gravelly and deeper than usual from all the yelling and crying.

"Here's some water."

I smiled, lighting up as much as I could as I reached for the offered plastic bottle. "Bless you."

"What happened, Pen?"

The bottle was to my lips, and I drank half of it before I could bring myself to stop. My stomach gurgled a warning as it prepped itself. "It was bad. Really bad."

She frowned. "How bad?"

"Apocalyptic." I sighed, mouth dry and heart wrung out. I took another drink to buy time and to attempt to mend my busted up body. "I drank about ten shots of tequila on an empty stomach, kissed Rodney, and fought with Bodie."

Her eyes blew open like I'd electrocuted her. "You kissed Rodney?"

she said way too loud.

I winced from the memory and the decibel. "Shhh! Fuck, you don't have to yell. Jesus."

Her face pinched in anger. "I cannot fucking believe you, Penny! How could you do that to Bodie? God, it's like I don't even fucking know you!"

My eyes squeezed shut as my head rang. "Seriously, you have to bring it down, or I'm gonna hurl. I didn't kiss him like that. Just calm down and let me explain."

She folded her arms across her chest, and I took a deep breath, taking another sip of water to fortify me, wishing it could bring my dried up soul back to life.

"We were at the show, and Bodie was acting all angry and weird and didn't seem to even want to be there. And at the end of the show, Rodney spotted me and called me up onstage to sing to me."

"He did not," she breathed, mouth open.

"He fucking did, that cockgobbler. He sang to me, and then *he* kissed *me*. Onstage. In front of everyone. Including Bodie."

She cupped her mouth with her hands.

"Yeah. So beyond fucked up. That stupid fucker with his stupid fucking hands on my ass, like he had any right to touch me. And what could I even do? A hundred phones were pointed at me, and frankly, I was stunned stupid. But the second I could get away, I chased Bodie out — because of course he'd left; I would have left me too — and we got into this huge fight. Then Rodney came out, and Bodie punched him in the nose."

She was blinking now, hands still over her mouth.

"And then he left us there, and Rodney was being *Rodney,* so I punched him in the eye."

"You didn't!" she said from behind her hands.

I held up my right hand, knuckles out, and rested my head against the headrest, closing my tired eyes.

"Get the fuck out of here. How are you going to work today?"

"I don't even know." All that water I'd had to drink hit my stomach and began to reverse direction. "Everything sucks. Literally everything. I just want to go home and die slowly, alone, in my bed."

"Are you gonna talk to Bodie?"

"I don't know, Ramona. I don't think he wants to see me again."

"You have to try. You can't just walk away. You can't just give up."

I shook my head, heartbroken and exhausted and worn down. "I don't want to talk about it, not right now."

"But—"

I held up a hand and burped with my lips closed. "Ramona. I need to get through today. And—" Bile raced up my throat, and I scrambled out of my chair. "I'm gonna puke."

I ran to the bathroom, hitting the john just in time for the volcano to blow, the mass quantities of alcohol I'd consumed leaving me in a burning rush. And the minute that hell was over, my stomach almost sighed, having exorcised the demon, leaving my body feeling frayed and threadbare but less like it was going to expire.

I only wished the same could be said for my heart.

- BODIE -

t was after noon by the time I finally woke. I'd slept like I was dead, a deep, dreamless sleep. But I woke feeling like I hadn't slept at all.

My stiff body creaked and groaned to life, and when I rolled over and slid my hand under my pillow, pain shot up my forearm and into my heart.

I'd clocked Rodney.

I'd lost Penny.

I flipped onto my back and hooked my arm over my face, sending me into darkness. Images flashed behind my lids like a horror show. Penny watching Rodney, her blue hair foreign, a change I'd known nothing about, a change that had felt like its intention was to isolate me, separating me from her. Penny up on that stage with Rodney's lips against hers, lips that were mine, lips that had been avoiding me. His hand on her ass and his face buried in her ear — that was the thought that hit me over and over. It had been the thought in my head when I put his face through the meat grinder.

I shouldn't have left her there with him on the sidewalk. I shouldn't have left her at all. I shouldn't have said what I had, but I didn't want to take it back either. I'd suppressed how I felt for so long that there was no holding it back, not after a fifth of whiskey and Rodney's hands all over her.

I was wounded, and I didn't know if I'd get over it.

The cold truth was that, over the span of the last week, since the wedding, I hadn't seen her. She'd blown me off, leaving my calls and texts largely unanswered, and then, when I'd finally seen her, it had been a nightmare.

The more I thought about it, the more my hope sank.

Penny hadn't said or done anything to admit that she cared for me, nothing concrete, nothing *real*. In fact, the way she'd been treating me over the last week only pointed to a simple, undeniable fact.

She just wasn't that into me.

Everything I'd thought I felt, I'd made up and imagined. I'd read too much into it, and here I was. If she wanted me, I'd know. There would be no cat and mouse, no games to play. No waiting to answer or avoiding each other. And at the end of the day, that had to be my answer.

Operation: Penny Jar was a massive failure after all. I'd knocked the jar off the shelf and it had shattered, leaving broken glass and shiny copper all over the floor of my heart. I was the asshole who had ended up getting hurt after all.

My heart hardened under my sternum, calcifying and shrinking at the realization that it was over. Maybe it had never gotten started. Maybe she'd never cared about me at all.

I flipped off my sheets and climbed out of bed, wanting to leave my thoughts on my pillow but they followed me around like a ghost.

Phil and Jude were already at their computers, and they turned when I shuffled in wearing nothing but sleep pants, rubbing my eyes.

"Morning, sunshine," Jude sang.

I humphed.

"How's your head?"

"Fine," I grumbled as I poured a cup of coffee. "I don't remember coming home." I took my mug with me to the island and sat on a stool, facing them, back against the cool counter.

Jude smirked. "You ate half of a cold pizza, drank a gallon of water, and ranted for two hours. I'd give you another high five for decking Roddy, but I don't want to hurt you."

I inspected my hand, bruised and cut up and aching, just like my heart. "Fuck that guy."

Phil watched me. "You gonna be okay?"

"Don't really have a choice, do I?" I took a sip of coffee when I should have let it cool off, and a scalding trail burned down my chest.

"I don't mean to be a dick," Phil started, which indicated he was about to be a dick, "but you've been gone, distracted, checked out, man. We're so close, but we need you to get to the end of this thing. I want you to be happy, but she's driving you crazy, and we don't have time for crazy right now."

I nodded, eyes down and heart sinking. "It's over. And I'm here.

I'm ready. No more distractions. *This* — the game, you guys — *this* is my priority. I'm sorry I've been tied up with her." *Mistakes. Regret. It's over.* "She's out of my system," I lied and stood. "So let's do this."

They smiled, though their eyes were sad, and I headed back to my room to put on a shirt.

When I picked up my phone, I found myself looking for her name, for a text, a call. Anything. But I only found the time. And the time said to move on.

So I powered it down and tossed it into my nightstand where it could stay in the dark.

Turn Back Icarus

-PENNY-

"**D**on't worry, Penny. Tacos will make everything better," Veronica said as she hooked her arm in mine.

This was untrue. Tacos could solve a lot of problems, but Bodie and I were not one of them.

The sun blazed down on the three of us, Ramona at my other side, as we headed toward a taco joint to pick up lunch for the shop, and I found myself frowning, eyes on the sidewalk in front of me, feeling like utter shit. Batshit, if I were being accurate, because my shit was crazy.

It had been three days, four texts, two phone calls, and a bottle of Patrón, and I found myself even further away from closure with Bodie than I had been on the night I last saw him.

His silence should have been enough to let me know how he felt.

But instead, I'd been driven mad with a thousand questions that only he could answer.

"Have you heard from him?" Ramona asked, reading my mind.

"Nope." I popped the P as my mood sank a little deeper.

"Ugh," she groaned. "This just doesn't even feel like him, does it?"

"No, it doesn't. But I seriously fucked it up. I just can't help but wonder if that's really it. Is it over? If I apologized, would it be okay? He won't answer me though, so there's not really anything I can do. I just wish I knew. I wish I had a chance to find out."

Veronica frowned but said nothing.

I rambled on. "I'm so frustrated and butthurt and mental over it. I wonder if he's doing it on purpose? Freezing me out to punish me?"

Veronica squeezed my arm. "Bodie wouldn't do that. I'm sure he's just busy. Don't they have that video game thing coming up?"

"Yeah," I conceded. "The whole thing sucks. I wish I could go back and do everything over again."

Ramona nodded. "Have you thought about going over there?"

I jacked an eyebrow at her. "He's not answering my texts, so you think I should stalk him?"

"Not stalk, just … face him."

"Showing up over there would be crazy, which I realize I am, but that's, like, next-level crazy."

"Pen," Ramona said as she hooked her arm in my free one, "you're not crazy. You're a mess, but you're not crazy."

I chuckled. "Thanks?"

"I mean it. And Bodie's not going to think you're crazy, especially if you apologize. I think he'll give that to you. I've said from the jump that you need to just talk to him, and I think this might be your last chance."

My heart burst apart like it had been stuffed with a lit M-80. "You think?"

"I do, on all counts. Go over there and talk to him. Tell him you're sorry. Either he'll tell you thanks, but no thanks or he'll take you back. Either way, you'll know."

"So either I'll be happy or miserable. That sounds super promising and not at all terrifying."

Veronica chuckled. "Penny, you're not afraid of anything but this *one thing*. I'm with Ramona. I say you should try so you can put it behind you. You're miserable. It's weird and very Four Horsemen."

"I know," I said on a soft laugh. "I'm sorry."

"Don't apologize for how you feel." Ramona leaned into me as we walked up to Taco Town. "But don't be afraid to do something about your feelings either."

She pulled open the door, and the smell of tortilla chips and greasy meat hit me like a wall of savory deliverance. I wanted to be with Bodie. I wanted to beg and grovel and get him back. And this was my last chance to do it.

"Okay," I said, standing up a little straighter. "I'll do it."

Ramona smiled, big and genuine and relieved. "When?"

And I sighed against the mounting pressure in my chest. "No time like the present. I've got a few hours — I'll swing by now. And maybe I'll bring tacos as a peace offering. He can't be mad at me if I'm holding tacos. It's a physical law of the universe."

Veronica laughed, and I only wished tacos were a guarantee.

- BODIE -

he game glitched. Again.

T I huffed and raked a hand through my hair, opening the code to comb through it. Again.

I'd done nothing for three days but work, sleep, and eat. My phone had stayed in my nightstand where I left it, and though I was fully occupied with the game, a little piece of my mind was always on Penny.

I was grateful for the distraction work provided.

Sorting through how I felt was too hard.

Numbers were simple. They didn't play games or lie — it was fact. You couldn't argue with math. It was unfeeling and logical and right.

It was a shame hearts didn't work the same way. They were the exact opposite of facts and reason. Hearts wanted what they wanted, regardless of the truth. And mine wanted Penny.

The sensible part of me — my brain — told me to just let it go. For the most part, I had. And the truth was, even though I wanted Penny, I didn't know if I wanted to be with her. Not at the status quo.

And that left me straddling the fence of her corral with no idea which way to go.

In any event, I had no time to expend on the decision. And that lack of time was a blessing, a bridge to put space between us that I desperately needed. So instead of thinking of the fight or how I missed her or how she'd hurt me, I filled my brain with ones and zeroes, a buzzing hum of logic that comforted me.

Well, not at the moment. At the moment, I was wrestling with the same string of code I'd been fighting since I woke up.

A knock rapped at the door, and when Jude answered and I heard the voice on the other side of the threshold, I spun around in my chair, stood numbly, and walked toward the sound.

The first and last person I'd expected to find on my welcome mat that day was Penny.

She stood in the hallway, sneakers turned in, shoulders rounded, red bottom lip between her teeth and eyes uncertain. She looked beautiful, sweet and beautiful and dangerous, with a bag stamped with the name *Taco Town* clutched in her hands.

Jude and I exchanged places at the door, and rather than moving to let her in, I stepped out and closed the door, leaving us alone in the hallway.

Somehow, she shrank into herself even more.

"Hey," she said simply.

"Hey," I echoed.

And then we stood there in the hallway with a thousand words hanging in the air.

She broke the silence. "I brought you some tacos."

Penny held out the bag, and I took it, opening it to look inside, not knowing what else to do. Five minutes ago, I'd been starving. Now I didn't know if I'd ever eat again.

"Thanks." I rolled the bag back up. "What's up?"

Her eyes were down, and she slipped her hands into her back pockets. "I … I'm sorry to just show up like this, but I hadn't heard from you, and …" She took a deep breath and met my eyes. "I'm sorry, Bodie. For everything. For bailing on you. For taking you to that stupid show. For hurting you. I'm … I'm sorry, and I was wrong."

I pulled in a deep breath through my nose and let it go. "Thank you."

Everything else I wanted to say piled up in my throat.

"I didn't want to go to the show, and I tried to argue, but I … I just wanted to see you so badly, and I didn't want to upset you any worse than I already had, not until I had a chance to talk to you." She took a breath and looked down again. "I know I don't deserve you, and I don't deserve another shot, but I need to know if I have one. Is there a way to go back? To fix things?"

I ran my fingers across my lips and tried to put the words together the right way. "Penny, I've gotta be honest. Right now, I am just … I'm so done. You're right; you hurt me, but I can't even blame you. But this isn't about the other night. This is about *us*. I can't keep up with you like I thought I'd be able to. You were always honest — you told me from the jump what you wanted, but I didn't listen. I thought … I thought I could tame you, convince you I was worth keeping. But I didn't think about what it would cost me. Play with fire and get burned, right? And, Pen — you are fire."

She took a breath but didn't say anything, just worked her bottom lip between her teeth, chin flexed like she might cry.

Please, God, don't let her cry.

"But the bottom line is that I can't deal with this right now. I've put so much on hold for you, for us, but now … now I need to go all in with the game, with my dream. Our meeting is tomorrow, and we've got so much to do that I don't have the bandwidth to figure out you and me. This game, Jude and Phil — this is my life. This is everything I've been working for, and it's happening *right now*. And I can't handle anything besides that. I'm sorry."

She nodded, her breath shaky. I could see she was definitely about to cry, and I wanted to scoop her into my arms and hold her, tell her I wanted her and needed her. But what I'd said was true. Penny was a white-hot flame, and I was made of wax. Holding her would ruin me.

"I'm sorry too," she said, looking up at me again with a smile meant to be brave.

That smile broke my heart into a thousand pieces, scattered on the floor with the broken glass of the penny jar.

She took a breath with shining eyes and said, "Hit me up, Bodie, if things change."

And I nodded and watched her walk away.

- PENNY -

I **hurried away from Bodie with** tears burning my throat and sneakers flying as I rushed down the stairs and outside, dragging in a breath so heavy with humidity and pain and regret that I felt like I was drowning.

It was over.

It was over, and it was my fault.

I wrapped my arms around my ribs and walked with no destination in mind, only desire to get as far away from my problems as humanly possible. Maybe I could find a cheap, last-minute flight to Tokyo. Or Budapest. Or Mars.

The exchange had been everything I'd feared, except somehow infinitely worse in reality than my imagination had been able to conjure. The look on his face, the resigned tone, the sadness in his eyes when he let me down gently.

But there was no amount of care that could have stopped me from breaking completely when I hit the ground.

The lump in my throat was sticky and hard, and I swallowed it down painfully only for it to bob back up.

Over, over, over. The word echoed with every footstep.

I'd come for closure and gotten it. I'd gotten it so hard, I might never get over it.

Avalanche

- B O D I E -

Phil **paced across the waiting** room of Avalanche's headquarters in Midtown, and I stared at my hands clasped between my knees with steam under the collar of my tailored shirt.

Jude seemed completely calm. The subtle façade of not giving a fuck in action. It was for show, though. He was just as nervous as the rest of us were.

We'd presented our demo to a handful of execs, which was weird to say since they were wearing jeans. One guy even had a T-shirt on with a binary joke on it that made me think of Penny. Because even then, even during our presentation, she'd found a way into my head.

I'd done all the talking, and when they had gotten their hands on the controllers and started to play, I'd found hope. Every one of them had gone wide-eyed, and as I'd pitched the story to them, their smiles had brightened just enough to betray their attempts to keep their poker faces on.

It had gone well. Very well.

But I counted on nothing as we waited for them in the lobby of their office.

My palms were damp and nerves shot as our hopes and dreams hung in the balance of a few quiet minutes.

It won't be the end if they don't take us, I told myself.

There were dozens more companies we could pitch to if this didn't work out, especially now that the demo was finished. But this … this was the holy grail, the absolute, the top of the list. The dream. The fact that we'd even gotten a meeting was unreal. The hopes of it getting better than that felt too slim to count on.

The doors to the conference room opened, and we were invited back, so we filed in and took seats. I was so nervous, I thought I might combust. But outwardly, I tried to keep cool, scanning their faces for some hint as to what they'd say.

Paul, the CEO spoke first. "I'd like to start by saying that we don't make a habit of keeping designers here while we talk, but I have to say — we were impressed."

Hope sprang, putting out the fear with a sizzle.

"You've hit all the high notes. The story is epic, and the twist … the twist just makes the whole thing sweeter. We see a three-game series over the course of six years. Breakneck, I know, but with our team and your brains, I think it's feasible. That is, if you're still interested in a partnership with us."

I blinked, trying to remember to breathe. "Absolutely."

Paul smiled. "Great. We've got to get with our team to put together the numbers, but we'd like to offer you a deal. This is one of the best demos we've seen — the hard work you've put into it is the real reason we feel comfortable taking the step — so we want you all to come in on lead positions to help us get the game produced just how you want it. You'll retain a level of control over everything — story, content, gameplay, UI — though it'll ultimately need approval. But I give you my word; this is your story, your vision, and because we like what we see, we'll put our trust in you. What do you think?"

I glanced at Phil and Jude, who nodded their approval. And then I smiled back at Paul. "I think you've got yourself a deal."

We beamed as we all shook hands, and with another meeting on the books to discuss details, the three of us headed out of the office. When we made it outside, we broke into jumps and laughter and back-clapping and bro hugs, and I thought my heart might blow from sheer joy. Because we'd done it. The hard work had paid off.

We'd just landed jobs at one of the best game design companies in America.

Once we caught our breaths, Phil pulled out his phone to call Angie, and Jude got his phone out too, wandering off to talk to who knew who.

Before I knew it, my phone was in my hand and my thumb was hovering over Penny's name.

I'd been so caught up that I'd forgotten we weren't okay. I'd forgotten I couldn't just call her, not without answering questions I didn't have a response for. Not without making a move I didn't know I was ready to make.

I pictured her face as she'd stood before me on my doormat, the smallness of her in the expanse of the hallway. She was all of a sudden the only person in the world I wanted to talk to, and the last person who I could.

The worst part was that I wasn't even mad anymore. I was hurt and sad and exhausted by her, but I wasn't mad. And I missed her.

A sick, masochistic part of me — my heart — wanted to give it another shot, wanted to hear her out and try again. The rest of me — my brain — told me I'd already slammed my hand in the door once, making a point of reliving the pain in an attempt to convince me not to do it again.

In the end, I figured they were probably both wrong. Because either way I looked at it, I was damaged, and I didn't know how or when I'd recover.

Moby Fucking Dick

-PENNY-

My *room was dark even* though it was after noon. Between the stormy day and my drawn curtains, I found myself happily miserable, buried in my sheets and blankets, listening to my Sad Panda playlist on repeat.

I'd done nothing but work and sleep for two days, and that morning, I'd woken up at seven, completely rested and still completely exhausted. I existed in that in-between — that state of mind where you couldn't physically sleep anymore, but you couldn't get out of bed either, folding in on yourself like origami until you disappeared. So I'd made plans to do absolutely nothing on my day off besides lie in bed and stare at my wall.

There was just so much to think about. I counted my mistakes and regrets in a loop like "99 Bottles of Beer on the Wall," though

less cheery and somehow infinitely more depressing and obnoxious. I'd exhausted my tears. At least, I thought I had. Every time I'd said it, they'd find their way back again, pricking the corners of my eyes.

It was over. And it was all my fault.

I sighed and rolled over, pulling a pillow into my aching chest.

My bedroom door flew open, and Veronica stood in the frame, hands on her hips like an unamused Wonder Woman. "Why are you still in bed?" she asked like she didn't know the answer.

I frowned and sank a little deeper into my blanket burrito. "Leave me alone, Ronnie."

"Nope." In three steps, she was at the foot of my bed with my blankets in her fists. She pulled, effectively subjecting me to the cruel, cruel world.

I scrambled to catch the covers before they were gone, but they lay in a pile on the floor, and Ronnie's hands were back on her stupid traitorous hips.

"Come on, smelly. You've been locked in here listening to Mazzy Star for days. You need a shower and a drink and a new playlist."

I covered my face with my pillow and curled up in a ball like I could hide. "Go away."

"Nope! Get up!" The bed dipped as she climbed on, stood up, and started jumping.

"Ugh!"

I flung a pillow at her, and she laughed, catching it midair to toss it behind her.

"Whoops, you lost another place to hide." She put a little more force into her bouncing, sending me jostling.

I grabbed another pillow and threw it but was thwarted again. "I hate you."

"Liar."

She giggled and stopped jumping, lying down next to me. Her face softened, her smile cajoling. "Seriously, though, let's go do something."

I pouted, curling up even tighter. "I don't wanna."

She rolled her eyes. "Real mature."

"Everything sucks."

"*Everything* doesn't suck," she corrected. "Just one thing."

I groaned. "But that one thing really, really sucks. I don't think he's going to call me."

She didn't answer right away. "Maybe not. Maybe so. You just have to wait and see."

"Waiting sucks too. Time sucks. Breaking up sucks. Everything sucks. See?"

"It's only been two days, Pen," she said gently. "Give him a little more time."

"He had his meeting. I wonder how it went. I wonder if he's okay." I paused. "I should call him."

She gave me a look.

"Ugh, don't look at me like that. Are you gonna slap my phone out of my hand again if I try?"

"Maybe."

I groaned. "But I can't call him. You're right. I'm trying to respect his space." My face bent under the weight of my conflict. "God, can't you just go sleep with Jude to find out what's going on over there?"

"Ha, ha." She pulled my last pillow out from under my head and pressed it over my face like she was going to suffocate me.

We laughed for a second, and then I groaned again. "This *sucks.*"

"All right, you win. Everything sucks."

"Thank you."

"But this is ridiculous."

My face went flat. "Thanks."

"What? It is, and you know it. Seriously, if I hear 'Fade into You' one more time, I'm going to open a vein. So let's get you cleaned up and out of the house. Even if just for a minute. Even if just for tacos."

"I don't want tacos."

One of her brows rose. "Wow. You really *are* fucked up."

"Told you."

"Okay, then call him."

"Oh, so *now* you'll let me call him?" I huffed. "I can't, and you know it. I literally just said that."

"I know, and I take it back. I'm changing my tune since my old tune is worn out, and you clearly don't want to hear it. If you want to talk to him, call him."

"He said he didn't have time to 'deal' right now." I made air quotes with one hand.

"I mean, I guess you can't really blame him."

"I don't," I said sadly. "I don't blame him at all. I blame me. I'm the one who did this. He's right; I kept all my feelings to myself, and this was the result. I hurt him, Ronnie. I don't even know if I deserve to have him back. So I'm at an emotional impasse."

She watched me for a second. "All right, then how about going back?" Somewhere in her twinkling eyes, I thought she might be baiting me.

I frowned. "What do you mean?"

"Let's get Old Penny back. The girl who doesn't do relationships because of exactly *this*."

A tiny sliver of hope shone on me as she continued.

"You're like this about guys because you don't want to get hurt. You just lived through a self-fulfilling prophecy. So, why not adopt the old rule again? Revive it. Bring it back from the dead."

I smiled for the first time in days as I relit the pilot light in my heart. "Yes. Yes! Old Penny is fucking smart. Feelings are dumb and stupid and ruin lives. I was so much happier when I had the rule and boundaries. You're right. I can't believe you're actually right. We should mark the calendar."

She laughed and pinched me in the arm. "Okay, so let's go out and prove how smart Old Penny is. We can go to Diesel and see Cody. Remember Cody? He always puts you in a good mood."

I sighed dreamily. "How could I forget? That's no man. That's a god, covered in tattoos. And he has that hair."

"Gah, that hair. That hair should have its own Tumblr."

I laughed, feeling less like my heart was going to fall out of my chest.

"Come on. It'll be fun. You can get back on the horse. Or the Cody. Whatever."

I laughed, but my insides knotted up at the thought of riding anybody but Bodie. "Okay. Let's do it."

She smiled and booped my nose. "Atta girl. It's gonna be okay, Pen," she said so softly and sincerely that I actually believed her.

My liner was winged, my heels were high, my shorts were short, and my mood was about as sturdy as piecrust — a thin, golden buttery façade over the gooey, messy, blood-red cherry filling. But I found myself strutting into that bar on a mission that felt awfully real even if it was bullshit.

Diesel was packed wall-to-wall with people. Everything in the bar was metal and brick and leather, dark and inky. The light fixtures were made of machine parts with naked bulbs and glowing filaments, and the bar itself was black brushed metal and my destination from the second we walked in the door.

We wormed our way up to the bar with smiles and arm touches, parting the crowd like Moses. Veronica pushed me in front, and I squeezed in between a couple of guys to lean on the bar, rack on display.

I spotted Cody at the other end of the bar, and he glanced at me and away before looking back to me with a whip of his head that was so fast, he might have sprained something. A slow smile spread across his face, and he jerked his chin at me in greeting.

Cody was one of those gritty, dirty tattooed types with the irreverent beard and hair a little too long, pushed back from his face with ruts from his fingers. The gauges in his ears were just big enough to be big without being obscene, and he not only had his nostril and septum pierced, but he also had snakebites — two rings on his bottom lip where, if he were a rattlesnake, his fangs would rest.

I'd had a boner for Cody since the first time I ever laid eyes on him, but he'd always had a girlfriend. I might love me some dick, but I'd never knowingly hook up with a guy with a girlfriend, so we'd kept it to flirting, but he was the number one reason why we used to come to Diesel. And when he made his way over, my insides went ballistic because:

1. He was gorgeous.

2. His eyes pinned me to the spot.

3. He wasn't Bodie, and him even looking at me like he was made me feel nineteen ways to wrong.

Cody leaned on the bar right across from me, ignoring everyone around me who'd been waiting.

"Damn, it's good to see you, Penny. Where the hell have you been?"

The guy next to me huffed and slapped a hand on the bar. "What the fuck, man? We've all been waiting longer than her."

Cody's eyes went hard as he glared at the guy. "You don't let a girl like *this* stand at the bar without giving her your full attention. And if you want a drink the rest of the night, I suggest you shut the fuck up and wait until I address you."

The guy pointed at Cody. "This is fucked up. Fuck this place!" And with that eloquent goodbye, he turned around and left.

Cody turned back to me, his gaze smoldering again. "Double Patrón, chilled?"

I smiled as discomfort twisted around in my stomach like snakes. "You remembered."

"Psh. You're impossible to forget, Pen," he said with a smirk, leaning a little closer. "Lean over."

I did, against my better judgment, and when I was half-bent over the bar, he leaned in close, his lips brushing my ear.

"Alley-oop," he said softly as he grabbed me by the waist and pulled.

I took the cue and lifted myself as he helped me onto the bar. I spun around on my butt until my legs were on his side of the counter and my feet dangled just outside the shelves of liquor and glasses tucked under the bar top.

My heart thundered its warning as I hung onto the edge and crossed my legs, locking my elbows and straightening my back. I felt like a pinup girl, and was pretty sure every eyeball in the bar was on me. A month ago, I would have been in hog heaven. In that moment, I'd rather be in a pig pen.

Cody kept on smirking, pouring well more than two shots of Patrón into a shaker. "How've you been? It's been too long since you've been in."

"Oh, I've been good. Just surviving." Surviving *Bodie* was the rest of that sentence, but, color me crazy, it seemed like the wrong thing to say in the moment. "How about you?"

He shook up my drink with his eyes dragging a path from my heels to the hem of my shorts, which were regrettably short. Sitting on a bar might sound sexy and brash and cavalier, but the truth was that it was sticky as fuck. I just hoped there was no grenadine. All I needed was a cherry stain on my ass to end the week on a high note.

"I've been waiting for you to come in. Sheila and I broke up."

My mouth popped open, and I blinked, noticing that he was shaking that shaker at his waist like he was pumping his dick.

"You're kidding." I had no idea what else to say.

He shook his head, not looking sad in the slightest, probably because he had me sitting on the bar like a trophy. "It's been over for a long time. Plus, I've had my sights set somewhere else."

Cody popped the top of the shaker and poured my drink, hooking a lime on the edge of the glass before handing it over. I took a sip, hands on my drink as he bracketed my crossed legs with his arms.

I'd been waiting for this moment for months, and here it was. The filthy, hot, tattooed, pierced bartender of my dreams had literally picked me up and set me on the bar to tell me he wanted to bang me. A month ago, I would have climbed him like a jungle gym. But when he ran his hand down the curve of my calf, I laughed awkwardly and chased his hand with my own, redirecting it.

"Straight to the point, huh, Cody?" I said, hoping I sounded cool. And then I swiveled around on the bar and hopped down, praying for that millisecond I wasn't going to break my ankle. I didn't, thankfully. "I'll see you later," I said over my shoulder with a smile.

"I sure hope so," he called after me as the crowd swallowed me.

My smile fell faster than a GTO hits sixty, and I stomped my way around the bar, scanning for Veronica.

I found her at a table. She was on her phone, texting so intently that she didn't even see me stalk up.

"Well, this is a fucking disaster," I shot and took a heavy pull of tequila. Too heavy. My face pinched up, and I shook my head to set it back to rights.

"What happened?" She eyed me.

"He fucking hit on me, that's what happened."

Her eyes narrowed. "And that's … bad?"

"Yes! I mean, no, but, yes! He and his girlfriend broke up, and he picked me up and set me on the bar and touched my leg and — ugh!"

That stupid look in her eye was back, the one that said she had me right where she wanted me. "You had the white whale in your clutches, and you didn't snag him?"

I took another drink, this time more moderate. "Yep. I had Moby Fucking Dick in my harpoon sights, and not only am I uninterested, but I'm ... what is this feeling?" My face fell. "Is this what it feels like to feel offended?"

She laughed — that asshole.

"Oh my God," I groaned as I plopped onto a stool next to her. "I'm broken. Bodie broke me, and now I'm ruined." My chest ached, and I slammed the rest of my tequila to burn the pain away. "I don't want to do this, Ronnie."

Veronica smiled at that, just a little, just enough. "Well, well. I'm not gonna lie. I kind of hoped this would happen."

I sucked in a tiny breath and gaped at her. "Did you fucking set me up?"

She shrugged. "I had a feeling you needed a push. I mean, you *definitely* needed a shower, so even if that was the only thing that came of tonight, I was going to call it a win."

I set my glass down with a clink and glared. "You dick."

But she reached for my arm, her eyes caring even if she was a douchebag. "Pen, you said you didn't want to do *this*, Cody, tonight, boy-hunt, whatever. So what other choice do you have? You want Bodie, right?"

"Yeah, I do." I didn't know why I wanted to cry, but I did. It had been at least ten hours. I was due.

"Then what are you gonna do about it?"

A tingle worked across my skin, either from the tequila or the realization of the truth.

I couldn't go back because Old Penny didn't exist anymore. Old Penny had lost her heart to Bodie.

He had changed me, rearranged me, and as I sat in that bar with an empty glass in my hand, I knew I'd never be the same. Even if I'd fucked it up, even if I'd lost him forever, I'd learned something very important.

I wanted to trust someone else with my heart.

Bodie had shown me what it was like to be with someone I trusted, someone who cherished me and whom I wanted to cherish. He'd taught me that letting someone in was a risk, but the reward was immeasurable. I'd let him in, and I'd gotten hurt because I'd fought the feeling. For a second there, I'd fallen into him and let myself go, and that second had been so glorious, so perfect, that all I wanted to do was get the feeling back. I wanted to get *him* back. I wanted to give him everything in the same way he'd given everything to me.

I loved the way he made me feel, loved his mind and body and soul, loved the way he cared for me, the way he'd let me breathe and given me exactly what I'd needed, even when it hurt him. Even when I hurt him.

The truth of the matter dawned on me like a ray of sunshine, illuminating what I'd known all along.

I didn't want to trust just anyone with my heart. I wanted to give my heart to Bodie.

It was already his.

Right then, I knew I would do whatever it took to get him back. Even if it didn't work and even if there was no way back to him, I had to try. I had to fight for him.

The sweet relief of decision knocked all the weight off my shoulders so I could breathe again, and that pilot light in my ribs fired up, igniting me with purpose. And as an idea came to me, I only hoped he would give me one last chance.

Bail

- BODIE -

I **dropped my hands into the** ocean on either side of my board
to wet them and ran them through my drying hair. Jude and I had
been waiting on a decent wave for long enough that I was ready to
call it.

I sighed and glanced down the line of surfers — all sitting on
their boards off Rockaway Beach looking bored — then at the beach,
dotted with sunbathers. It was my first session in New York, and if
things had gone differently, Penny would have been one of those dots
on the beach. She would have been my dot on the beach.

I imagined her letting me teach her how to surf, imagined her on
a board laughing, and my mood sank even further.

"Ugh, man. Quit being so fucking mopey."

"This sucks. Let's just go."

He rolled his eyes. "Quitter."

"Bro, this is bullshit. We rode the subway for an hour to get here with boards and wetsuits, and it's nothing but closeouts. I told you to check the fucking reports, man."

"I did," he said with a huff.

"Liar. Nobody's getting a decent ride today. It's not happening, so why the fuck are we still sitting here? I mean, I appreciate you trying to cheer me up and all, but the longer we sit here, the more pissed I am."

"You're just bitchy because of Penny."

I narrowed my eyes at him.

He held up his hands. "Look, I'm not judging. I'm just saying."

"I'm not calling her, dude," I said for the hundredth time.

"I don't see why not. We were busy before, but we did it. It's over, so now you can figure out what you want to do about her. It couldn't hurt to just talk to her."

I rested a hand on my thigh and turned to him, making a face. "Seriously? Because if I talk to her and she says the right thing, I'll be right back where I started."

"Why's that a bad thing?"

"Because I don't know if I can trust her. Don't you think I want to call her? Don't you think I want to go right back to the way things were? Because I do. I want to so bad, I can't even stand it. But the problem is that there *is* no going back, and I don't know if Penny's capable of going forward."

"What if she is and you just don't know it?"

I sighed and shook my head. "I dunno, man. I don't know if I'm ready to put myself through that again. I'm scared of her. I care too much *not* to be scared. Maybe I just need a little more time. Space."

"Yeah, because that's going so well for you."

He wasn't wrong. I'd been reserved and in my own head ever since the concert, even worse since she'd come over with tacos.

I ran a hand over the smattering of stubble across my jaw. "I almost call her every day. I just don't even know what to say or how to handle her. I don't know what she wants from me or if I can even give it to her anymore. Because if she wants to pretend like we don't care about each other, I'm out. I want her. I want her for keeps, and I'm through playing games."

"Then you need to tell her."

"Man, you don't fucking get it. I can't just tell her. I can't guide her through this; she's got to figure it out and let me know. If I tell her what I want, who's to say she won't agree without really understanding what I'm asking of her? I can be patient, but I can't teach her this. I can't tell her what to do or what she wants."

"Don't you think she deserves the chance? She's waiting on *you*."

"Yeah, well, she shouldn't," I said, my throat tight as I lay on my belly and paddled away, angling for a wave that wouldn't last more than six feet, but I didn't care. I didn't want to talk. I didn't want to participate. I just wanted it all to go away.

I popped up onto my feet and rode the wave until it folded in on itself. When the barrel disappeared, I bailed, diving off my board and into the ocean, opening my eyes underwater to watch the wave roll away from me upside down, taking my hope with it.

What Part of $\sigma = \lambda(\nabla \cdot \acute{u})I + 2\mu\varepsilon$ Don't You Understand?

- BODIE -

The whiskey in my hand was cold, but it went down warm as I walked around the party the following night, trying to have a good time and failing miserably.

Jude had the idea to throw a party to celebrate our dreams coming true, and maybe if I'd lived in New York for more than a month, I would have been having a better time. Maybe if I knew anyone in New York besides Jude, Phil, and Penny, I'd have someone to talk to. But Jude was busy working the crowd, Phil was busy with Angie, and Penny was, of course, not there.

I paced through the people scattered all over the roof of our building, a common space strung with lights and dotted with islands of chairs. Everyone seemed to be having a good time — we'd even sprung for a DJ who spun actual records and a bartender who we'd tipped extra to get everybody tanked.

I walked to the edge of the patio, looking toward Central Park, the strip of darkness cradled in the light of the city with Penny on my mind, as she always was.

Jude and I had come home from Rockaway the day before with almost complete silence between us. Well, Jude had talked a lot, and I'd listened and responded when I was supposed to. But the whole way, I had thought about what he'd said, and when I had been alone in my room, I'd held my phone in my hand for a long time, thinking about calling her.

Because he was right; she deserved the chance to tell me what she wanted, and I needed to know. I just didn't know if I was really ready to hear it if it wasn't what I wanted to hear.

And that was the real truth of it. It was easier to leave that door open and wonder than to hear that she didn't want me like I wanted her.

But Penny had bolted after all, and I couldn't make her stay. In the end, she'd bucked me off and left me stranded.

She was wild, and I should have known better than to try to hold on to her.

Of course, the other thing about loving something wild was how it changed you. And I'd found myself changed for the better — having held her for a moment — and for the worse — the wounds from my grip on her still fresh and tender.

A deep sigh did little to vent the pressure in my chest, and I turned to head inside, exhausted beyond measure.

Jude was striding toward me looking suspiciously subversive, and my eyes narrowed. He'd been barring me from going downstairs all night.

I held up a hand. "I'm going down. Don't try to stop me."

He smiled. "It's cool. I won't. You've fulfilled your obligations tonight, so go ahead and mope all by yourself while we party until dawn."

I shook my head and rolled my eyes. "That trick doesn't work on me."

Jude shrugged. "Had to try."

He clapped me on the shoulder, and I headed for the stairs, lost in my thoughts, grateful to be alone as I trotted down to our apartment.

Except when I walked inside, I wasn't alone at all. And when I saw her standing before me, time stopped.

Penny stood in front of our computers next to a blank chalkboard on wheels looking afraid and hopeful and absolutely beautiful. Her hair was purple again and spilling over her shoulders, her fingers toying with the short hem of her gauzy black dress that was sweet, almost demure, though she hung onto her edge with the deep V and strip of broad lace around her waist where her skin peeked through.

My heart jumped in my chest like it was reaching for her, and my throat closed up, jammed with a hundred things I felt and wished for and wanted. A question was on my lips, and I opened them to speak, but she took a breath and beat me to the punch.

"They call me Pi because I'm irrational and I don't know when to stop."

A single laugh burst out of me, and she smiled, relaxing just a little as she stepped closer to the chalkboard.

She drew a line with a shaky hand, then drew another perpendicular line in the center to make a right angle. "I'm not always *right*." She drew another line at about the one hundred twenty degree mark. "And I know I've been *obtuse*." Her final line was at around the forty-five degree point. "But luckily I'm *acute* psycho, which makes me a little easier to deal with."

I folded my arms and squeezed, heart thudding, smile on my lips, disbelieving as my eyes and ears sent signals to my brain that my heart had always known.

"It's all fun and games until someone divides by zero, which I did when I took you to that godforsaken concert and that zero came between us. But even before that, I should have told you something I was too afraid to admit," she said as she drew two right triangles, backed up to each other to make a whole. "You and I are so right."

She drew a box on the chalkboard underneath the triangles with an anatomical heart inside without a single mistake, like it was second nature.

"I can't let you go, not without telling you how I feel, but I had to think outside the quadrilateral parallelogram to figure out how. Bodie, you're like a math book; you solve all my problems. And like decimals, I have a point."

She turned and moved toward me with her eyes so full of questions and answers and secrets and love that it broke my heart and healed it. My hands fell to my sides, my breath shallow, when she stopped just in front of me.

"I'm sorry. I'm sorry I was afraid, and I'm sorry I hurt you. You're the best thing that has ever happened to me, and I want to return that gift. I want to be your everything if you'll take me back. Because there's no equation in my heart that doesn't put you and me together and end in infinity. I'm all in, Bodie. All three hundred sixty degrees of me."

I took a breath and stepped into her, bringing her into my arms as my lungs filled with air, filled with her.

"You are one well-defined function, Penny," I joked quietly, holding her against my beating heart, searching for words. "This was all I needed — to know how you felt. If we're going to work, you've got to tell me. You've got to trust me."

"I do," she said softly. "Does this mean …"

I gazed down at her, drunk on her, smiling. "You know," I said as I brushed her hair from her face, "they say the best angle to come at something is the *try*angle."

"Do they say that?" She smiled, her eyes shining as she leaned into me, her breaths short.

"They do," I answered, thumbing her cheek, searching her eyes. "I don't want to lose you either, Pen. So I'll take your three-sixty and give you mine. It was already yours," I said against her lips.

And with the smallest of shifts, we connected, breathing out relief and breathing each other into its place.

Her lips were so sweet, the feel of her in my arms so much better than I'd been daydreaming about since I'd held her last. And all my fears fell away. All except one.

Slowly, reluctantly, I broke away slowly.

"You changed your hair again," I said as I slipped a lock through my fingers.

She nodded, smiling lips together. "It was a complete science experiment of pink-to-blue ratios, but it worked out. I really like this color after all. I think I'm gonna stick with it for the long haul."

"Penny," I started, looking down at her, hoping this was it, that she was mine for good, "I need to know you're not going to run when it gets hard. Because it will get hard, and I … I can't hang around on the fence waiting to see which way you'll go."

She nodded. "God, I hate that I've done this to you, that you'd question it. So I'll tell you now, and I'll prove it as we go." She held my jaw in her hands and looked into my eyes. "I'm here to stay. I'm not going to run, and I know it'll get hard. And you're right; we can't pretend like everything's fine when it's not. I can't be afraid to tell you how I feel, and you can't either. I promise to be honest with you if you do the same."

"I promise. But that's not the only reason you bugged out."

She took a breath and looked down. "No, it wasn't the only reason. I've never felt like this before, Bodie. For so long, I've suppressed all of this, hid from it, stopped it before it started, and now that I'm letting go of that, it's like learning how to walk. And I want this. I want you. But I'm scared."

I cupped her cheeks and tilted her face up to meet my eyes. "I know," I said softly, gently. "But I'm not going to hurt you, Pen. I want to protect you. I want to love you." My chest tightened as the word passed my lips.

"I want to love you too," she said as the fear left her eyes, "and I know you won't hurt me. All you've ever done is try to make me happy. So now it's my turn."

And when she stretched onto her toes, when her lids closed and lashes cast shadows on her cheeks, when she pressed her lips to mine, I knew without a doubt that it was true.

She opened her mouth and opened her heart, and I slipped in, holding her against me. She held onto me like she never wanted to let me go, and I did the same. Her hands found their way into my hair, her tongue sliding past mine, her back arching her body into my chest, bringing us almost as close as we could be fully clothed.

She seemed to notice the same thing as she brought the kiss to a close and ran her hands down my chest, tilting her chin to watch them.

"I missed you," she said.

I pressed a kiss to her forehead. "I missed you too."

My heart chugged under her palm.

"Should we go to the party?" she asked.

I knew for a fact it was the last thing she wanted to do.

I smirked. "How'd you know about the party?"

She smiled back. "Jude. I had his number. He helped me set this all up."

"No wonder he wouldn't let me come down," I said with a laugh.

"He told me they want the game, that you did it. You got the job. You chased your dream down and caught it, and I'm so proud of you. I wish I could have been here for you."

I held her close, full of gratitude and reassurance and utter joy. "You're here now. That's all that matters."

She smiled. "We should go up and say hi."

But I bent to grab her around the waist, picking her up as I stood. "Not a chance."

She wrapped her legs around my waist and smiled, and I slid my hands up her thighs to her bare ass.

I groaned and squeezed. "Fuck, Penny."

And all she did was laugh and kiss me.

I made my way into my bedroom, lit only by a lamp next to my bed, kicking the door closed behind me before tipping her onto the bed to kiss her, to press her small body into the bed with mine. And for a long time, we lay together in my bed — my hands in her hair, on her face, reverently brushing her collarbone, and her hands in my hair, on my jaw, riding the backs of my fingers as they traced the curves I'd thought I'd never touch again.

I could have kissed Penny forever. If I was lucky, maybe I would.

But our hands and lips and bodies weren't content with that and moved on their own. Her hips rolled gently against mine, stroking her body against the hard length of my cock, and my hips flexed in answer, my lips harder, my hand roaming to cup her breast through the thin fabric of her dress. When I thumbed the peaked flesh of her nipple between her barbell, she cupped my neck and whimpered. And that was all it took to lose my patience.

I backed off of her, and kneeling at the foot of the bed, I tugged off my shirt and flung it, hands moving for my belt and eyes on Penny shifting on the bed, watching me.

I popped my button and lowered my zipper, hooking my thumbs in the waistband to push my jeans over my ass and down my thighs, shimmying out of them with the help of Penny's feet.

I nestled my hips against hers, the fabric between her clit and my cock thin enough that I could feel everything — the balls of her piercing, the soft, warm flesh waiting for me. But I left her dress where it was between our hips and kissed her again. I kissed the sweetness of her lips and silently told her I'd take care of her. I kissed her neck and promised her she was safe. I kissed the space between her breasts, her heart thumping against my lips, and vowed I'd never break it.

My fingers pushed the strap of her dress over the curve of her shoulder until her breast was bare, and I ran my hand over the sweet, supple flesh, pressing myself into her with an ache in my chest from the weight of all I wanted and wished for and held dear. And my lips found hers again as our bodies wound together, a knot of arms and legs and hands whose purpose was only to bring us as close as we could get.

Her hips moved with intention, inching her dress up until we were skin-to-skin. She sighed through her nose against my cheek, gave the smallest of hums against my tongue in her mouth, and I wrapped my arms around her and squeezed. She tilted her hips to press the slick center of her to the length of my cock, and it was my turn to hum.

It had been too long without her, without *this*. And now that I had her in my arms again, it was beyond what I'd dreamed of. Because now, she was mine.

With every flex, she angled for my crown until I gave her body what it asked of me, backing up until the tip of me rested just inside her. I waited for only a moment before I slipped into her slowly in a motion that pushed a breath from both our lungs with every aching millimeter.

I pulled out and slid in easier, faster than before but still slow, deliberate, as if I could prolong it. As if I could make it last forever. And when I hit the end of her, when our bodies were a seam, she lay underneath me, bracketed in my arms, lids heavy and eyes full of love, and I committed every sensation — mind, body, and soul — to memory.

And when I kissed her again, it was with more emotion than I knew what to do with.

I pushed the other strap of her dress over her shoulder, wanting her skin on mine, and she wiggled her arms out and pushed the dress down her ribs. Every stroke of ink on her chest was brushed by my fingertips. The feel of her metal barbells and the soft flesh between impressed themselves in my palm. Her hood piercing pressed into the skin just above my cock, giving me a target, and I ground against it with every pump of my hips until she muttered my name, hooking her legs around my waist to twist us.

I let her guide me onto my back, our bodies still connected, hers rocking as she reached across her body and grabbed her dress, pulling it off, leaving her naked. And then she braced herself on my chest and raised her ass, dropping down on me achingly slow, working my body with hers, hips rolling.

Every time I disappeared into her, my pulse raced faster until my heart hammered against my ribs, and I sat, reaching for her, winding my arms around her, burying my face in her breasts, my hands cupping her ass to lift and lower her.

She clenched around my cock once, gasped my name — the sound sweet and right and everything — and her body tensed as she squeezed me so tight, so hard that when she came, I did too with a growl and a moan and the nerves in my body so raw and connected to her that I vibrated like a tuning fork.

My hands flexed, holding her against me, rocking her gently as the last flickers worked through us. She curled into me, arms tucked into her chest and head under my chin. I wrapped my arms around her, so small and right and mine.

She was mine. I was hers. And that was it.

My fingertips skated the length of her back while we came down, and when she sighed — a heavy, satisfied sound — I lay back, taking her with me, pulling out of her. And as we lay there on our sides together, wrapped up in each other, I found myself so content, so happy. I knew right then and there that I'd do anything to hang on to that, hang on to her. I cursed myself for ever walking away.

Of course, as I slid my hand into her hair and kissed her, I realized I couldn't have stayed away. Penny and I felt inevitable that way. I hadn't stopped thinking of her any more than she had of me. And even though I'd been hurt, I couldn't imagine ever *really* walking away. We would have found a way back to each other.

The alternative hurt too much to even think about — I'd have lost my chance at *this*. Because holding Penny, I knew I could spend a thousand nights like this and never get my fill.

She stirred against my chest and kissed my collarbone. I kissed her forehead in answer and whispered I'd be right back before climbing out of bed to dart across the empty hallway to the bathroom. And when I came back with a washcloth and a smile, it was met with hers. She was curled up in my bed like a cat, looking sated and content and just as happy as I was.

I crawled to her, kissing her bare hip before rolling her over onto her back to clean her up, and she watched me with a purple strand of hair between her fingers and her lip between her teeth.

"I missed you," she said, her voice husky. "I was a mess without you."

I chuckled. "You're a mess with me."

"That's true. But so, so much worse without."

I shook my head, marveling over the night. "I can't believe you did all this. Where'd you get all the math material?" I tossed the washcloth in the general direction of my closet.

"Mostly the internet, but I asked one of the girls on set who's a real math whiz."

She reached for the covers tucked under my pillow and slipped between the sheets, and I followed her in.

"And you memorized it and everything," I said, still smiling as I pulled her back into my chest and our legs scissored together. I wondered absently if I'd ever stop smiling.

"Mmhmm. Ronnie made flashcards."

I laughed at that.

"I just … I'm sorry I didn't try harder sooner. I'm sorry I didn't tell you how I felt from the start."

"It's all right," I said quietly.

"But it's not. Bodie, I know it's no excuse, but I've been this way for a long time and for a lot of reasons that seem really stupid now." She took a breath. "You remember how it was with me and Rodney in high school?"

My fingers dragged across her shoulder blades and back again. "I remember."

"He used to manipulate me, gaslight me to make me think I was crazy, which made me crazier. It was like a self-fulfilling prophecy. And even at that, I never left him."

"Penny, you aren't responsible for what he did to you. And plus, we were just kids then."

She backed away and propped herself up on her elbow. "But see, it changed me. I looked at what happened with him and knew I didn't want to feel that way anymore, ever again. And in my brain, that meant not letting myself care about anybody. So I conditioned myself over eight years. And everything went along shipshape, until I met you. You came along with your dimple and torpedo cock and sank my battleship."

A laugh burst out of me, and she smiled.

"But then I was drowning. Clearly, I do not know how to swim. It was cruel really," she teased.

"I'm not sorry I sank your battleship, and neither is my torpedo."

I propped my head on my hand.

Penny giggled, her cheeks rosy and smile warm. "I ain't mad atcha. That ship was a bucket of bolts." She paused, perking up. "Oh, I meant to ask you how your hand was."

I showed her my knuckles, which were almost fully healed. "All better."

She held hers up with a smirk— they were a little scraped up. "Mine too."

My brow quirked, and I reached for her hand to inspect it. "What happened?"

"Well, I couldn't let you be the only one to get licks in on Rodney."

A surprised laugh shot out of me. "You're kidding."

She shook her head. "He called you a loser, and I punched him in the eye."

I laughed even more and kissed the back of her hand.

"And then he called me a psycho, and I kneed him in the balls."

That one earned her a kiss on the lips.

"God, I wish I'd seen that."

"There might be a YouTube video out there somewhere. Who knows?"

I chuckled. "Well, I have a confession to make since we're confessing things."

One of her brows rose. "Oh?"

"Mmhmm." I watched her, smiling. "I knew from the jump that I wanted to be with you, and I knew I'd have my work cut out for me when it came to convincing you to let me stick around longer than a few dates."

Her mouth opened in a red O that wasn't at all serious. "You fucking sneak! Heart-ninja sneak, with your heart-ninja stars that make girls fall for you. I've been tricked."

I chuckled and rested my hand on her hip under the blanket.

"More like lion tamer than a ninja."

She lit up. "Ooh, do you have a whip?"

"No, but I can get one." I leaned forward to kiss her, laughing through my nose.

"I like it. I'm the lion. How are you gonna keep me from eating your face off?"

"Just gotta keep you well fed." I pulled her hips into mine to show her just what I could feed her.

She laughed. "That'll do."

I smiled at her for a minute. "Scared?"

"Fucking terrified."

"Trust me?"

And she leaned into me, cupping my jaw as she said against my lips, "Without a doubt."

Donut You Know?

-PENNY-

The sun broke in through Bodie's window, shining a ray of light across his nose and lips, illuminating them from behind and casting them in shadows in the same feat of physics.

I didn't know how long it had been since I'd woken — not overly long, I didn't think — but I didn't care to move. I didn't care if my phone had a bazillion texts or if the world was on fire. All I wanted to do was lie there next to Bodie.

I watched him sleep with a smile on my face. His hand rode his chest up and down as he breathed slow and deep, and his hair was mussed, his face soft and young and beautiful. And in that moment, I swear I was the luckiest girl on the whole planet.

Somehow, he'd taken me back. Somehow, we were going to be together, and as scary as that was, I had no fight-or-flight urge at all.

I had the love-and-snuggle urges instead, which was far preferable.

He pulled in a loud breath and shifted as he woke, and I lay there, practically bouncing as I waited for him to open his eyes.

When he did, they found mine, and he smiled.

"Hey," he said sleepily.

"So, whatcha doing today?"

He chuckled and rolled over to grab me and pull me into him, nuzzling into my neck. "Hopefully, you."

"That's a guarantee. Wanna spend the day together?"

"Mmhmm." He kissed my neck, slipping his thigh between my legs. "I wanna take you on a date."

"Ooh, fancy." I wrapped my arms around his neck and hitched my leg onto his hip.

"Fancy date for my shiny Penny."

I smiled and pulled him even closer. "Can we go by my place and pick up some stuff?"

"Yep," he said against my skin as his hand roamed down my ribs to my ass, his fingertips grazing places that made my heart speed up and hips squirm against his very morning wood.

I hummed and slipped my fingers into his hair. "Good. And can I stay the night again?"

"Pen, you can stay as long as you want." He licked the skin of my neck and kissed the hollow behind my jaw.

"You won't get sick of me?"

"Not possible," he whispered in my ear.

"But maybe it is; you don't know," I said as he cupped my breast, thumbing my nipple while he kissed my neck as if it tasted like honey.

"You're probably right," he muttered between kisses, shifting his hips to angle for me. "I'm sure today will be awful. All that talking." *Kiss.* "Hanging out." *Kiss.* "Eating." *Kiss.* "Fucking," he said as he pressed his tip against my pussy and flexed, filling me up with a *kablam* that made fireworks go off behind my eyelids.

I had no words after that. My lips were too busy with his. My body was too busy processing the feeling of him sliding in and out of me, full and then empty, over and over. My mind was too busy with the realization of just how gone I was over him. And my heart was too busy opening up to let him in.

Bodie fucked me slow and sweet in the golden morning sunshine, and I wished for a hundred more mornings just like it. My whole life, I'd been missing this, missing him, and now that I had him, I wouldn't give him up so easily. Maybe not at all.

A few hours later, we were laughing and holding hands and walking back to his place from mine. I'd packed a bag and gotten nailed good and hard in the shower, and found myself starving, so we ducked into a donut shop to grab a dozen.

He assured me it wasn't our date.

Just saying — I would have given him an A-plus if it had been.

By the time we got back to his place, I'd convinced him through begging — whining — to let me play his video game demo. He actually had the nerve to ask me if I knew how to use the controller.

Fortunately, he had Mortal Kombat, and I blew his mind up with all the things he thought he'd knew about me but had no idea. Nobody fucked with Sub-Zero. Not even Bodie, video-game-genius-of-the-world-and-my-heart.

And then I played his game.

It was glorious. For twenty too-short minutes, I ran through a temple solving puzzles and watched cut scenes that looked almost like they were out of a movie. While eating donuts and getting cinnamon sugar all over everything. While Bodie watched me like I was a goddess.

He made me feel like a goddess.

It was in the small moments — him smiling down at me as he

opened the door to the restaurant that night, holding my hand across the candlelit table while we ate, the look in his eyes when he told me how happy he was.

But Bodie made me feel like *more*. He made me feel loved and treasured.

And the best part was that I loved and treasured him too.

At the time, in the moment, I couldn't place the feeling, the whisper of premonition. I just knew that my life would never be the same. I knew I didn't want to be without him. I knew he'd take care of me, and I knew I'd take care of him too.

That night, we made love in the moonlight. That night, I lost my heart to him forever, and I never wanted it back.

I had his instead.

Epilogue

It *was June in New* York, which meant it was hot as fuck, but things were looking up. A double scoop of salted caramel was in my hand-slash-mouth, and Bodie was smiling at me from across the table of the ice cream shop where I'd seen him for the first time since high school.

I moaned as I took a long lick of my ice cream, eyes rolling back in my head, hand resting on my very pregnant belly.

"Jesus, fuck, that is *so good,*" I mumbled around a full mouth, not even swallowing before I went back for more. "I swear, everything tastes better when you're knocked up."

He chuckled and licked his ice cream. "Feel better?"

"Mmhmm." I swallowed. "I'm sorry I've been such a raging bitch. It's just so fucking hot and I'm so fucking fat and I'm so fucking hungry. But this ice cream is *so fucking good.*"

"You're not a bitch, Pen."

I barked out a single laugh. "That's funny. I nearly slit your throat this morning for leaving your shoes in the living room after I almost tripped and fell and broke my neck. You know I can't see anything past this." I gestured to my stomach. "I haven't seen my feet in a month. Who even knows what my bush looks like."

He laughed. "Trust me, it looks perfect."

"Psh, you say that now. Wait until I push your baby out of it. God, my vag is gonna look like a roast beef sandwich." I frowned, bummed out. And just like that, I thought I might cry.

"Penny," he said sternly, "your pussy is pink and perfect and mine and nothing will change that."

I sighed and reached for his hand. "I fucking love you."

He smiled. "I fucking love you too."

"Even though I've spent a small fortune on fancy stretch-mark lotions?"

"Yep."

"Even though I'm crazy?"

"Especially because you're crazy."

I sighed and licked my ice cream. "You're the best, babe. You're like a unicorn."

"A sex unicorn?"

"I dunno what that is but clearly, the answer is yes." I pointed to my stomach.

"Hmm, well, the sex unicorn is horny." He took a lick, eyes twinkling.

I laughed, and the baby shifted and stretched. My hand flew to the spot. "Whoops. I woke Coco up. Sorry, cupcake." I patted the spot that I thought might be her butt as I took a full-on bite of my ice cream. My teeth stung, and I couldn't even care — I moaned like I was in a porno.

Bodie laughed and took a bite of his cone.

"This is all your fault, you know," I said, motioning to my belly.

"You and your super sperm. Only I would be in the zero-point-one percent of the population who gets pregnant on birth control."

"Psh, that was all you. And the stomach flu. You puked your pill up three days in a row."

I shook my head. "I'm going with super sperm. Lucky for me, you're a hottie. Our baby is gonna be so pretty."

"Rock the Casbah" played over the speakers, and I lit up. "It's our song!"

He smiled at that, and I saw a little secret behind his eyes.

"Know what today is?"

My brow quirked. "June something?"

"Two years ago today, we sat right over there while you ate your ice cream just like that. And that night, we went to—"

"Circus!" I grinned stupidly as my lovesick heart sprouted daisies and butterflies. "I didn't even know what day that was."

He shrugged and ate his ice cream like it was no big deal. "I remember stuff like that."

"I can't even remember what I had for breakfast this morning," I said in utter awe. Why a guy like him wanted anything to do with the likes of me, I'd never understand.

"Bagel with strawberry cream cheese, lightly toasted."

I shook my head, giggling. "You're my dream guy, you know that?"

"I'm glad you feel that way."

He pushed a black velvet box across the table at me, taking another lick of his ice cream like it was a totally normal day and he wasn't giving me one of *those* boxes with what I was pretty sure was one of *those* things in it.

"Bodie," I breathed, my eyes on the box and ice cream dripping onto my hand.

"Penny," he said softly, a lightness to his voice that betrayed the heaviness underneath.

When I looked up at him, his face was soft and beautiful and perfect and made my insides turn to goop.

"I love you, and I don't want to be without you. Not ever. I've wanted you to be mine every day for the last two years, and I want you to be mine for every day for the rest of my life. I've had this ring since we found out you were pregnant, but I figured it would be best to wait until you were so big and dependent on me for foot rubs that you couldn't say no."

I laughed through a sob.

His voice softened. "I've been waiting for the perfect day, and I found it. Open the box."

I shoved my ice cream at him and wiped my hands off before picking up the box with trembling fingers. And when I opened it, the most beautifully simple ring lay inside, shining with diamonds and gold and promises of forever.

"Marry me, Pen."

I breathed for just one second, one savored moment where the man I loved told me he wanted me always, when the life we'd created stretched inside me, when everything was right and perfect and an absolute dream.

And then, I jumped out of my seat and into his arms as best I could weighing a metric ton, and he caught me as best he could with his hands full of ice cream cones.

"Of course I'll marry you," I said with my throat tight and heart singing. "I might be crazy, but I'm not stupid."

He laughed, and it was only then that I realized I was crying, my cheeks soaked and warm and aching from smiling.

And when I kissed him, he tasted like mint chocolate and love and forever.

Acknowledgments

No book is written without the help of a massive support system, and here are some acknowledgements to some of those who were a part of this story.

Jeff Brillhart — You are a king and a savior, and without your love and support, I just couldn't even get through it. I don't think I'd want to. Thank you for always providing inspiration for these books. You're the reason I believe in love.

Kandi Steiner — How much hand holding could a hand holder hold if a hand holder could hold hands? I think we found the answer. #Freakoutcentral. Hopefully everyone finds Penny as amusing as you and I do. I love you more than tacos, sunshine.

Karla Sorensen — There has never in the history of the world been a better critique partner than you. You know exactly what I need to hear when I need to hear it. You know how to cheer me on and bark at me like a drill sergeant in a way that is always genuine, always just what I need to get motivated. When it's hard, you're there, and in a handful of rambling voice messages, we can solve pretty much anything. Maybe we should try our hand at world peace.

BB Easton — Beastie, you're my hero, my soul sister, my brain twin. I had more fun plotting this book with you than should be legal. Every day you're here for me to pet my hair and tell me I'm pretty, even when I'm a smelly, bloated sack of garbage. How I ever got so lucky to find you, I'll never know, but I'll never stop thanking the universe for you.

To my many, many beta readers — You are all so appreciated. Your feedback shaped this book, shaped these characters, and that influence is as much of a part of the story as my heart is.

Penny Reid and Sara Ney — Here's to writing characters people hate with our chins up and our hearts behind them. Your pep talks gave me the courage to put my sassy, irreverent character out into the world, and I can't thank you enough for that.

Marcus Diddle — Thank you for your moniker. I'm sending Janet a T-shirt that says "I got Diddled by Diddle." She'll probably use it to clean toilets, and I'm totally cool with that.

To my editors, Ellie McLove and Jovana Shirley — you've once again made my story as clean and perfect as humanly possible. Thank you for your hard work and dedication to your work and mine.

Lauren Perry — You are a magical unicorn who finds me magical unicorns and produces magical unicorn photos for my covers. If you ever stop doing cover shoots, I might actually die.

To the bloggers — You make the book world go around. I see you, I appreciate you, I love you, and I thank you for everything you do.

And to you, reader, thank you for your love, your support, and for reading my words. I wouldn't be where I am without you all, and I love you for picking this up, for following me, just for being.

About Staci

Staci has been a lot of things up to this point in her life: a graphic designer, an entrepreneur, a seamstress, a clothing and handbag designer, a waitress. Can't forget that. She's also been a mom to three little girls who are sure to grow up to break a number of hearts. She's been a wife, even though she's certainly not the cleanest, or the best cook. She's also super, duper fun at a party, especially if she's been drinking whiskey, and her favorite word starts with f, ends with k.

From roots in Houston, to a seven year stint in Southern California, Staci and her family ended up settling somewhere in between and equally north, in Denver. They are new enough that snow is still magical. When she's not writing, she's gaming, cleaning, or designing graphics.

FOLLOW STACI HART:

Website: Stacihartnovels.com
Facebook: Facebook.com/stacihartnovels
Twitter: Twitter.com/imaquirkybird
Pinterest: pinterest.com/imaquirkybird

Made in the USA
Middletown, DE
10 December 2019